SHOW

Special Books by Special Writers

The Book:

BAREFOOT IN THE GRASS

A warm, poignant and humorous story about real-life problems and real-life solutions. Definitely a winner!

The Writer:

Judith Arnold is one of Harlequin's most popular and prolific romance writers. Her stories have captivated readers around the world and are sure to linger in the hearts and minds of anyone who reads them. *Barefoot in the Grass* is no exception!

"A sizzling hero, a poignant heroine—and a story about a problem only love can solve."

—Jennifer Greene

"Every character (is) exquisitely drawn and unforgettable. Judith Arnold's heroines will be your life-long friends, her heroes your dream lovers. Reward yourself with the very best. You deserve it!"

—Suzanne Forster

"Sometimes funny, sometimes poignant, always wonderful, *Barefoot in the Grass* is guaranteed to make you laugh, cry and best of all, think. Judith Arnold, who is always wonderful, too, has outdone herself."

—Emilie Richards

Dear Reader,

Romance novels are women talking to other women about the things that matter to us: nurturing and communication, freedom and responsibility, anger and lust—and, of course, *love*. Through our books we explore the power of love to wound and to heal, to strengthen us, to make us better people.

I decided to write *Barefoot in the Grass* because, like every other book I've written for Harlequin, it's about all these things that matter to us. It tells the story of a woman who faces a challenge too many women face every day—and she faces it with the kind of indomitable spirit and humor we expect in a true heroine. Beth Pendleton is a breast-cancer survivor. She's been given a second chance at life, and she's determined to make the most of it.

Luckily for her, fate throws Ryan Walker into her path. Ryan is everything we want in a romance hero—he's smart and sexy and fiercely independent. But he has no idea how strong he is or how much love he has to give until he meets Beth and learns the real meaning of beauty, honesty and hope.

Writing *Barefoot in the Grass* was emotional, inspiring and a great deal of fun for me. I hope you enjoy it. Please send me your thoughts c/o Harlequin Books, 225 Duncan Mill Road, Don Mills, Ontario, Canada M3B 3K9.

Judith Arnold

Judith Arnold

BAREFOOT IN THE GRASS

Harlequin Books

TORONTO • NEW YORK • LONDON
AMSTERDAM • PARIS • SYDNEY • HAMBURG
STOCKHOLM • ATHENS • TOKYO • MILAN
MADRID • WARSAW • BUDAPEST • AUCKLAND

ISBN 0-373-70715-0

BAREFOOT IN THE GRASS

Copyright © 1996 by Barbara Keiler.

This edition published by arrangement with Harlequin Books S.A.

® and TM are trademarks of the publisher. Trademarks indicated with ® are registered in the United States Patent and Trademark Office, the Canadian Trade Marks Office and in other countries.

Printed in U.S.A.

This is for my sister, Carolyn.
My cousin Judy.
My mother's friend Adele.
My grandmother's friend Hannah.
And all your sisters and mothers and cousins
and friends.

CHAPTER ONE

EVERYTHING WOULD have been fine if a car hadn't backfired.

The explosion ripped through the midday tranquility of downtown Devon like a rifle shot, leaving an acrid scent in its wake. By the time Beth spotted the car responsible—a dilapidated station wagon rattling along the street, trailing smoke from its exhaust pipe—Missy was frenetic with fear, barking and straining at the brand-new leash Beth had just clipped around the puppy's furry little neck. Missy lurched this way and that, straining at the strap, scampering wildly around the sidewalk until the leash circled Beth's ankles. One sharp tug yanked her legs out from under her, spilling her into an undignified sprawl on the sidewalk.

She let out a shriek and dropped the leash. Missy took off at a gallop.

Okay, Beth chanted, swallowing the expletives that crowded her mouth. *Stuff happens. Don't panic.*

Staying calm was important. Denying stress its due, maintaining a perspective, enjoying every minute of every day... She was not going to fall to pieces just because her beloved puppy—whom she'd adopted from the Devon Animal Shelter less than ten minutes ago—was bolting down Main Street, darting past shops and shoppers and dragging the fancy new leash along the pavement like an extra tail. Beth was not going to let any of this get to her.

"Missy!" she yelled, pulling herself carefully to her feet. A cursory inspection of her ankles and knees—and a delicate pat-down of her behind—revealed no serious damage to her body. She lifted her purse and scanned the street in time to see Missy slipping through the hands of a preschooler who'd just stepped out of the bakery with her mother. The child giggled as the puppy charged ahead, yipping and yapping and loping to the corner with surprising grace, considering that her paws were much too big for her fuzzy football-size body.

Beth shook her head in amazement. In Manhattan, people would have flattened themselves against the buildings to avoid touching a runaway dog. In Devon, they actually tried to catch the beast.

She didn't have time to reflect on the cultural differences between her old address and her new one. Sliding the strap of her purse higher on her shoulder, she raced after her new pet. The fleeing puppy caused a teenager on in-line skates to bank into a lamppost, then eluded a UPS delivery man who had attempted to snag her with one hand while balancing an unwieldy carton in the other. Missy sprinted to the curb, leapt into the street and miraculously avoided being hit by an elderly man pedaling a bicycle.

Beth accelerated her pace, but her sandals weren't designed for track-and-field events and her stamina wasn't what it used to be. The balmy June day suddenly felt steamy; perspiration glued her hair to the nape of her neck, and her breath seared her throat.

She swore, more at herself than at Missy. What had she been thinking of, to take on a headstrong, madcap mongrel? What Beth knew about dogs wouldn't fill a thimble.

She had moved to Devon to begin a new life. She had traded her Upper East Side co-op for a charming antique saltbox colonial on a weaving, winding road in the hills of southern New Hampshire. She'd traded her high-power job with a top-tier Park Avenue law firm for a partnership with Cindy Miller and her husband, Jeff, in an office where Beth would be able to do law on weekdays from nine to five and have the rest of her time to herself. And she'd traded her solitude for a dog, because an antique saltbox colonial on three rocky, wooded acres in rural New England cried out for a pet.

Besides, the instant she'd peered into the spacious cage of dogs available for adoption and seen one frisky puppy scrapping and scampering and dominating all the others, Beth had fallen in love.

Right now, love didn't come close to describing what she felt for the runaway mutt. So what if Missy had soulful brown eyes and ears as soft as velvet? Beth's bottom was aching from her tumble, and the dog was bounding toward the next block at a speed Beth couldn't possibly maintain.

The driver's-side door of a dusty gray pickup parked at the curb swung open, obscuring her view of the man who climbed out. He jogged around the rear of the truck to the sidewalk, and Beth watched as his huge, thick-soled work boot slammed down on the looped end of the leash, jerking Missy to a halt.

Arms akimbo, lungs pumping, Beth willed her pulse to beat slower and lifted her gaze to view the man who'd come to her rescue. His smile stunned her.

Granted, there was more to him than just his smile. Her gaze took in his tousled brown hair, his chocolate-brown eyes bracketed by laugh lines, his angular chin and sharp nose and the dimples framing his mouth. But his smile... It governed his face, illuminated it, defined and informed it in an astonishing way. Not just the dimples and the laugh lines, but his eyes themselves were smiling. As were his cheeks, his nostrils, his eyebrows. Every aspect of him seemed to contribute to the smile—his sun-darkened complexion, his solid stance, the angle of his head, the sinewy grace of his arms, exposed beneath the short sleeves of his T-shirt.

Could arms smile? she wondered. Well, *everything* about the man was smiling. Why not his arms?

And what on earth was he smiling about, anyway? Her pet's shenanigans? Her embarrassing crash landing outside the animal shelter? No doubt her jog down the sidewalk had left her disheveled and flushed, but honestly, the man didn't have to be smirking as if she were the headliner clown in a two-bit circus.

"Lost something, did you?" he asked. His voice carried the flavor of his smile.

Pursing her lips, she made a futile attempt to smooth her blouse into the waistband of her skirt, then ruffled her short-cropped hair with her fingers, as if by neatening herself she would give him less to laugh at. It wasn't as if he were a paragon of impeccable grooming himself. His jeans were worn and faded, practically white at the knees. His navy blue T-shirt was flecked with pale dust along the shoulders and across the chest. And those heavy boots looked as if he'd recently worn them on a fifty-mile hike through mud.

Given the old truck from which he'd emerged, she concluded that he was a laborer of some sort. An absurdly handsome one. She wasn't averse to admiring a gorgeous guy... but not one who considered her a joke because she'd let her dog have the upper hand—or, more accurately, the upper paw.

She scowled, annoyed that she should find him attractive. She shouldn't even have noticed his rugged build, his lean physique. Physical perfection wasn't a particularly worthwhile quality. It simply was or wasn't. It was a gift, not something a person could earn through hard work or a noble attitude.

The man reached down and scooped the puppy up into his arms, shifting his foot to release the leash. His hands were thick and strong, so large he could cradle the dog in the curve of one palm.

Missy nestled snugly into his hand and emitted a whimper of contentment. The man scratched her behind her ears and she closed her eyes, clearly smitten with him. Barely minutes ago, Missy had been licking Beth's fingers, panting and drooling and giving her the canine version of an adoring smile. But now the fickle little mongrel had apparently found true love with this stranger.

Beth sighed. If she were a dog and had to choose between a skinny blond lady and a luscious hunk of masculinity, she'd choose the hunk, too.

The man lifted Missy to eye level and peered into her rapturous face. "So tell me, pal—is this lady your pet person?"

His playful comment caused Beth's resentment to ebb. How could she resent the man just because he was strong and quick and healthy looking and had developed an instant rapport with her dog? Beth probably deserved to be laughed at for her public ineptitude. "I'm hoping to reverse the owner-pet power structure in the near future," she admitted with a grin. "Thanks for your help. I'm not a very fast runner."

The man glanced at her legs, his smile changing slightly. Her flowing cotton skirt fell several inches below her knees, so he couldn't see much, but his gaze lingered a bit longer than she would have expected. "No problem," he said as he turned his attention back to her face. His voice carried the distinctive New England flatness she wasn't yet accustomed to. "The way that car backfired, it sounded like the shot heard round the world. If it freaked me out, I can't blame a puppy for getting freaked out, too."

"I guess puppies can't handle that kind of noise," she agreed. His eyes seemed focused on her—more than friendly, but not in the wolfish way of a sidewalk stud in Manhattan. Evidently small-town men weren't as flagrant about ogling women on the street. Or else *this* small-town man didn't consider Beth worth ogling.

Not that she blamed him. Her bony feet and ankles had failed to impress him. As for the rest of her...well, that would also fail to impress him.

Still stroking the fur at the nape of the puppy's neck, he continued to study Beth, his gaze unnervingly potent. "You're new in town, aren't you?"

"Yes."

His left hand taking the full weight of the dog, he extended his right. "Ryan Walker."

"Beth Pendleton." His long fingers practically swallowed her narrow hand as she slipped it into his. His palm was leather-hard and smooth—a laborer's hand.

"And this little guy is—?" He peered down at the dog.

"That little troublemaker is Missy."

Ryan Walker's smile faltered. "Missy?"

"I just came up with that name. She looks like a Missy, doesn't she?"

Ryan let out a guffaw. "He looks more like a mister to me."

"A *mister?*"

Ryan lifted the puppy to eye level once more, as if to peek under its belly. When he lowered the dog to rest against his chest, he appeared to be choking on a laugh. "I hate to break the news to you, Beth Pendleton, but this dog is no Missy."

Beth considered hauling her dog out of Ryan Walker's huge hands and having a look for herself. But she'd already humiliated herself enough for one day. Missy, or Mister, or whatever name Beth finally attached to the cur, had caused her more trouble in less time than she could have possibly imagined.

That the dog seemed so damned comfortable cuddled up to Ryan Walker only made her feel worse. Not only was it the wrong sex, but it had apparently fallen in love with a man who was not quite succeeding in his all-too-obvious effort to keep a straight face.

She had always stayed on top of things in the high-energy, high-stress world of Manhattan. How was it that in this sleepy New Hampshire village she was totally out of her depth? "I could have sworn the clerk at the shelter told me I'd picked a she," she mumbled, glowering at the dog.

"You didn't bother to look?"

"Of course not. That would have been rude."

Ryan chuckled. "Yeah, I guess it would have been. Most dogs are pretty rude, though. Especially male dogs." Ryan's easy tone informed her that he was aware of her embarrassment and didn't intend to add to it.

She appreciated his effort, but she couldn't quite meet his gaze. "I feel like a fool," she muttered, focusing on her wretched pet. "I was so excited when I saw her—I mean, *him*. It's my very first dog, and I guess I wasn't paying attention. I used to be so good at details, but—I don't know, the clerk gave me all the papers while I was writing a check, and I didn't pay much attention. Things just get past me these days. I don't know where my mind is sometimes, and I..." Aware that she was babbling, she clamped her mouth shut and kept her eyes on the dog.

Ryan took a moment to digest her words. "You've never had a dog before?"

Attempting a glum smile, she shook her head. "Isn't it obvious?"

"Well, there's a first time for everything."

"Not necessarily. If I'd given this pet business a little more thought, there probably wouldn't have been a first time for me to own a dog."

"Sometimes it's better not to think too much."

"Oh?"

"When it's your first time at something, for instance. I can remember a few first times in my life that wouldn't have happened if I'd stopped to think. And I don't regret any of them."

She dared to meet his gaze, and the smoky intensity of his smile informed her that they weren't discussing dog ownership anymore. They were talking about something else, the sort of first times that occurred between men and women.

Of course, she could be misreading him as badly as she'd misread her puppy. She was so out of practice when it came to dealing with men in anything but a professional context that she could no longer tell whether or not a man was flirting with her.

Beth had sworn that in her new life she would try to live as normally as possible—and normal, for a single, healthy thirty-two-year-old woman, was supposed to include social interaction with members of the opposite sex. But maybe she wasn't ready to interact with a member of the opposite sex like Ryan Walker. He was just too physically flawless. Too dauntingly male.

She watched as he scratched Missy's belly. She hadn't known dogs could make such noises, but the sound emerging from her pet sounded an awful lot like purring. She imagined that Ryan Walker's callused fingers felt glorious on the downy white fur of the puppy's abdomen as they caressed him with a gentleness that seemed to contradict the man's tough, work-hardened appearance.

The noon sun made her feel terribly hot—or else it was Ryan Walker's hands, his eyes, his smile that caused her blood to simmer in her veins. She really, really hoped he wasn't coming on to her. She definitely wasn't ready for this.

"The clerk must have given you a license," he said, his eyes remaining on Beth's face, his smile never faltering. "Doesn't it mention his sex on the license?"

"I'm sure it's there. I didn't read everything, though. I just saw the puppy and lost my mind."

Ryan's dimples intensified. "Sounds like love at first sight."

No doubt about it—Ryan was flirting with her.

She mulled over her options. One part of her—the sensible part, or perhaps the frightened part—wanted to tell him the truth, to set him straight, to stop this episode before it had a chance to start. But another part of her wanted to take a chance and flirt back, just to see if she remembered how to, just to prove that, at least on the outside, she could pass for normal.

Why not? she thought. It wasn't as if she and Ryan Walker were ever going to be anything more to each other than a couple of Devon citizens discussing a dog. Beth ought to take advantage of the opportunity to test her reflexes and practice her old moves. Someday they might come in handy.

Bravely she met Ryan's unwavering stare. She felt momentarily swamped by the rich, seductive intensity of his eyes. "I didn't believe in love at first sight until fifteen minutes ago," she said, then smiled at how calm and poised she sounded.

"And then?"

"And then..." She glanced down at her dog and then lifted her gaze to Ryan once more. "Then I met Missy."

He chuckled. "This dog's going to develop a complex if you call him Missy. He'll be in therapy for the rest of his life, struggling with his gender identity."

"Oh, heavens. I'd hate to cause him that kind of pain."

"Are you sure this is really the dog you want?"

"Absolutely." She refused to look away from Ryan— to do so would signal some kind of defeat. She liked feeling daring and capable and interesting to a man, even if the man knew nothing about her beyond these few minutes on a sidewalk in Devon's business district. She stroked the soft fur behind the puppy's ears, aware of how close her fingers were to Ryan's. She didn't have to look down at their hands to know. She could feel the movement of the dog's fur; Ryan's fingers caused little waves in the tawny hair that rippled against her fingers. "I chose this dog—or maybe this dog chose me. Either way, we bonded."

"That definitely sounds like love at first sight." Ryan's smile, his husky voice and his relaxed Yankee accent were too potent a combination. Even at her best, a few years ago, Beth would have felt overwhelmed by a man endowed with such an abundance of sex appeal. She ought to ease off now, before she lost her emotional footing and took another graceless dive. "You're much better off with a male," he told her. "But you knew that already, didn't you?"

"A male dog, you mean?"

His smile eased, as if he were aware that the conversation had gone as close to the edge as she would let it. "Male dogs never get PMS," he pointed out, safely sticking to pets. "Male dogs are strong and stalwart and loyal."

"Sexist hogwash," she argued, relieved that he'd backed off a bit. "I'll bet female dogs are just as stalwart and loyal. And I'll bet they don't get PMS, either. And they're probably much better behaved than male dogs."

"Oh, sure," he concurred with fake solemnity. "Female dogs wiggle their bottoms and whine. Male dogs guzzle beer and love the Three Stooges."

"I'll bet they track mud through the house, too."

"Tons of mud. Always right after you've just mopped the floor."

The last of her tension waned. She stroked the puppy's ruff and he let out blissful sigh. "What am I going to call you?" she asked the dog in a cooing voice.

"Chuck," Ryan suggested.

"Chuck?" She shot him a horrified look. "You want me to name this sweet, cute, cuddly little puppy *Chuck?*"

"Don't you think he looks like a Chuck?" Ryan lifted the puppy to eye level again. "What do you say, Chuck?"

The traitorous dog licked Ryan's chin.

"There, you see?" he said. "He told me himself. He likes Chuck."

Beth scowled, unable to come up with a better name. "Chuck it is," she said, capitulating. She reached for the loop end of the leash. "If that's what he told you, who am I to question it?"

Ryan lowered the puppy to the sidewalk and straightened. "So," he said, eyeing Beth up and down. "What brings you to Devon? Other than your search for the ideal pet, of course."

The question was asked lightly, without ulterior motives. Just more flirtatious small talk. Ryan couldn't possibly know how difficult it was for her to answer.

Many things had brought her to Devon. One particular thing. Ryan didn't need to know—and if she told him, he would probably wish that she hadn't. "I was ready for a change," she said vaguely.

"A change from what?"

This question also sounded innocent. But if she answered, he would ask another question, and another. "City living," she said laconically.

"A city's no place to raise a dog," he commented, once again picking up her cue and steering the conversation back to the relative safety of her pet. "Especially this dog."

"Why do you say that? I'm sure he'd do all right in the city."

"In an apartment? Not a chance. He's going to be a horse by the time he's done growing."

"A horse?" she asked incredulously, glancing down at her puppy, who was sniffing Ryan's boot with great gusto, as if the dirt-encrusted leather smelled like a prime rib.

"By Christmas he'll be bigger than you."

She laughed at Ryan's exaggeration. "He's not going to be that big."

"He's going to be enormous. Look at the size of his paws. They're huge! I'd figure he's got some golden retriever in him, and a whole lot of Saint Bernard. He's no wussy lap dog, that's for sure."

Terrific. She'd thought she was getting a cute little female. Instead she'd wound up with a male destined to mature into a canine King Kong. "He's going to eat me out of house and home, isn't he?" she lamented.

"I hope you've got some land for him to run around on," Ryan continued, sounding awfully knowledgeable—but then, anyone who knew anything about dogs would have to know more than Beth did. "Big dogs need lots of space."

"My property measures about three acres. Some of it is forest, but there's a nice yard, too."

"Oh, yeah? You bought that old saltbox on Loring Road?"

"As a matter of fact, yes," she told him, startled. "How did you know?"

He shrugged. "It was on the market for a while."

"You follow the real-estate market?"

"I do construction." He waved at his work clothes, then at his truck. "You get to know what's getting built, what's getting rebuilt, what's available. That house isn't bad. Old, but sturdy."

"Yes." It was old, sturdy, and radically different from the chic, sterile co-op apartment she'd owned in New York City. That difference had been what had drawn her to the house. She'd been enchanted by its weathered roof tiles, its clapboard walls, its six-over-six windows and its stairway. She wanted to run up and down the stairs in her own home. She wanted to step outside and feel grass beneath her feet, and maybe see a garden carved out of a corner of her yard, and beyond the garden she wanted trees. She wanted to stand at her front door and view not just another towering apartment building, but the sky spread wide above her.

"That *is* a nice piece of property," Ryan conceded. "Chuck'll love it."

"I think he and I both will," she said.

"Just you and Chuck, huh?" Ryan assessed her speculatively. She could guess what he was thinking...that she was single, childless, on her own.

All of which was true. She wondered what he intended to do now that he'd reached the right conclusion about her. Flirt some more? Lure her back into a discussion about gender issues and love at first sight?

"Not to presume or anything," he said, "but since you're new in town, someone ought to alert you to Martha Strossen. She's the town matchmaker. It's a compulsion with her."

Beth smiled to disguise her wariness. He *was* presuming, even if his presumption happened to be correct. At least superficially she had the qualifications to make a compulsive matchmaker's heart beat quicker. "Thanks for the heads-up."

"If you're looking to link up with a guy, Martha's your ticket. Give her half a minute, and she'll pair you with someone."

"It appears I've already got a man in my life," Beth noted, smiling down at Chuck, who abandoned Ryan's boot and peered up at Beth, his tail wagging eagerly.

"Oh, yeah, you've got yourself a real man, there." She heard the humor in Ryan's tone—but she also heard other things. Exploratory things. His smile seemed personal, his gaze probing. Apprehension nipped at her, making her want to wrap her arms tightly around herself.

She'd thought she had overcome the fear that everyone in the world was gawking at her, noticing. Objectively she knew she looked fine, but inside, in the tender, vulnerable part of her soul that wasn't quite healed, she couldn't shake the belief that everyone who saw her knew. Particularly men.

Could Ryan Walker see? Did he know?

Her thoughts were like a cloud passing in front of the sun, causing a chill to ripple across her skin. Perhaps in time she would be able to relate to a man without suffering from doubts and inhibitions. But that day was a long way off, and the realization saddened her.

"Well," she said, forcing levity into her tone, "I should be on my way. It was nice meeting you," she added, not just to be polite. It *had* been nice until she'd started to feel self-conscious.

Ryan's beguiling smile made her profoundly aware of exactly how nice it had been. "So. Welcome to Devon and all that."

"Thank you," Beth said, looping the leash around her wrist and adjusting the strap of her purse on her shoulder. She turned from Ryan and started down the sidewalk. Chuck took a few steps, then balked. Twisting around, he whined plaintively at Ryan.

"A choke chain would be a good idea," Ryan commented. "You could train him to heel."

Beth frowned. "A choke chain?"

"To train him. So he doesn't go running off in traffic."

"This—" she waved toward the sporadic vehicular activity on Main Street "—is hardly what I'd call traffic."

"You'd call it traffic if Chuck wound up under someone's tires. Get a good training leash for him. Teach him not to run away. You don't want to have to depend on me to catch him every time he bolts."

True enough. Beth certainly didn't want to have to depend on Ryan Walker or any other man. "All right, I'll think about a—a choke chain."

"And let me know if you need any work on that house you bought. Antiques can be tricky."

Beth stifled a groan. All her schooling, her pricey education and her professional acumen didn't make her smart. She'd bought an antique house without recognizing that it could be tricky, and she'd adopted a puppy without recognizing how big he was going to grow. Maybe she ought to give Ryan the house and the dog and go back to New York.

No. She wasn't going to let anything defeat her ever again. She'd faced her worst test and she'd passed. She could handle whatever else life tossed her way.

She wasn't going to let fear win. She was going to enjoy life, learning from her fumbles and foibles as she went along. She had money, a good job and health. Whatever else she needed to thrive in Devon, she could learn.

She could probably even learn how to deal with a man like Ryan Walker. She *had* dealt with him, and she'd done all right.

As she gave him a farewell wave and started down the street once more—this time yanking the leash until Chuck reluctantly fell into step beside her—she decided she was doing better than all right. She was doing fine. Just fine.

RYAN HAD ALWAYS believed that a woman in a long skirt was more interesting.

Miniskirts or shorts were good for a quick, hot charge. He was a red-blooded American man, and he would never avert his eyes if a woman with great legs passed through his field of vision. But a skirt that concealed as much as it revealed got a guy to thinking about how much he'd like to see what was hidden. It didn't force him to view anything. It didn't impose on him. Rather, it made him consider the possibilities.

Long after Beth Pendleton and her dog had vanished around the corner, Ryan was still considering the possibilities.

One thing Devon could definitely use was a new woman—especially a pretty, unmarried woman with a functional brain and no dependents. Ryan had spent most of his life in this town. He knew just about everybody, which was nice, but also pretty limiting. His social life tended to center south of town, in the cities of Manchester and Nashua. But while he knew how to navigate a city, and how even to enjoy himself there, he was a hometown guy. He liked Devon. He was a part of this place. He belonged here.

And now a lovely new lady, determined to put city living behind her, had shown up. A lady in a long skirt that whetted his curiosity. A lady with breezy blond hair and pastel-blue eyes and a mouth that could turn up into a smile or narrow into a prim little scowl and then widen once more in a shy, unexpectedly sexy way.

He didn't have time to be loitering on Main Street, fantasizing about a woman's smile. Beth Pendleton

hadn't come to Devon in search of male companion-
ship, canine or otherwise. If she was in the market for
a boyfriend, she wouldn't have transplanted herself to
this small, out-of-the-way dot on the map of New
Hampshire.

Climbing into the cab of his pickup, he shoved aside
the deli bags stuffed with sandwiches and sodas for his
crew and jammed his key into the ignition. And found
himself wondering what *had* brought Beth to his particular dot on the map. It wasn't as if Devon were
teeming with job opportunities. For that matter, he
couldn't really tell from Beth's outfit if she'd been
dressed for work or was just passing through. But if she
was just passing through, she wouldn't have bought the
house on Loring Road.

So she was planning to stick around. She'd gotten
herself a dog and a house. Not just any house. That
colonial was a good hundred years old, built to last but
showing its age in ways Ryan's trained eye could see
better than most people. It sat on a terrific piece of
land—the property might be worth more than the
house, although Loring Road could be a bitch to navigate in the winter. Did a city slicker like Beth Pendleton know how to handle icy mountain roads? Did she
have a four-wheel drive?

Was it any of his business? No.

But she owned that house now, and she was going to
be living there, up the hill, all by herself. Correction—
with a big, clumsy puppy in need of some serious training. The lady knew squat about dogs. She'd certainly set
herself a few challenges when she'd decided to plant her
suitcase in Devon.

And she didn't even know the biggest challenge facing her, Ryan contemplated as he turned north, head-

ing for the ten-acre lot off Rainor where a very rich Boston widow had decided she wanted him to build her a New Hampshire version of the Winter Palace. Beth Pendleton might think she had her hands full with an old house and a new dog, but she didn't even begin to know what she'd gotten into when Ryan had slammed his foot down on her little mutt's leash.

What she'd gotten into, he thought with a quiet chuckle, was Ryan's sights. And he happened to be a damned good shot.

CHAPTER TWO

LYNNE WASN'T at her desk when Beth entered the shingled Victorian that housed Miller, Miller and Pendleton, Attorneys-at-Law, on a side street off Main. The law firm's receptionist, secretary and resident know-it-all was still at lunch. As far as Beth could tell, Lynne was an expert on everything. The firm would collapse without her, but she sometimes took a bit too much pleasure in displaying her superior wisdom.

She was sure to ride Beth mercilessly about her stupidity concerning dogs—and Beth would deserve the scolding. But she didn't need Lynne telling her what a ninny she was. She already felt sufficiently foolish.

She also felt exhilarated. She'd managed to behave like a normal, ordinary, unselfconscious woman with a handsome stranger. Just the way she used to, before everything had changed.

Yet accompanying her exhilaration was a whisper of doubt, rather like the odd blend of pride and panic she'd experienced when she'd taken her first solo trip in her father's car after receiving her driver's license. The freedom was immeasurably exciting—but it was accompanied by an almost oppressive sense of dread.

But Beth hadn't totaled her father's Buick sixteen years ago, and she'd survived today's outing more or less unscathed, her ego intact, her spiritual bumpers undented. And she had her very own dog to show for it.

"Come on, Chuck," she urged, denying him the chance to sniff every square inch of the mock-Persian rug that covered the floor of what had once been a parlor but was now the law firm's reception area. He seemed obsessed with one particular corner of the faded rug; he circled back to sniff it again and again, ignoring Beth as she yanked the leash and called his name.

A choke chain, she recalled. That was what Ryan Walker had recommended. When Chuck refused to acknowledge her after three sharp tugs on the pretty leather leash, the idea of choking him into submission held a certain perverse appeal.

She jerked the leash once more. Chuck sent her a doleful look, then reluctantly turned his back on the rug and followed her toward the back hall. It led past a stairway, the former dining room—now a conference room—and Cindy's and Jeff's offices, to Beth's office at the rear of the building. Chuck's hesitancy vanished a few steps into the hallway, where he picked up a new scent and barreled past her. Surprised, Beth raced to keep up with him. Unlike her stubborn dog, *she* didn't need to be choked to respond to a sharp pull on the leash.

With a spirited yelp, Chuck practically flew across the threshold of Cindy's open office door. Lacking a choice in the matter, Beth followed him in.

Cindy smiled at her from the small sofa near the window, where she sat nursing Erica. Cindy's suit jacket hung over the back of her desk chair, and her blouse was unbuttoned. A receiving blanket lay across her lap to protect her skirt. Despite the chaos of infant paraphernalia scattered around the room, she looked serene.

Chuck fell silent, as if aware that the baby was half asleep. Erica's eyes were closed, her plump legs motionless in the summer-weight pink coverall she wore. Her only signs of life were her mouth pumping as she suckled and her tiny, perfectly shaped hand flexing against the curve of her mother's breast.

The sight transfixed Beth. Only a heartless boor could fail to be moved by the beauty of a mother nursing her child. Even Chuck subsided. He flopped onto the floor, his tail thumping quietly against the carpet and his eyes riveted on the drowsy infant.

Beth lifted her gaze from the baby to Cindy, whose hair was mussed, her eyes shadowed from a lack of sleep. Yet she looked peaceful, as if her soul were as swollen with love as her breast was swollen with milk. Beth felt privileged to witness such an intimate moment between a mother and child—Beth's best friend and Beth's goddaughter.

Beth and Cindy had met each other their first day of law school and had been as close as sisters ever since. They'd shared an apartment during their student years and double-dated. Beth had introduced Cindy to Jeff Miller, the friendly, bespectacled third-year law student whose study carrel in the law library was across from hers, and when he and Cindy got married, Beth had served as Cindy's maid of honor.

When Beth had been ill, Cindy had telephoned nearly every day and had flown down to New York to be with her after the surgery. Cindy had urged Beth to leave her old job and join the small-town practice she and her husband had established in Devon. They really needed her, Cindy had insisted. There was so much construction going on in the area, and neither Cindy nor Jeff specialized in real estate and contract law, so they were desperate for Beth's expertise. And with the arrival of Erica, the exhausted parents needed a third partner to help carry the load.

Beth hadn't had to think long before accepting their offer. She'd been earning more at the firm in New York, but money didn't go as far in Manhattan. The pace was too hectic in the city, the demands on her too burdensome—and too impersonal. When death threatened, a person had to reassess her life, to reorder her priorities. Making partner and accumulating billable hours had come to seem a lot less important to Beth than walking barefoot in the grass and observing the shapes of clouds.

So she'd moved to Devon to walk in the grass and study the clouds and witness the many miracles of Erica's first months of life. She'd moved to a town where she could relax, slow down, restore herself.

Standing quietly in the doorway, watching Cindy feed Erica, Beth felt a sweet, sad pang. She doubted she would ever become a mother—the doctors said it was possible, but she simply couldn't imagine it. And even if by some odd chance she did have a child, she would never hold her baby the way Cindy held hers, cuddled to her bosom, offering nourishment from her own body.

It simply wouldn't happen. It couldn't. That was one of many blunt realities Beth had come to terms with in the past year.

Cindy grinned at the unexpectedly demure puppy and then at Beth. "He's adorable!"

Beth tried not to agree. "He's despicable," she grumbled. "He swept me off my feet—literally. He tripped me with his leash and I landed on my butt on the sidewalk, in front of half the town."

Cindy let out a hushed laugh, struggling not to jostle her daughter. "Maybe he's despicable, but he's also really cute." Her gaze shifted to Chuck, who remained at the center of the room, panting quietly, staring at the baby and—Beth could tell from his large, damp eyes and poignant canine smile—falling in love with her, just the way he'd fallen in love with Beth and with Ryan Walker. When it came to giving his heart away, Chuck obviously had no concept of fidelity.

Despite his utter faithlessness, he *was* cute. "He's a complete twit, but what can I do? He stole my heart," she confessed, leaning over to scratch him behind the ears. He sent his passionate smile toward her. So much for his love affair with Erica.

"Well, I'm proud of you, taking such a big step and getting a dog. Another week or so and you're going to lose that Noo-Yawk accent and buy a willow wreath for your door. And then you'll be a genuine Devonite." Cindy rose slowly from the sofa, cushioning Erica in her arms, and carried her to the stroller parked near the desk. She lowered the back of the stroller into a reclining position and placed Erica in it slowly, gently, managing not to jostle her. "The baby-sitter's supposed to be back in five minutes to pick her up," she told Beth. "I've got to be in court at two, and there's an ice-cube's chance in hell Jeff'll be back here by then. He went down to Manchester to take a deposition. I'll be lucky if he gets back in time for dinner."

"I can keep an eye on Erica if you have to leave," Beth offered.

Buttoning her blouse, Cindy snorted. "Right. You're going to take care of a dog and a baby while you work."

"I can do anything," Beth joked, striking a body-builder pose. "Haven't you noticed? I'm a super-woman."

"So, tell me all about this little fellow you've adopted." She smiled down at Chuck, who decided to fall in love with her, too, if his moony expression meant anything. "What's his name?"

"Chuck."

"Chuck?" Cindy had been about to lift her jacket from her chair, but she paused and scowled. "You would never name a dog Chuck."

Laughing at how well Cindy knew her, Beth lowered herself onto one of the chairs facing Cindy's desk, keeping the loop of the leash around her wrist. "Okay," she conceded. "What would I name a dog?"

"Something classy. Charles, at the very least. Charlemagne."

"I didn't name him."

"Oh?"

"Things got a little crazy. After he tackled me, he ran away. A man jumped out of his truck and caught him for me. He told me I had to name him Chuck."

"And you listened? Ms. I'll-Do-It-My-Way Pendleton? I'm shocked, shocked!" In fact, Cindy looked intrigued. Sliding her blazer up onto her shoulders, she asked, "Who was this strange man who got you to bend to his will?"

Beth sighed. If she downplayed her encounter with Ryan, Cindy would become suspicious and interrogate her endlessly. "A construction worker," she said. "His name was Ryan Walker."

"Ryan!" Cindy let out a hoot. A quick, anxious glance at the stroller informed her she hadn't awakened Erica, but she lowered her voice anyway. "You met Ryan Walker?"

Beth unexpectedly felt the midday heat at the nape of her neck again. She recalled Ryan's warm, dark eyes and his magnificent physique and the way the sunlight sifted through his hair in search of tawny highlights. And the way he'd talked about love at first sight.

"I take it you know him," she murmured, sitting a little straighter.

"Not as well as Jeff does. They grew up together. Ryan's a sweetheart."

"Is he?" Beth wished she weren't so interested.

"Actually, he's a rascal. A very charming one, though." Cindy slid some folders into her briefcase. "He's Devon's Most Wanted. Every single woman in town has the hots for him. Probably more than a few of the married women, too."

"Including you?" Beth asked slyly.

Cindy laughed and shook her head. "But you're a single woman in Devon . . . and you're blushing."

"I am not. It's just a little stuffy in here."

"It's not stuffy. You're blushing." Cindy snapped the briefcase shut and eyed Beth curiously. "What happened? Did that naughty man make a pass at you?"

"No. He only implied I was an ignoramus when it came to dogs."

"You are."

"He gets a point for being perceptive. As a matter of fact, he was perceptive enough not to make a pass at me." She hated lying to Cindy, but honestly, Ryan's palaver hadn't meant anything. It wasn't even worth thinking about.

Cindy pursed her lips. "Don't you dare put yourself down, Beth," she scolded.

"I'm not putting myself down."

"You're implying that he wouldn't make a pass at you—that you aren't worthy of a man's attention."

Beth bristled. From everyone else in the world she got tact. But she and Cindy knew each other too well not to speak frankly, sometimes brutally. "Give me a break, Cindy. I'm sure Ryan noticed I'm a woman. But I'm not the kind of woman someone like him would pursue."

"Why not? You're smart, you're attractive—why wouldn't he go after you?"

"You damned well know why."

"Because you've got an attitude problem?"

Cindy's taunting carried an edge of criticism. No one but Cindy would push Beth like this, and usually Beth would be able to accept the push—or ignore it, or push back just as hard. But today the needling drew blood— probably because her few minutes with Ryan had made her painfully aware of what her problem actually was.

She kept her anger out of her voice, only so she wouldn't rouse the baby or alarm the dog. "My attitude is fine. It's the rest of me that's the problem, and you know it."

"Your attitude is what makes the rest of you seem like a bigger problem than it has to be."

"Is there some maximum size on this problem of mine? A scale to measure it on? In case you forgot, Cindy, I happen to be missing some significant parts."

"You're missing one part, and it's not that significant."

Beth gripped the arms of her chair and took a deep breath. Only Cindy could aim so accurately at Beth's insecurities, her fears and vulnerabilities. Only from Cindy would Beth take it.

In theory, of course, she was right. Beth was no less feminine than any other woman. Just because where she used to have a left breast she now had a four-inch scar slashing the skin across her chest didn't mean she wasn't desirable.

Most men would beg to differ with that opinion, however. To them, appearance was, if not everything, then certainly a large part of everything. It was what drew them to a woman in the first place. Ultimately, they would all swear a woman's personality was more important than her looks. But *ultimately* was a long way off from first impressions.

As long as Beth was dressed, she looked normal. But naked, she looked like a freak. And somewhere between the first meeting and the *ultimately,* a woman usually got naked. Surely a man like Ryan Walker, with his sexy build and his sexier gaze, would expect a woman to disrobe. Surely a woman like Beth would want to. And then . . .

Once again, she felt a cloud move across the sun, depriving her of warmth, making her feel exposed and afraid and incomplete. She *was* incomplete. That was her reality, and it wasn't going to change.

Cindy couldn't possibly understand. She had never stared at her reflection in a mirror and wept. She, with her two big, lovely milk-filled breasts, couldn't possibly know what Beth had gone through, what she was still going through.

"Don't you dare tell me what I feel," she muttered, taut with suppressed rage.

Cindy attempted an apologetic smile. She reached across the desk as if to pat Beth's hand, then thought better of it. "You're right. I don't know how you feel.

But I know how you look, Beth, and you look wonderful. You shouldn't be so uptight."

"I'm not." Like hell she wasn't.

"And I'll bet Ryan *did* make a pass at you. If he didn't notice what a terrific-looking woman you are, then he needs to have his eyes checked." Her smile grew mischievous. "Of course it's possible that *you* were the one who didn't notice what a terrific-looking man *he* is."

"You got that right," Beth grumbled. The air around her felt steamy again. Merely thinking about how terrific-looking Ryan was caused her nerves to hum. She crossed her legs and coiled the leash around her finger, avoiding Cindy's probing gaze.

Cindy knew better than to believe her. "This is incredible," she said sarcastically. "Ryan didn't make a pass at you, you didn't notice that he's gorgeous enough to pose for Calvin Klein underwear and—"

"And we came up with a name for my dog," Beth said with finality.

"Uh-huh," Cindy scoffed. "Nobody noticed nuthin' except the dog."

"That's right," Beth said tersely.

Cindy laughed. "Well, I hate to have to break it to you, Pendleton, but you and Ryan Walker are going to be not noticing each other a lot more. Jeff handles all Ryan's legal work."

"Isn't Jeff lucky."

"The luck is about to become yours. Jeff's going to pass Ryan's business over to you."

Beth groaned in protest. "Why?"

"You're our real-estate expert, remember?"

"Ryan Walker is a construction worker."

"He owns a construction company," Cindy corrected her. "You should be glad to add him to your client list. Walker Construction is a major client. His father and uncle founded the company thirty-something years ago, and now Ryan and his cousin Larry run it. They're the best builders north of Manchester. They did that new subdivision out on 101—those ski lodges. Ten vacation homes, and the asking price is half a million a unit. Jeff's been handling those closings so far, but you'd do a better job than Jeff any day."

A strange blend of dismay and panic assailed Beth. "I can't work with Ryan Walker," she protested.

"Why not?"

"Because." Because she'd flirted with him, that was why. Because he *had* made a pass at her and she'd enjoyed it. Because he had seen her mishandle her dog and might conclude she would mishandle his legal business. Because every time she thought about him, the air around her grew uncomfortably hot.

"News flash, Beth. You're a partner in this firm. If we lose clients, you lose money. Devon is a small town. We take any business that comes our way and we're grateful for it."

"All right. Fine." Beth struggled to keep her wits about her. Hadn't she worked with single male clients at the firm in New York? Hadn't there occasionally been some mutual sexual awareness in her dealings with them? If there had, she'd paid it no mind—just as she would pay no mind to any undercurrents flowing between her and Ryan Walker.

"This is exactly what we needed a real-estate expert for—clients like Ryan. You'll do wonders for him, Beth." Cindy considered her words, and her smile grew sly. "Who knows? Maybe he'll do wonders for you, too."

"I don't want him doing anything for me. He's too..." Handsome. Tempting. *Physical.*

Cindy chuckled. "Okay. 'Fess up, sweetie. Ryan Walker came on to you, and you loved every minute of it."

"Not every minute. Just about three-quarters of them." Beth sighed glumly. "It won't happen again, Cindy. It can't, not if I have to work with him."

"You don't have to worry about getting involved with Ryan. He's a confirmed bachelor. Although maybe you could be the woman to change that," Cindy teased. "Any man can be redeemed, you know."

"I have no interest in redeeming Ryan Walker. If he wants to be a bachelor for the rest of his life, hooray for him."

"But you know..." Cindy lapsed into thought for a minute, tapping her index finger against her temple as if to jar loose an idea. "This could be your opportunity." She shuffled her stockinged feet into her shoes and pulled a tube of lipstick from her purse. "You haven't been with anyone for a couple of years, right? You were diagnosed and that toad Peter ran screaming into the night—"

"He couldn't handle it. I don't blame him."

"You *should* blame him," Cindy retorted. "If he was a real man, he would have stood by you. But he was a coward, so he ran."

"Most men would do exactly what Peter did," Beth observed wearily.

"Maybe, maybe not. But here's the thing." Cindy tapped her temple again, making Beth progressively more nervous. "You haven't been with anyone for a long time, and you're obviously skittish about becoming involved with a guy now. Horny but skittish.''

"I'm not—"

Cindy plowed ahead blithely. "Now, Ryan Walker isn't the sort to get serious about a woman—which makes him ideal for your purposes. You could kind of experiment with him. You know, stick your toe in the water, get a feel for things. You could practice on him."

"Oh, for God's sake!" Beth laughed in spite of herself. "You make him sound like an exercise machine."

"Not an exercise machine, a lo-o-o-ve machine." Cindy stretched the word out, making it sound hilariously lewd. "You've got to start somewhere. Why not start with Ryan?"

Beth shook off her laughter. "I'm not starting anything with anyone," she insisted. "Certainly not with him. Only a very special man would be willing to have a relationship with me. You know that. It's going to take time and trust. It can't just be any old guy."

"Ryan isn't old. What you need to do is dive back into the pool and swim some laps. When was the last time you had sex?"

Beth blushed. Even though she and Cindy had always been able to talk frankly about anything, some subjects flooded her face with color, the curse of her fair coloring. "I guess it's been a while," she admitted. "I've had other things on my mind."

"Well, now those things are no longer on your mind. You're healthy, you're here and you're ready for a roll in the hay. Why not roll with Ryan?"

"You're mixing your metaphors," Beth argued. "Two minutes ago you had me swimming laps. Or maybe drowning in the deep end."

"Okay, forget the hay. Dive in. Get wet. If ever there was a man worth getting wet over, it's Ryan Walker."

It was definitely too hot in the room. Beth could practically feel steam rising off her skin.

"And if it doesn't work out," Cindy continued, "no harm done. He isn't a forever kind of guy anyway." She glanced at her watch and started toward the door. "I really hate to do this to you, but if I don't leave for court now, I'm going to be held in contempt. Could you keep an eye on Erica till the baby-sitter gets here?"

"Of course."

"Lynne should be back from lunch soon. I'm really sorry, Beth—"

"Go."

"And think about it. Ryan could be just the guy to get you back in the swim of things."

"Go!" Beth nearly shouted, then glanced at Erica. The baby sighed but didn't wake up.

With a wave, Cindy departed. Once she was alone, Beth sagged in her chair, closed her eyes and let out a long, tired breath.

Cindy *should* be sorry—not for racing off to court but for browbeating Beth into considering Ryan Walker as a possible sex partner. Getting wet with him? Honest to God.

If Beth ever got close to Ryan, he would discover the truth about her. As she'd told Cindy, only a very special man would accept her, and for all his abundant sex appeal, Beth doubted that Ryan was special—at least not the way he would have to be if he and Beth were ever to get wet together.

The likelihood of rejection—by him or anyone else— was enough to make her wrap herself in the heaviest emotional armor she could muster. She was still fragile, still healing. To have a man like Ryan Walker shrink from her with revulsion was, quite honestly, more than she could take.

A small, high-pitched whimper from Chuck caught her attention. She opened her eyes and smiled at her dog.

Maybe he was fickle and faithless, but right now he appeared to be profoundly in love with her. Chuck would never notice her imperfections. He would never view her as less than a whole woman. He might be a troublemaker, but he offered unconditional love.

She smiled at the puppy, who tapped his tail against the floor and peered adoringly up at her. She couldn't expect unconditional love from a man. Any man. Especially a man like Ryan Walker.

That was why she'd gotten herself a dog.

"OH, RYAN! There you are!" Mitzi Rumson chirped, tottering over to him on her spike-heeled sling-back shoes. Her smile was wide, her body lush and the high angle of her shoes made her hips sway suggestively with each step.

Shoes like Mitzi's were impractical at a construction site—worse than impractical, they could be dangerous. The area was full of equipment, rocks, ruts and debris. Even if his insurance company hadn't demanded it, Ryan would have insisted that his crew wear steel-toed boots on the job.

But Mitzi Rumson didn't work for Ryan, and he had no say in her choice in footwear. He had to admit, though, that those spike-heeled shoes showed off her legs in a great way. Mitzi Rumson's legs were definitely worth showing off.

So was the rest of her, a fact of which she seemed well aware. Today she had on a slim-fitting, above-the-knee leather skirt, a green silk blouse with the top three buttons undone, a pair of rhinestone barrettes holding back her luxuriant auburn hair, and a gold charm bracelet that drew attention to her by jangling whenever she moved her left hand.

Ryan remained by the truck, bracing himself for her approach. What she lacked in modesty she made up for in sheer guts. He didn't know too many voluptuous twenty-seven-year-old women willing to parade around a dusty, dirty construction site in a minimum of clothing and a maximum of jewelry. The adornments spangling her various appendages had to be worth thousands of dollars—glittering earrings, a multitude of gold strands circling her neck and dipping into her cleavage, a Rolex watch, a gold chain belt curving suggestively toward her hips, and an ankle bracelet that glinted whenever a shaft of sunlight caught it.

Not too much sunlight reached Mitzi's ankle. The site still held a lot of trees, mostly pine and spruce, which created a mesh of needles for the light to trickle through. Bulldozers had knocked down a few of the evergreens, but Mitzi was very particular about which ones were to be sold for lumber, which ones transplanted and which ones left in place.

The men on Ryan's crew must have seen Mitzi mincing over to him, because they shut down their equipment and jogged to the truck. He hoisted the bulging deli bags from the passenger seat and handed out the sandwiches and cans of soda, saving two of each for himself and Mitzi.

"Oh, for heaven's sake," she coyly chided him. "You didn't have to bring me a sandwich."

"Well, you've been out here as long as we have," Ryan said, unhooking the tailgate of his truck and arranging an almost-clean tarp over the metal bed. "I figured you might be hungry. Want a seat?"

She smiled and let him help her up. Her skirt was too short and tight to offer her much mobility, but somehow Ryan managed to get her settled on the tarp without having to clamp his hands around her waist and give her a heave.

He got an eyeful of her, though. Her hips were soft and round and alluring, and until a half hour ago, Ryan would have appreciated the view she offered. Mitzi was the sort of woman who flaunted what she had: voluptuous curves, voluptuous hair and a whole hell of a lot of money, thanks to the generous last will and testament of Winston Q. Rumson, who had died last year—with a smile on his face, no doubt—at the age of eighty-four, after seven years of marriage to Mitzi.

Ordinarily Ryan didn't want to know the details of his clients' lives. But when Mitzi had hired Walker Construction to build her a million-dollar dream house on a magnificent parcel of land about half the distance from her Boston penthouse to her lodge on Lake Winnipesaukee, she'd told him everything—about how much she'd loved Winnie, about how terribly she missed him, about how happy she'd made him during the autumn of his life...and about how very, very wealthy he'd left her.

There were times in the months since Mitzi had first sashayed into Walker Construction's office when Ryan had believed she could bulldoze the world more efficiently than the bright yellow earthmover parked near a cluster of doomed trees on the northeast corner of the lot. The woman had moxie, she had a smile that could blind lesser mortals and she had a chest most center-folds would kill for—and she used all her assets to get what she was after.

At least she tried. Ryan hadn't fallen for her antics, although he'd been amused by the way her bosom seemed to arrive everywhere a full two seconds before the rest of her and the way she could modulate her voice through the entire range of feline expression, from sexy purr to threatening roar. If nothing else, Mitzi Rumson knew how to keep a man on his toes.

She accepted the tuna sub he handed her, then spread a napkin daintily across her lap and smiled. "It isn't exactly a candlelight dinner for two, but what can you do? We'll have to have dinner some other time."

"Sure," Ryan said, his smile disguising his wariness. Mitzi's goo-goo eyes and boom-boom body weren't pushing his buttons. Ryan was simply unable to give her the attention she coveted. He was too distracted by thoughts of a slim blond woman with an unruly dog.

Tucking into his sandwich, he nodded absently while Mitzi chattered about her landscaping schemes for the property. "Rhododendrons here, pachysandra there," she rambled on while his mind strayed to images of Beth Pendleton, her elegant cheekbones, her blue eyes sharp and savvy one minute, cool and guarded the next.

"I wonder if we're too far north for wisteria here," Mitzi mused. "I just love wisteria, don't you? It's so Japanese...." And he thought about Beth's delicate ankles, her creamy complexion, the neatly cropped blond hair framing her narrow face.

"I just used to love our place in Boca Raton," Mitzi enthused. "It was so tropical, all those palms and hibiscus...." And he thought about Beth's hilarious obtuseness on the subject of dogs. Mitzi yammered on about wanting the Palladian window in the house's library to overlook a topiary arrangement of yews and azaleas, and Ryan thought about how, if someone didn't explain to Beth Pendleton the ins and outs of training a dog, she was going to be in major trouble. He thought about how much he'd like to rescue her from that trouble. He thought about how much more intriguing a woman was when she didn't advertise her physical assets the way Mitzi did.

"What do you think, Ryan? The architect said it wouldn't be a big problem to put a solarium off the kitchen."

"What?"

"Haven't you been listening to me?" Mitzi sighed. "I was just telling you, I want a solarium off the kitchen. The architect said it would be easy to add one."

"But the kitchen is on the north side of the house. You can't have a solarium with a northern exposure."

"Why not?"

He ignored her cute pout. "Not enough sun. It'll suck the heat out of the house—and in the winter, that's a real problem. If you want a solarium, it's got to face south."

"Yes, but the architect said you could tack on a solarium right off the back of the kitchen. It would be so beautiful, all those plants, and maybe I could have a little indoor herb garden—"

"Your kitchen is on the north side of the house," he repeated. "Listen to me, Mitzi. You can't put a solarium there."

"I'm sure there's a way you could do it," Mitzi declared, leaning toward Ryan just enough to let him glimpse the hollow between her breasts. "We'll go over the designs together and figure it out. I just know you could do anything if you put yourself into it. Maybe you could just turn the whole house around or something. You're so brilliant, Ryan, I know you'll figure out a way to make this house exactly the way I want it."

Ryan was in no mood to argue with her. He studied her smile objectively, trying to figure out whether her teeth had been capped or were naturally that even and white. Her lipstick was a coral shade, so subtle it looked like her own lip color, only more so. He imagined Mitzi working out her smile at a facial gym the way other people worked out their abs and pecs.

He could wipe that smile off her face by telling her how much it would cost to turn the house around and add a solarium. Mitzi was obviously used to getting her way, on her own terms. But today, Ryan just didn't feel like accommodating her. He was too distracted by his memory of Beth Pendleton's quiet wit, her self-deprecating humor, her determination....

Who was she? How had she gotten such a tight lock on his imagination? Why did she fascinate him so much more than the bold, brassy woman seated next to him, who was eyeing him coquettishly above her can of soda? Why was Ryan becoming fixated on a pale stranger, a transplanted city slicker who hadn't done anything in particular to encourage his interest?

What the hell. He knew where Beth Pendleton lived and he knew her dog. He supposed there would be no harm in stopping by her house, maybe inquiring about her dog and hopefully getting a sense of whether, under the right conditions, he could make her as interested in him as he was in her.

She was new in town and probably didn't know anybody. She could use a pal to show her the ropes—and the dog leashes. Why not pay her a call that evening after work and see if she might want some help with her puppy?

They said the way to a man's heart was through his stomach—although Ryan would argue that point— but . . . wasn't it just possible that the way to a woman's heart was through her dog?

CHAPTER THREE

"YOU SHOULDN'T wear blue in June," Lynne said, eyeing Ryan up and down from her seat behind a broad oak desk in the reception area of Jeff's law office. "It attracts blackflies."

"Like hell it does." Ryan snorted. Blackfly season had just peaked in southern New Hampshire, the bloodthirsty bugs continuing their migration from Massachusetts to Maine. As far as he could tell, any and every color attracted them. They'd sucked enough blood from him to keep a hemophiliac alive for a decade.

"I read that in a scientific journal," Lynne said, pursing her lips disapprovingly at his royal blue T-shirt and his faded blue dungarees. "Blue attracts them, just like red attracts bulls."

"*I* read that bulls are color-blind, and what attracts them is the fluttering of the toreador's cape."

Lynne bristled, and Ryan smiled in triumph. He had no idea whether that bit about bulls being color-blind was true, but he'd tossed the factoid out just to shut Lynne up. He had known Lynne for years; she'd graduated from the regional high school two years ahead of Ryan and Jeff and she'd always been a pompous know-it-all. She hated it when anyone dared question her superior wisdom. Jeff always swore that if she weren't the best damned secretary he'd ever employed, he would fire her in an instant.

The best damned secretary decided to abandon the science of color and do her job. "What brings you here this morning?" she challenged Ryan. "You haven't got an appointment."

"I was hoping I could borrow a minute of Jeff's time."

"Time can't be borrowed," she lectured, segueing smoothly into philosophy. "It can be stolen, it can be wasted, but it can't be borrowed, because once you've taken it you can never return it."

Lynne's speechifying tried his patience—but if he didn't humor her he might never get past her and into Jeff's office. "Tell you what," he wheedled, assaulting Lynne with his most high-potency smile. "I'll borrow ten minutes from Jeff now and I'll give him fifteen of my minutes when he needs them. You can't beat that, Lynne. Even a loan shark wouldn't demand fifty percent interest."

Lynne pursed her lips again. Although she wasn't much past her mid-thirties, she projected late middle age in a maiden-aunt kind of way. Whenever Ryan sent a seductive grin in her direction, she acted like a virgin, huffy and chagrined and deep-down flattered. Her face flushed crimson and the tight curls of her permed brown hair shivered like springs under pressure. "He's really got a busy day today," she insisted.

"We've all got busy days. Look, Lynne—your printer's finished."

Lynne swiveled in her chair to observe the laser printer on a counter behind her. As soon as she rose from her chair to turn off the machine, Ryan made a break for the hall beyond the reception area.

The door to Jeff's office stood slightly open, and Ryan could hear Jeff's voice emerging loudly, as if he were delivering an oration. Ryan edged the door wider so he could peek inside. He saw Jeff blindly trying to adjust the knot of his necktie at his throat while simultaneously shouting into the speaker phone on his desk. "But none of that matters," he was saying when he caught Ryan's eye and beckoned him inside. "I've got the documents right here in front of me—" he emptied a packet of no-calorie sweetener into the mug of coffee on his desk "—and I'm telling you, Roger, this is the best deal we're going to come up with. Let him plead it out. Time served plus community service. You get a notch on your belt and my client promises never to bilk lonely widows again. Okay? Type up the papers and we'll sign them. I'll see you at nine-thirty."

He hit the disconnect button on the console, took a loud slurp of his coffee and smiled at Ryan. The round lenses of his eyeglasses fogged up from the steam of the hot beverage. "What a case," he groaned, pulling off his glasses and wiping them clear with the end of his tie. "Personally, I'd like to string the guy up by his thumbs for ripping off little old ladies the way he did."

"Why are you representing him if you want to string him up?" Ryan asked, flopping onto one of the chairs across the desk from Jeff.

"I was assigned by the court. You wouldn't believe how little they're paying me to defend this creep either. Ah, justice in America." He took another sip of coffee, frowned and nearly crossed his eyes trying to view his tie. "What are you staring at?"

Ryan hadn't realized he was staring. He'd momentarily zoned out, that was all. He hadn't slept well last night, and this morning he was suffering the consequences. He'd done his own coffee slurping before he'd left his house, and a thermos of liquid caffeine sat in his truck. But he remained bleary, his gaze unseeing, his mind drifting.

Drifting to thoughts of Beth Pendleton.

She was what had kept him up all night. Every time he'd started to nod off he was jolted awake by his memory of her slim, trim body, her wide blue eyes alive with secrets, her alluring lips that made him think of strawberries, both sweet and tart.

It wasn't like Ryan to lose sleep over a woman, particularly a woman he barely knew, and especially when a woman he *did* know—a woman whose assets, both physical and financial, were awesome—was sending him all sorts of signals that she was available. Mitzi Rumson gushed over him, she fawned over him, she wiggled her hips at him, and Ryan was perceptive enough to appreciate what she was offering. But...

Beth Pendleton.

He'd driven to her house yesterday evening, after a long, tedious afternoon of haggling with Mitzi over the placement of the solarium she wanted to add to her dream house. Twilight had fallen, transforming the dense woods bordering Loring Road into a shadow-land and giving the sky the appearance of a watercolor painting, dark blue bleeding into pale gold along the horizon. The air had been mild and scented with pine, and he'd been feeling mighty confident as he'd cruised the twisting road past a couple of truck farms, past a subdivision of colonial reproductions and more undeveloped forestland until he reached Beth Pendleton's home.

The house had sat square and solid and comforting in the dying light, her windows glowing amber. One of them had been open, and through the screen he'd heard her puppy barking and the lilting cadence of her voice. He hadn't been able to make out her words, but it had sounded as if she and Chuck were doing just fine without his help.

He might have pretended he'd gone to her house to help her with her dog. But the truth was he'd gone because he'd wanted to get to know her better, because he'd wanted to find out if her pale blond hair felt as soft as it looked, if her eyes looked as blue in artificial light, if her lips tasted like strawberries ... or like hot, sweet sex.

But he'd lost his nerve.

That had startled him. He wasn't in the habit of holding back. When he was interested in a woman, he made overtures. If she was as interested as he was, great. If not, no big deal.

Somehow, as he'd sat in his truck at the mouth of Beth Pendleton's gravel driveway, he had sensed that if she rejected him it would be a very big deal. So he'd driven away. And spent the rest of the night lying awake in bed, trying to figure out why he hadn't just marched up to her front door and asked if he could come in.

"What?" Jeff goaded him, abandoning his tie for his belt. "Is my fly open?"

"Sorry." Ryan gave his head a sharp shake to clear it. "Listen, Jeff, I need some legal advice. I'm having a hard time with Mitzi Rumson."

"Why doesn't this surprise me?" Jeff asked. He'd met Mitzi once, when she and Jeff had signed a preliminary contract covering the development of her property. After the meeting, he and Ryan had spent more time discussing Mitzi's attitude—and her attire—than the contract. "What has that fine Boston woman done to you?"

Ryan groaned, partly from annoyance with Mitzi and partly from exhaustion. "She wants to change her house around. We're ready to start digging and pouring the foundation, and all of a sudden she's got this screwball idea that she wants a solarium on the north side of the house."

"I take it that wasn't in the original blueprint?"

"Of course not. If it had been, I would have told her what a lousy idea it was before we went to contract."

"So tell her that now."

"I did, but she seems to think I can do anything. And it's not like I couldn't put the solarium there—it's just that it's going to turn her house into an igloo if I do. But she doesn't care. It's got something to do with her late husband's estate in Boca Raton. I've tried to explain to her that New Hampshire is a little different from Florida, but she just keeps batting her eyes and telling me to put the solarium next to the kitchen. I don't know what to do."

Jeff shrugged. "Hey, don't look at me. I don't want her batting her eyes at me, either."

"Well, give me some counsel. You're my lawyer."

"Not anymore, I'm not. I'm passing you along to my new partner."

"What new partner?"

"Come on, Ryan—I told you we were taking on a new partner."

Ryan shook his head. "Nope."

"I'm sure I did. You were probably tuning me out, as usual."

"I wasn't."

"Sure you were. You were probably fantasizing about Mitzi's millions—or Mitzi's whatever." Jeff grinned slyly, then gestured toward the window, which overlooked the front of the building. "Didn't you notice our new sign outside?"

"I'm half-asleep," Ryan complained. "I'm lucky I noticed the other cars on the road." Even fully awake, though, he would have been surprised by Jeff's taking on a third partner. He'd always thought of the Millers as a self-contained shop, two like-minded lawyers who could handle everything that needed handling.

"Well, there's a third name on our sign now. We lured an old law school friend into the business. And she's going to take care of all your problems." Jeff checked his watch, lifted his briefcase from the floor beside his desk and started toward the door.

"What do you mean, she's going to take care of my problems?"

"She's your attorney now," Jeff informed him as he started down the hallway toward the back of the building. "I'm handing you over to her."

Growing edgy, Ryan followed him. "I like the way *you* do things, Jeff," he muttered. "I don't want your old law school friend."

"You'll want her," Jeff said. And then Ryan heard a familiar sound through the door at the end of the hall— a puppy yapping.

Beth? Beth Pendleton was the third partner?

Well, maybe he *did* want her. Not necessarily as his lawyer, though.

Jeff tapped on the door and opened it. "Beth, I've got a client for you. I've got to go tie up a plea bargain." He gave Ryan a firm nudge, shoving him over the threshold, and then waved farewell and headed down the hall, calling over his shoulder, "Treat him right, Beth. Don't let your dog bite him."

Ryan scowled after Jeff, then turned and surveyed the office. It was far from settled; moving cartons were stacked in a corner, the teak shelves occupying an entire wall were only half-filled with books, the floor was bare wood, and several framed prints—abstract stuff, brightly colored but lacking recognizable shapes—stood propped against the wall, waiting to be hung. Only her desk seemed set up, a massive rectangle of teak with a high-backed leather chair behind it.

Beth wasn't in the chair. She was perched on a small stepladder, her arms laden with leather-bound volumes that were obviously destined for an upper shelf. Her dog was barking enthusiastically and running in circles around the legs of the ladder, causing it to vibrate beneath her feet.

Ryan quickly shut the door so Chuck couldn't escape and then raced toward the ladder to snag the dog. Chuck jostled the ladder, and Beth let out a shriek, dropping her books onto the shelf in front of her. Startled, Chuck charged at Ryan, who tripped and stumbled into the ladder. If he hadn't grabbed the shelves on either side of it, he would have knocked it—and Beth— over.

If he hadn't grabbed the shelves on either side of the ladder, he wouldn't have wound up with his arms sandwiching her knees and his cheek resting against her bottom.

He locked his arms, seeking stability, and then eased his face away from her. She was wearing a skirt of soft blue linen, and beneath the fabric he'd felt the firm curve of her flesh. He would have liked to rest against her, to slide his hands from the shelf to her hips and pull her fully into his arms.

But according to Jeff, she was now Ryan's lawyer, and guys didn't haul their lawyers into their arms, at least not during business hours. Besides, her lunatic dog was gnawing at the edge of his jeans, trying to pull him away from the ladder.

"Are you okay?" he asked her, jerking his leg free of Chuck's mouth.

"Just a little shaken up," she answered breathlessly.

"Thanks for not dropping those books on my head. They look pretty heavy." He stepped back from the ladder, then bent over and lifted Chuck, leaving her plenty of room to climb down. His eyes, however, were trained on her hips, her waist, the modest swells of her breasts beneath the conservative white blouse she wore. Ryan noticed a blazer, the same soft blue as her skirt— the same gentle shade as her eyes—draped across the arm of her leather chair.

"They are heavy," she said, moving around her desk and lifting her jacket from the chair. "They're crammed with the weight of legal thought." Not until she'd donned the jacket did she meet his gaze, as if she considered it essential to look like a proper lawyer before she formally acknowledged Ryan as a client. She ran her fingers through her hair, just the way Ryan would have liked to, then smiled. Her cheeks were rosy. "Hello, Ryan."

Chuck let out a bark and wriggled in his grasp, trying to break free. Ryan lowered him to the floor and he dashed off toward the cartons. "Not that it's any of my business, Beth," he noted, "but most people don't bring their dogs to work with them unless they're blind."

She laughed sheepishly. "I wanted to leave him home. But every time I closed the door he whimpered and whined. He looked so sad...and I was afraid he'd chew the furniture. Yesterday he kept gnawing on the legs of the kitchen table and the sofa. Is that normal for a dog?"

"Only a dog that isn't trained." A strand of her hair had wound up on the wrong side of her part, and his fingers itched to fix it. The collar of her blazer was slightly askew, and he longed to smooth it out. Hell, he just wanted to touch her. She presented such an enticing mixture of sophistication and bewilderment. Her jewelry was elegant—tiny gold hoops in her ears, a simple gold necklace circling her throat, nothing that would jangle and clank like Mitzi Rumson's jewelry.

She glanced at her puppy, who was shredding a wad of packing paper with his paws and teeth. She looked utterly overwhelmed.

"You don't have to leave him in your house all day," he pointed out. "On a sunny day like today, you could keep him outdoors."

"But then he'd run away. I hate the thought of chaining him up all day," she said, bending over and pulling the tattered paper from Chuck. He let out a bark of outrage.

"You've got to get him a chew toy—or an old sock. Something you don't mind having him rassle with. And you've got to get him a runner leash."

Pinching the soggy paper delicately between her thumb and forefinger, she rolled her eyes in mock exasperation. "Yesterday you said I had to get him a choke chain. Now you're telling me I have to get him an old sock and a runner leash," she muttered, carrying the paper to a wastebasket and dropping it in.

"Nobody ever said raising a dog was easy."

"I take it you've got a dog?"

"Not at the moment. I had one when I was growing up, and another one who died about a year ago. I haven't replaced him yet. Every time I think about it—" he smiled slyly "—I remember how much work it is to train in a new puppy and I come to my senses."

"It *is* a lot of work, isn't it?" she murmured. "If I'd realized how much..."

"You wouldn't have gotten Chuck?"

She shook her head and laughed. "I would have gotten him anyway. He's such a cutie."

"And you're such a softie."

She flashed Ryan a quick look, then shrugged. "Raising Chuck may be a challenge, but I've always welcomed challenges."

Ryan welcomed challenges, too. Particularly the kind of challenge a smart, classy lady lawyer like Beth posed. But of course he couldn't say so. Instead, he said, "Well, here's a challenge for you. I need a lawyer, and I guess you're it." He leaned against the ladder, frowning as a new insight struck him. "You don't seem surprised that I'm here."

"Cindy told me that Jeff had been handling your legal work," she admitted, "and that I'd probably take you over as a client, since I'm the firm's contracts expert."

"You and Cindy were talking about me, huh?"

She smiled. "I told her about Chuck's little escapade yesterday. Your name came up."

"I hope you told her I was your knight in shining armor."

"I think I said you were a helpful guy in an old truck."

"Gee, that sure sounds gallant." He returned her smile, wondering why, just like last night, he was suddenly feeling a little less certain than usual. What was it about Beth that undermined his confidence? Why couldn't he just flat out ask her if she was busy for dinner?

"So," she said after his silence had lasted a full minute, "what can I do for you?"

He decided not to tell her all the interesting possibilities that filled his mind. In her office, here for legal advice, he ought to maintain a professional tone. "I've got a problem with a contract. But you don't look as if you're open for business yet," he observed, surveying the clutter of cartons and unshelved books.

"I'm getting there." She produced a folding metal chair from a corner and dragged it toward her desk. "I know things are messy in here. If you want, we could go into the conference room—"

He didn't want to go anywhere. He wanted to stay right where he was, shut up inside the mess with Beth. "This is fine," he said, crossing the room to help her with the chair, which she was having trouble opening. He found himself only a couple of feet from her, fighting the stubborn hinges, his hands just inches from hers. He caught a whiff of her perfume, a subtle, spicy fragrance.

The chair was really stuck. He eased it from her grip, got a better purchase on it and yanked the seat and the back apart. "Thanks," she said, her cheeks growing rosier.

"Once again, your noble knight to the rescue," he joked. "Chairs and dogs I can manage. Legal hassles are beyond me."

"You probably think I'm inept at everything," she lamented. "I *can't* manage chairs and dogs. But if it's a legal hassle, you've come to the right person."

"I trust you." He said it so bluntly, so reflexively, he knew it was true. If Jeff trusted Beth with legal matters, she had to be good. But Ryan's trust for her seemed more than just intellectual. It had to do with the intelligence he sensed inside her, her courage, her humor. He wouldn't be surprised if dogs and chairs were the only things in the entire universe she couldn't manage.

She circled the desk and took her seat. Enthroned in the high-backed chair, she looked professional, smart—and surprisingly alluring, in spite of her demure outfit. "You shouldn't wear blue during the blackfly season," he warned her, lowering himself carefully onto the rickety metal chair.

She burst into laughter. "Not again! Lynne harangued me about that this morning!"

He tapped his blue shirt with his thumb. "She chewed me out, too."

"I like blue," Beth declared, grinning defiantly. "Blackflies be damned. If I want to wear blue, I will."

He took advantage of the opening. "It looks good on you. It matches your eyes. They're an amazing color." He caught himself, unsure if whether by complimenting her he was breaking a rule—and even more unsure why he cared about the rules at all.

She reached for the pen in the onyx stand on her desk and fiddled with it, glancing everywhere but at him. "So, you're having a problem with a contract," she said a little too briskly.

So much for compliments. Obeying her unspoken reproach, he explained, "It's like this. I'm supposed to build a mini-estate for a lady named Mitzi."

"Mitzi?"

"Margaret Rumson. She told me to call her Mitzi."

Beth nodded, her gaze returning to him, her beautiful eyes as clear and piercing as blue topaz. Not that he would dare to point that out to her again.

At least not now, in her office. He would see her another time, in another place, when conversations about her eyes and her sweet pink mouth and all the rest of her would be appropriate. "Mitzi's decided that she wants to add a solarium off the kitchen of this house I'm supposed to build for her. The architect altered his designs so she could have the solarium. The problem is, the kitchen faces north. I told her she can't put a north-facing solarium on a house. I explained about heat loss, and if she wanted a solarium she'd either have to have the architect redesign the ground floor so her kitchen faces south, or else we'd have to site the house differently."

"And she said . . . ?"

"She said she believes I can do *anything*." He grimaced to indicate that he didn't exactly agree with Mitzi's assessment.

"Then you'll need to indemnify yourself," Beth said.

"How do I do that?"

"We'll have to make sure your contract covers any and all alterations in the design and construction. If necessary, we'll write up a new contract. Do you have your original contract with Ms. Rumson?"

Ryan shrugged. "I have a copy on file at my office, but I didn't bring it with me. I came straight here from my home this morning. Jeff probably has a copy, though."

Beth lifted the receiver of her desk telephone, pushed a button on the console and said, "Lynne? I need a copy of a contract Jeff drew up for Mr. Walker regarding a construction job for Margaret Rumson. Could you locate it for me?" She listened for a minute, then said, "Oh, really? Well, thanks for telling me." She hung up and grinned. "Lynne thought I should be made aware of the fact that Ms. Rumson is worth quite a lot of money."

"Rumor has it."

"Lynne knows everything."

"Rumor has it." Ryan laughed. Beth joined him. Not to be left out, Chuck howled and began jogging laps around the office.

"So tell me, Ryan—what's a runner leash?"

It amused him that she could breeze through his legal problems with complete mastery, yet be such a dolt when it came to dogs. "It's a leash that gives a dog running room outdoors. One version is kind of like an old-fashioned clothesline on pulleys. The leash attaches to the line, and the dog can run from one pulley to the other, plus the length of the leash. He can cover lots of territory without leaving your property."

"Would I have to put stakes in the ground to install it?" she asked.

"Not if you've got a couple of well-placed trees to hang the pulleys on. I could put one up for you if you'd like."

"Oh, no, that's all right. I'm sure I can figure it out."

"I'm not sure of that at all," Ryan argued, still smiling. "Let me do it for you."

"You really do think I'm an idiot, don't you?" She was smiling, too, but he heard grit in her voice.

"I think you're a lawyer," he answered honestly. "Probably a top-notch one if Jeff made you his partner." He'd played by the rules long enough, and he felt like taking a chance. "I also think," he said, "that you're a great-looking lady. And when it comes to runner leashes for dogs, yeah, I think you're an idiot."

Ryan watched her reaction play itself out on her face. Her eyes widened. Her cheeks darkened. Her lips parted slightly in surprise. Was she reacting to his having called her great looking or an idiot?

A knock at the door prevented him from apologizing—as if that had ever been an option. He wasn't sorry for either of the things he'd called her. And anyway, she'd seemed more disconcerted by his compliment than upset by his insult.

The instant Lynne opened the door, Chuck leapt at her, barking exuberantly. "This is not going to work," Lynne chided, nudging Chuck out of her way with her knee. "Cindy with her baby, you with your dog... This is an office, not a zoo. You're going to have to make other arrangements for your animal."

"I will," Beth promised, shooting Ryan a conspiratorial look. "I'm going to put up a runner leash for him so he can stay home." She rose from her desk to take the file from Lynne, who was barricading the doorway with her body to keep Chuck from slipping out of the office.

Ryan reached around behind his chair to snag the hyper puppy during one of his circuits. Still barking, Chuck squirmed and slobbered all over Ryan's fingers.

Lynne clicked her tongue in disapproval. "He needs exercise. Dogs have to develop their cardiopulmonary systems, just like humans. There's a book out now called *Aerobics for Pets.* I think you ought to read it." With that, she left, closing the door behind her.

Beth clapped her hand over her mouth to stifle a laugh. *"Aerobics for Pets?"* she whispered.

Ryan wagged a remonstrative finger at her. "You should also read *Isometrics for Pets.* And that great classic of animal exercise, *Hot Dog Buns of Steel.*"

She laughed out loud, then, a deep, throaty laugh that stroked his nerves and made them quiver. It was the first time he'd ever seen her let go—throw back her head and abandon herself to a laugh that seemed to start somewhere in the vicinity of her soul and rattle every cell in her body before spilling into the air. It was the kind of laugh that made Ryan wish he could see her cut loose in other contexts. Romantic contexts. X-rated contexts.

This was a dangerous train of thought. Fortunately, the train got derailed when Chuck nipped his wrist with his small, sharp teeth.

"Hey, cut that out!" Ryan scolded, closing his hand firmly around Chuck's snout and glaring at him. "No! No biting! No!" He set the dog down on the floor, his hand still clamped around Chuck's mouth for a moment. "No," he said, a final warning before he released the dog, who dropped his head into his paws and whimpered.

Beth gasped and stared fretfully at her dog. "What did you do to him?"

Ryan checked his wrist for damage. No blood, no broken skin. Just a few red marks where the teeth had pinched. He peered over at Beth, who seemed much more concerned about Chuck's well-being than Ryan's. "It's called discipline," he said.

"But—you could have hurt him!"

"He could have hurt *me*." When Chuck lifted his head, Ryan glowered at the beast and shouted, "No!" Chuck promptly lowered his head to his paws and whimpered some more.

Straightening up, Ryan noticed that Beth had finally turned her attention to him. He almost wished he *was* bleeding. It might make her feel guilty. She'd fuss over him and go out of her way to make him feel better. He'd really enjoy having her go out of her way for him.

Luck wasn't with him. She appeared less solicitous than curious and perplexed. "Shouting at him just frightens him, doesn't it?"

"You've got to train him so he won't bite people. You've got to teach him what 'no' means. If he won't obey, you've got big trouble. People will sue you if your dog bites them. You're a lawyer—you ought to know that."

"But screaming at him . . . I mean, he's just a little puppy!"

"You don't have to scream at him. You just have to be firm. Some people might advise giving him a little whack on the rear end with a newspaper."

She shook her head emphatically. "Absolutely not. I would never hit him."

"Fine. Then train him some other way. Use the choke chain and voice commands."

Beth looked as if it were all just a bit too much for her. "I had hoped I could train him with doggy treats."

"Sure, positive reinforcement when he does something right. With this dog, though, God knows if he'll ever do anything right."

"Oh, well, then, I suppose I'll just choke him with that chain you told me to put on him," she muttered.

Maybe it *was* too much for her. He decided "softie" described her perfectly. A soft touch. A tough lawyer with a marshmallow interior.

"Hey," he said gently, aware that she was in dire need of reassurance, "I'm not talking about cruelty to animals. It's just discipline so Chuck doesn't make a habit of biting your clients. Maybe you could train him so he only bites other lawyers."

"Are you all right?" she asked belatedly, reaching for his hand to inspect his wounds. Her palm was cool and silky against his knuckles, her fingertips whispering lightly over the skin of his wrist. There wasn't much to see—just a few faint pink marks. But Ryan didn't want her to let go of him.

She rotated his hand, then moved her fingers over his wrist once more. Her fingernails were polished with a clear gloss and filed into neat ovals. Her thumb stroked against the tendons in his wrist, and he held his breath at the sensations she created inside him with her innocent touch. It would be so easy for him to shift his hand to capture hers, to pull her closer, to press her hand to his lips or his hand to hers. It would take so little for them to turn this moment into something unrelated to dogs and discipline.

Abruptly she released him and retreated a step, regret shadowing her face. She lowered her gaze to her guilt-stricken puppy. "You mustn't bite my clients," she admonished. "Or other lawyers, either."

"Keep it simple," Ryan advised. "Just shout *No!*"

"I don't want to have to yell at him," she said sadly. "I want him to love me."

Her statement puzzled Ryan. Of course she wanted Chuck to love her—which he obviously did. And she loved Chuck, too. Yet she almost sounded as if she felt unloved—and unlovable.

He decided his safest route was to make this about the dog, not her. "Chuck wants to be trained. If you teach him how to behave, he'll love you for it."

"Do you think so?"

Her gaze was dubious but hopeful. There was definitely something else going on with her, something he couldn't begin to guess at. It intrigued him, though. He wanted to find out what it was. He wanted to so much, he had the awful feeling he was going to be facing a few more sleepless nights trying to psyche her out.

"Tell you what," he suggested. "Why don't I take Chuck for a walk while you have a look at that contract? Have you got his leash here?"

"You don't have to do that," she said.

Actually, he did. He had to put some distance between her and himself for a few minutes, to regain his balance. He had to give some careful consideration to whether he really wanted to solve the mystery of Beth Pendleton. Would it be worth the effort? Should he commit his time and energy to finding out what made her smile and what made her tick and what made her beautiful blue eyes look so sorrowful sometimes?

He waved toward the file on her desk. "It'll probably take you a while to plow through the Rumson stuff. You don't need me and Chuck distracting you."

She didn't argue. The leash was lying on a shelf behind some cartons, and when she handed it to him she smiled hesitantly. "Thank you," she murmured. She seemed on the verge of saying more, but she only turned from him to the dog. She bent down and rubbed Chuck's back tenderly, as if to buy a little extra insurance that the dog would love her.

"He's going to be fine," Ryan insisted, because she seemed in such desperate need of reassurance. "A little discipline won't scare him away."

Beth peered up at Ryan. "I hope you're right. Some people scare very easily."

Chuck isn't a person, Ryan almost blurted out. *Chuck is a dog.* But then, Ryan already knew that whatever was going on with Beth, it wasn't just about her dog.

Chuck gave a lively bark and jumped at the leash. Ryan clipped it to Chuck's collar, then lifted his gaze to Beth once more. She looked oddly fragile to him, less like a lawyer than like a lost little girl, unsure of where she was or what she was doing.

Evidently aware of Ryan's scrutiny, she forced a smile and returned to her desk, where the Rumson file awaited her. Another, more certain smile communicated that she was ready for Ryan to take the dog and go.

He headed out of the office with Chuck. By the time he reached the front door, his head had cleared. He felt himself escaping from her spell, from the strange aura of sexiness and sorrow that emanated from her. Ryan liked things simple, and he liked his women simple. Beth Pendleton was *not* simple.

He should forget about helping her with her leash and her dog. He should forget about wheedling his way into her life in the hope that he could wheedle his way into her bed. There were other women in the world—even in Devon. Mitzi Rumson sure seemed hot to trot. And if Ryan looked around, he was sure he'd find others.

But he *did* like a challenge. And Beth *did* need some help with the dog.

And damn it, Ryan was never one to run from a dare, especially one that promised such a fine reward if he could stick it out.

So maybe he wouldn't back off from Beth just yet.

CHAPTER FOUR

SHE WOULD SEE him Friday, and she would see him Saturday.

Two plans. Two days in a row. She was already getting nervous.

As she filled Chuck's water dish and set it on the kitchen floor, she recalled a time, not too long ago, when the thought of seeing an appealing man didn't send her into paroxysms of terror. And she wasn't really terrified about meeting with Ryan, she assured herself. She was just...insecure.

The Friday meeting would be business. While Ryan had taken Chuck for a walk that morning, Beth had vetted the Rumson contract he'd signed and decided it needed a major overhaul. Jeff hadn't done a bad job with it, but he didn't know the best way to phrase certain clauses, the best way to stipulate certain protections. As the contract currently stood, Ryan could be held accountable for damages that resulted from Ms. Rumson's transient whims. The woman could ask him to build her a greenhouse on the wrong side of the house, and if he complied with her request and the heating system proved insufficient, he could be required, at his own expense, to install a larger heating system than had been in the original specifications.

Beth wanted to tighten up the contract, but she hadn't been sure Ryan would agree to let her take over. How could he have any faith in her skill as a lawyer when she acted like such a flake around him? Nevertheless, she knew her stuff when it came to contracts. As she'd told Ryan once he and Chuck had returned from their jaunt around the block, "Jeff's good at most things, but contracts aren't his strong point."

"That's what he keeps telling me," Ryan had admitted. "My cousin Larry is in charge of the books at Walker Construction. He found us a lawyer to use down in Manchester because Jeff insisted he wasn't up to it. But the guy in Manchester retired last year, so I forced Jeff to take Walker as a client."

"You forced him?"

"I used threats. I used blackmail. I told him I was going to have a witch place a curse on his unborn child. He's no fool—he came around."

"And promptly offered me a job," Beth had noted, unable to resist Ryan's smile.

"So, you think you can do better with this thing than he could?"

Beth had seen no need for false modesty. "I know I can. As a matter of fact, I wouldn't mind having a look at what this lawyer down in Manchester did for you. If I'm going to represent Walker Construction, I'd like to know what other contract terms you've agreed to."

"Meaning, what other booby traps you're going to have to get us out of." Ryan had grinned. "Sure. Just come on over and tell Larry you want to walk your fingers through the files. Meanwhile, what are we going to do about Mitzi Rumson?"

Ryan had listened to her as she worked her way through the contract, clause by clause, explaining each section she wanted to reword or clarify. Then she'd asked Lynne to set up a time when Beth and Ryan could hammer out a new contract with Ms. Rumson. A meeting had been scheduled for Friday at nine-thirty.

Beth was certain she could handle the meeting. At the firm in New York, she'd hammered together much more complicated agreements, and never had a client complain about a contract she'd negotiated.

But those clients hadn't seen her at her worst. Ryan Walker had.

And he would see her at her worst again on Saturday, when he came to her house to install a runner leash for Chuck. She wouldn't be able to hide behind a contract then. She would be with him as a friend—and as the owner of a dog, which meant she'd probably make a hash of things.

She shouldn't care so much about what Ryan thought of her. This was why she'd adopted Chuck—to have someone she could love without reservation, someone who would return that love without giving a damn about who she was or what she looked like.

She watched as her puppy lapped up his water, splashing droplets onto the floor and making a rhythmic slurping sound with his tongue. The evening was hot and they'd walked more than a mile. She was pretty thirsty herself.

She crossed to the refrigerator and pulled a bottle of mineral water from the top shelf. She briefly considered being civilized and pouring her drink into a glass. Chuck wasn't going to be dazzled by a display of good manners, though, so she took a slug directly from the bottle.

She wished it was a diet cola. She hadn't had one in nearly two years, and she missed the flavor, the fizz and the kick of caffeine. But one of the deals she'd made—with God or with herself, she wasn't sure which—was that she would give up diet **so**da and all its ominous-sounding chemical ingredients if she was allowed to survive. God had done His part; now she had to do hers.

She took another long drink, then screwed the cap back onto the bottle and returned it to the refrigerator. Chuck was still chugalugging his water. He had lost plenty of fluid during their hike, emptying his bladder one tedious squirt at a time throughout the entire walk. She'd once read somewhere that that was how male dogs marked their territory. If that was true, Chuck obviously believed he owned half of Loring Road.

She doubted he had anything left in him, but given the way he was guzzling the water, he would probably want to mark some territory again soon. Too tired to take him for another walk, she spread several sections of newspaper across the floor in one corner and hoped he would limit his marking to the sports and business sections. The floor was a scratched, ugly beige linoleum, and Beth planned to replace it with something nicer once Chuck was potty-trained. But ugly or not, the kitchen floor was *her* territory, and she didn't want Chuck leaving a mess on it the way he had last night. Starting the day with a mop and pail wasn't her idea of fun.

Why in the world had she gotten a dog?

When he lifted his cute little face to her, she knew why. He was so happy, so playful. So enviably uninhibited.

"I'm working on it," she said to Chuck. "I'm trying to be less inhibited, too."

His bark sounded a lot like encouragement to her.

Smiling, she filled his other bowl with dry puppy food, then mixed in some gravy from a jar and what was left of the hamburger she'd cooked for him yesterday. He buried his face in the food, his tail wagging at twice the speed of sound.

She watched him for a moment, then headed out of the kitchen. Her T-shirt was damp with sweat from their brisk walk. With food to distract Chuck, she figured he wouldn't get into any trouble during the few minutes it would take her to shower.

Or if he did, his trouble would be limited to that one room, she assured herself as she closed the kitchen door tightly. It was almost as ugly as the kitchen floor, an old, unevenly stained slab of wood, nicked and dinged near the floor as if someone had kicked it shut on a regular basis. When she got around to redoing the kitchen, she would definitely replace it with a French door.

And she'd add a ceiling fan—or two, one in the kitchen and one in the den. Even with the windows open, the house held the early summer heat, making the air stuffy. She would get one of those broad-bladed fans—like the ones in *Casablanca*—for the den, and for the kitchen something that would match her oak table and chairs. On the other hand, a ceiling fan might blow her napkin off the table. Maybe she'd be better off with another window fan there, like the one in her bedroom. But ceiling fans looked so nice.

She laughed at her newly awakened decorating urges. In New York, she had never bothered to fix up her apartment. Given how much time she'd spent at the office, decorating her apartment hadn't seemed worth the effort. It had merely been an address, a place where she sacked out after a twelve-hour workday.

But in Devon, she could imagine herself transforming her house into a real home, buying a peacock screen for her fireplace, selecting a colorful area rug for the living room, perhaps painting the dining room walls a soothing green. She wasn't sure she had any flair for interior design, but that didn't matter. She had no flair for rearing dogs, either, and that hadn't stopped her from adopting Chuck.

As soon as she entered her bedroom, she raced to the window to turn on the fan. Staring through the window, she surveyed her backyard and thought about her puppy, about Saturday...about Ryan Walker.

She honestly wasn't convinced that he ought to come to her house, but he'd insisted on it. He had pointed out, with irrefutable logic, that she didn't know beans about how to put up a runner leash—indeed, that she didn't know beans about dogs, period.

But if Ryan was her guest, she would have to offer him a drink, and he would come indoors, and there would suddenly be a tall, virile man in her home. He would gaze at her with his devastating brown eyes and smile his rakish smile, and she would remember how he'd felt pressed up against her when she'd nearly fallen off the stepladder and into his arms. She would recall what Cindy said about getting wet with him, and she would wish such a thing could be possible.

It *wasn't* possible. It wouldn't happen, and she was going to have to stop torturing herself about it. Ryan Walker was her client. He had the potential to be her friend, and that was that.

If only he weren't so damned sexy. If only she were a little more sexy. If only her life hadn't taken such a drastic detour two years ago.

Yet if it hadn't, she wouldn't be here. She wouldn't have purchased this charming old house and gotten a dog and needed a runner leash. She wouldn't have met Ryan Walker and had temptation thrown in her path.

Turning from the window, she wriggled out of the T-shirt and denim shorts she'd donned after coming home from work. Once she was showered, she would feel refreshed. None of this would matter.

She removed her bra, slid the prosthetic pad out of the left cup and glimpsed herself in the mirror above her dresser. Over the past year, she had grown accustomed to the way she looked. She rarely hesitated or recoiled from the sight of her lopsided body, her scar, the odd flatness where the disease had been cut away. She had learned to avoid self-pity by viewing the scar as if it were a war wound—and reminding herself that she'd won the war.

Tonight, as she spied her reflection in the silver glass above her dresser, war wounds weren't on her mind. Rather, she stared at herself as a woman. And she didn't like what she saw.

Every other part of her was adequate, she supposed. She actually preferred her hair short, something she would never have realized if it hadn't all fallen out during her chemo treatments. Her face was the same face she'd always had—a bit too lean and angular, but acceptable. Her shoulders were horizontal, her arms and legs thin. As a child, she'd taken ballet lessons for a few years, and her teacher had always exclaimed over the fact that Beth had the perfect build for a ballerina. Unfortunately, she'd been singularly lacking in talent.

All in all, though, it wasn't a bad body. Except for the left half of her chest.

What would a man think if he saw her? Not a medical professional but a *man,* a real man. Peter hadn't stuck around long enough to look at her after her surgery; two weeks after she'd told him her diagnosis, he'd decided he couldn't deal with it—as if dating a woman with breast cancer were more difficult than *being* a woman with breast cancer.

She remembered the women in her support group back in New York talking about how the men in their lives reacted to them. Evelyn's husband was perfect; he still brought her flowers every day and swore she was the most beautiful woman in the world. Tammy's boyfriend rivaled Peter for turkey-of-the-year honors; he'd broken up with her the morning after her surgery. The partners of the other women in the group fell somewhere in the middle—supportive but uneasy, loving the woman but not crazy about her body.

After all, most men in America came of age reading *Playboy*. As teenage virgins, they lived for the chance to grope a girl's bosom in the back seat of a car. As adults, they probably considered push-up bras the greatest invention since penicillin. Breasts were a big deal.

Closing her eyes against the image in the mirror, Beth pictured Ryan. He was funny, he was patient, he had a way of laughing *with* her instead of *at* her, even when she was screwing up—and he was a man. And if the suggestive curve of his smile and the tantalizing glimmer in his eyes told Beth anything, it was that he was a man with ideas.

Of course he would expect a lover to come with a matched set. Beth couldn't blame him. In all honesty, the first thing she'd noticed about him was his physique. If she could be so conscious of his appearance, she couldn't condemn him for taking an interest in hers.

With a sigh, she turned and stalked to the bathroom.

Beth had every hope of living life to the fullest—and that included sex. But a man like Ryan... No. Beth wasn't going to test the waters with him. She wasn't going to give him the chance to turn tail and run the way Peter had. Ryan Walker was never going to see what she'd just seen in the mirror.

For the time being, she thought as she reached into the tub and twisted the faucets, the only way she was going to get wet was by taking a nice, cool shower.

HE ARRIVED at Miller, Miller and Pendleton ten minutes early.

By Friday, Beth had made great strides in her office. All her books had been shelved, her rug laid, her pictures hung. She'd taken on two new clients thanks to the advertisement Jeff and Cindy had placed in the local newspaper announcing the addition of a new real-estate specialist to their firm. And that morning, for the first time all week, she hadn't had to mop the kitchen before coming to work.

Clad in a suit of pearl gray linen, she had passed inspection with Lynne, who stared at her outfit for a long, critical minute and said, "Gray projects authority. I would predict that you were going to have a successful meeting this morning—except that you brought your dog along."

"I've been trying to train him," she apologized, giving Chuck's leash a tug when he zeroed in on his favorite corner of the rug in the reception area, his moist nose sniffing vigorously at the nap. "He actually went twenty-four hours without using my kitchen as a latrine. But I couldn't take a chance on leaving him in my house all day. He'd wreak havoc with the place."

"So you've brought him to wreak havoc here." Lynne clicked her tongue reprovingly.

"Only for today. Tomorrow I'm putting up a runner leash so he can stay outdoors while I'm at work." She didn't bother to go into detail. If she mentioned that it was Ryan who would be putting up the leash, Lynne would work over that news the way Chuck worked over the old wool sock she'd given him to chew on at home. Lynne might salivate just as much as Chuck did, too.

"Well. If you confine him in your office, he might develop claustrophobia. Dogs—particularly those who don't get enough aerobic exercise—can become neurotic in enclosed places. I advise you to tie him up on the porch outside the back door while you have your meeting."

"The porch?" The idea didn't sit well with Beth. What if he broke loose? What if he ran away—or worse, what if he ran into traffic as Ryan had warned?

"I'll do it," Lynne said, less an offer than an order. "I carry some spare rope in my trunk. There's coffee in the conference room, and a pitcher of ice water. Rumson *et alii* are going to be showing up any minute."

Of course Lynne carried spare rope in the trunk of her car. She probably also had a blowtorch in there, as well as a week's supply of canned soup and all thirty volumes of the *Encyclopedia Americana*. Not only did Lynne know everything, but she was prepared for everything.

"Okay." Reluctantly, Beth handed Chuck's leash over and watched as the puppy trotted cheerfully down the hall and out the back door with Lynne. She turned from them in time to see Ryan saunter in through the front door. The sight of him momentarily made her forget all about her dog. If he looked fantastic in a pair of work jeans and a T-shirt, he looked lethally handsome in a jacket and tie.

She thought about the men she used to work with in New York. Compulsively fashionable, they showed up at the office in their elegant suits—Armani if they were younger than fifty, Brooks Brothers if they were older. Their shoes were buffed to a high gloss, their hair manicured, their necks graced with hundred-dollar ties.

Ryan looked nothing like they did—for which Beth was grateful, yet irked. Grateful because he was such a pleasure to look at, and irked for much the same reason.

His jacket was old, an oatmeal tweed, slightly baggy at the elbows and slouching over his broad shoulders. His shirt was a wrinkled brown linen, his striped narrow tie a relic from a previous decade, his trousers khaki and his shoes whipstitched leather moccasins. He had apparently put some effort into parting and styling his hair, but it was still far too long. The effect was of a wicked boy forced against his will to dress up for church.

Perhaps in some past life Beth had had a thing for wicked boys in their Sunday best, because merely looking at Ryan made her blood run hot.

"Hi," he said as casually as if he were standing by his truck in his dusty workclothes. "Are you going to make me rich today?"

She discovered that smiling relaxed her, making her less susceptible to his outrageous good looks. She was his lawyer, nothing more. "I may not make you rich, Ryan, but I'll certainly keep you from going broke," she promised.

"That sounds good. When do we start?"

"As soon as Ms. Rumson gets here. Would you like some coffee?"

"Isn't it Lynne's job to bring us coffee?" he asked, following her into the conference room. "Or is serving coffee beneath her?"

"Lynne is taking care of Chuck," Beth confessed.

"He's here?"

"He's outside with her. She's tying him up on the back porch. I would have left him home, but I didn't think he could handle it. Or maybe it's my house that couldn't handle it."

"After this weekend, leaving him home won't be a problem," Ryan said, shoving his hands in his pockets and sending her an unnervingly personal smile, one that reminded her he would be coming to her house, spending a morning with her, being alone with her.

Unbelievable. There she was, thirty-two years old, a veteran of one of the top New York law firms, a triumphant survivor of several kinds of hell, and she was afraid to attempt pouring a cup of coffee because Ryan's sensual smile made her palms slick with sweat. She felt less like the legal eagle she was than like a smitten schoolgirl who'd somehow wound up alone in the supply room with the class hunk.

She was supposed to be composed around him today. She was supposed to dazzle him with her confidence and expertise. Saturday she could act like a giddy fool with him, but not today.

Collecting her wits, she crossed to the sideboard, a beautiful mahogany built-in dating back to the conference room's previous incarnation as a formal dining room. After drying her hands discreetly on a paper napkin, she placed a cup on a saucer, lifted the coffee-pot—and nearly spilled it when she was jolted by Cindy's chipper voice shouting a greeting from the doorway. "Ryan Walker, look at you! Don't you look spiffy today!"

Beth repressed a twinge of envy that Cindy could behave so breezily with Ryan Walker when she herself was suffering from a terminal case of the jitters. She carefully set down the coffeepot and turned to greet her friend. "Hi, Cindy. Where are you off to?"

Cindy rolled her eyes. "I've got to put asunder what God has brought together. A divorce case." She augmented her eye-rolling with a bit of nose-wrinkling. "I hate divorces. I always want to grab the client by the shoulders and shake her hard."

"You don't sound too sympathetic," Ryan commented, sharing a smile with Beth.

"I can't help it if I lose patience with these people. They marry in haste and repent at leisure, or whatever the saying is. I really wish people would think before they made the commitment and messed up their lives." She shook her head, then allowed herself a brief grin. "Then again, I get paid very nicely to clean up their messes."

"Well, you tell that daughter of yours that if she agrees to marry me, I won't divorce *her*," Ryan said. "I'm willing to wait for her if she'll have me."

"You're going to have to stand in line, just like every other man who meets her," Cindy predicted. "She's going to break hearts. I can tell. She's already got Jeff wrapped around her little finger."

"She's got me wrapped around her other little finger. What do you think, Beth?" Ryan asked. "Don't you think Erica and I make a great couple?"

"It sounds like cradle-robbing to me," Beth muttered, finding it hard to join in their banter. It wasn't that she was jealous of Cindy's baby daughter—that would be absurd. But she sensed a strategy behind Ryan's teasing. He was hinting that he was a romantic, a suitor, one half of a potentially great couple. He was reminding her that he was a man who was keenly aware of women.

Faking a smile, she addressed Cindy. "Do you have time for a cup of coffee before you leave?"

"No. Gotta run. You two have fun now, okay?" Cindy winked and vanished from the doorway, a blur of navy silk, fluffy hair and leather briefcase.

Thanks a heap! Beth wanted to shout after her. It was bad enough that she was so conscious of the fact that she was alone in a room with a man who looked good enough to make the word *celibate* miraculously disappear from most standard dictionaries. She didn't need Cindy to remind her of the kind of fun a woman could have with a man like him.

She commanded herself to remain poised. "Cream or sugar?" she asked, filling a cup with coffee for him.

"No, thanks."

"Why don't you have a seat while I go get my files?" She lifted the cup and turned, nearly flinching when she discovered him standing right behind her, much too close.

When he took the cup from her, his hand brushed hers and she again had to stifle the impulse to flinch. She remembered the way their hands had touched yesterday, when she had inspected the skin of his wrist. Suddenly she wanted to take his hand in hers and examine it again.

For heaven's sake. She wasn't used to acting like a ninny, getting all worked up over the thought of touching. "I'll go get my files," she repeated, desperate to escape from his enigmatic smile, his coffee-colored eyes, his fresh-lime scent.

She hurried out of the conference room.

In her own office, she leaned against her desk and took a few deep breaths—in through her nose, out through her mouth, the way the social worker who led her support group in New York had trained her. "You've all been through a great deal of stress," she'd explained, "and you need to learn how to purge yourselves of tension. It's part of the healing, part of what gives you the strength to reclaim your lives. Inhale...hold your breath...exhale."

Beth inhaled, held her breath, exhaled. Slowly the anxiety drained from her body. She was a lawyer again, a mature professional, an advocate about to draw up a new contract for a client. *Okay,* she murmured to herself. *Don't panic. You're all right.*

She lifted her files and laptop from the desk, took one last deep breath and strode out of her office feeling reasonably composed. She entered the conference room, where Ryan stood near one of the open windows, talking through the screen. "Hey there, big guy—remember me? Of course you do!"

"Is Chuck over there?" Beth asked, setting her paraphernalia on the conference table and frowning. "I thought Lynne said she was going to tie him up on the back porch."

"She gave him a lot of rope. It's almost as good as a runner leash."

Beth approached the window and peered out. Sure enough, her puppy had stretched the rope to its limit—which placed him almost directly under the window. Seeing her, he let out a joyful bark.

"Sorry, Chuck," she told him. "You've got to stay out there."

He barked again, letting her know in no uncertain terms that he didn't agree. But she was bigger than he was—at least temporarily, she thought as her gaze dropped to his gigantic paws—and for now she was the boss.

With grim determination, she turned her back on her beloved puppy. Guilt nibbled at her, but she didn't make the mistake of turning back to him. If she did, he would look at her with his sad, glistening puppy eyes and she would probably wind up climbing through the window to rescue him.

Lynne materialized in the doorway. "Ms. Rumson and her lawyer, Mr. Beebe, are here."

"Please show them in," Beth said, walking away from the window and ignoring Chuck's aria of whines and moans.

She sent Ryan a smile that said, *Don't worry, this is going to be a piece of cake,* and strolled toward the table. She uncoiled the power cord for her laptop, bent over to plug it into the socket near the floor, straightened up and saw Mitzi Rumson looming in the doorway. A good measure of her confidence drained away once more.

Mitzi Rumson was...daunting. She was statuesque, she was lush and she was dressed in a tailored hot pink suit, the skirt of which ended several risqué inches above the knee. The jacket was held shut by a sash belt, and as far as Beth could tell, Mitzi wasn't wearing anything under it. Not a blouse, not a camisole, not a bra. Nothing but Obsession, which wafted up from her deep cleavage in aromatic fumes.

Beth dragged her gaze from Ms. Rumson's chest. A strand of perfectly matched pearls, each a half inch in diameter, circled her neck. Matching pearls, enhanced with chunks of diamond, tipped her ears. The necklace and earrings alone would be enough to finance the addition of a solarium to her house.

Beth arranged her mouth into a courteous smile and extended her right hand. "Ms. Rumson? I'm Beth Pendleton, Mr. Walker's attorney. Please come in."

Mitzi Rumson slipped a silky hand into Beth's. "So very pleased," she said, her voice only marginally less husky than Beth had expected. "This is Herman Beebe, my attorney from Boston. Hermie? Come meet Ryan's new attorney."

Apparently most of the participants were already on a first-name basis. Beth didn't mind. Margaret Rumson's nickname suited her perfectly.

Herman Beebe's name suited him, too. He was tall, thin and bland, tilting toward sixty, his complexion almost as gray as his hair. "How do you do?" he said as he shook hands with Beth. Then he shook hands with Ryan. When Ryan turned to greet Mitzi, she kissed his cheek.

Ryan shot Beth a quick look. She labored hard not to let her irritation show. She suspected that by the time she was done reworking the contract in Ryan's favor, Mitzi wouldn't be in much of a kissing mood.

Lynne followed Mitzi and Herman Beebe into the conference room and busied herself at the sideboard, pouring coffee. Then the foursome arranged themselves around the table, the two lawyers squaring off and Mitzi facing Ryan. Perhaps Beth was only imagining it, but Mitzi seemed to position herself deliberately to afford Ryan a clear view of the gap where her jacket lapels intersected.

Of course Beth was imagining it, she chastised herself. Mitzi's perfume might be Obsession, but breasts were Beth's obsession. Even before Beth had had her original equipment reduced by half, she had never been in Mitzi's league.

That went for the rest of Mitzi, as well. The woman was astonishing, her hips deliciously curved, her waist marvelously trim and her face aggressively gorgeous. Compared to her, Beth's appearance was as bland as Herman Beebe's.

She couldn't believe she was letting herself get hung up on something as irrelevant as Mitzi's breathtaking beauty. Even as a typically insecure teenager, Beth had never wasted time comparing herself with other girls and fretting over where she fell short. Self-inflicted ego-battering had never been her hobby.

Now she was in a law office, in her element, prepared to do what she did best—and she was shriveling inside from insecurity. No one—not even Mitzi Rumson—should be able to do this to her.

Mitzi wasn't doing anything, Beth acknowledged grimly. Her insecurity was caused by Ryan, seated beside her but gazing only at the magnificent woman across the table from him, his dark eyes just sleepy enough to put Beth in mind of beds and sex. Ryan, with his unfashionable clothing, his long hair and his roguish smile directed at Mitzi, was the one who disturbed her most.

The hell with it—and with him. She would satisfy his legal needs. Mitzi could satisfy any other needs he might have.

"Well," Beth said crisply, as Lynne distributed cups of coffee around the table. "Shall we get started? This contract—"

"This contract was entered into by your client," Herman Beebe said. His voice was as dry as sawdust. Listening to it made Beth itch. "There's no reason to rewrite it."

"It has to be rewritten because Ms. Rumson has requested alterations in her building plans, and these alterations weren't covered by the original contract."

"The original contract has several clauses that call for alterations in the design," Beebe insisted.

"Minor alterations. Not alterations that, in the long run, are going to cause a significant devaluation of the property. My client needs to protect himself from liability for that devaluation."

"He signed this contract," Beebe persisted, waving his copy of the original document at Beth. The gesture was dramatic, but his voice remained soft and scratchy.

"Now, Hermie," Mitzi purred. "If we have to redo the contract, we'll redo it. It's no big deal."

Beebe scowled. "I'm sure you could find another builder who wouldn't renege on a contract he signed of his own free will."

"I don't want another builder," Mitzi said, pouting and turning to Ryan. In an unnervingly sultry voice, she said, "I want Ryan."

Beth coughed. The corners of Ryan's mouth twitched upward. Through the screened window behind her came a plaintive howl.

"Oh, my lord!" Mitzi jumped to her feet. "There's an animal out there!"

"That's just Chuck," Ryan told her.

"Chuck?" Mitzi pressed a hand to her throat and gasped. "A *man* made a sound like that? He must be hurt!" She stalked around the table, surefooted in her towering high heels.

Beth rose from her chair, also alarmed at the sound her poor, tethered pet was making. "Chuck is my dog," she explained, joining Mitzi at the window and trying not to choke on the woman's overpowering perfume.

Seeing the two women, Chuck let out an excited bark. "Oh, look at him!" Mitzi cooed, pursing her lips and batting her eyes. "He's so cute! Isn't he a little lovey! Hello, there, my sweet!" She waved at him through the screen.

Naturally, Chuck fell in love with her. He immediately lapsed into his aren't-I-adorable? routine, making his eyes shimmer with moisture, cocking his head, flexing his ears and whipping his tail back and forth.

"Do you want to come in? Does Chuckie want to come inside and be with Aunt Mitzi?" Mitzi offered.

"He's not trained yet," Beth warned.

"Oh, that's okay. I don't mind messy little boys as long as they're cute. And you're so cute!" she murmured through the screen. "Let's get you inside here so you can help me and Hermie make a good contract, okay?"

Beth bit her lip. If she fought Mitzi on this, Mitzi would fight her on the contract. And frankly, Beth would prefer not to have Chuck tied up with a rope like a criminal heading for the gallows. "I'll have Lynne bring him in," she said at last, turning from the window.

On her way to the door to summon the secretary, she caught Ryan's eye. He was still smiling indolently, still looking unbearably handsome.

This time, however, the full force of his seductive gaze was on Beth, as if she were the only woman in the room, the only one he saw. As if she were the only woman who mattered.

CHAPTER FIVE

HE COULDN'T TAKE his eyes off her.

She was incredible. Phenomenal. Sexier than any straitlaced, business-minded lawyer had a right to be.

The negotiations had gone on for more than an hour, and Ryan still hadn't grown tired of watching Beth do her thing. She exhibited no flash, no fury—just the sort of composure that made a man want to burrow beneath her poise and find out what she could be like when she let go.

She wasn't letting go at this meeting. Mitzi was doing her usual razzle-dazzle, batting her eyes, pursing her full pink lips and imploring her own lawyer to get her some more coffee at regular intervals, then telling him, "I really like that clause, Hermie. I really don't think that clause is going to hurt me." For his part, Hermie appeared long-suffering and utterly ineffectual, although he poured coffee nicely.

And of course there was Chuck. Lynne had put up a bit of a fuss when Beth asked her to bring in the dog, and she'd delivered an uninvited lecture on medieval courts, which she claimed used to be held in grand public halls with beasts roaming about and clumps of straw and animal droppings scattered across the stone floors. "We've come a long way since then—but evidently some of us haven't come far enough," she'd muttered before literally unleashing Chuck into the conference room.

Chuck had zoomed straight toward Mitzi, who had immediately taken him into her lap. He'd sniffed her skirt, planted his paws on her shoulders and given her a slobbery kiss on the chin. In her chair beside Ryan, Beth had tensed up, coiled to spring at her puppy. But Mitzi hadn't minded Chuck's crude behavior one bit. On the contrary, she seemed quite taken with him. "Well, aren't you the cutest!" she'd gushed.

"I'm sorry," Beth had murmured. "He needs training."

"All little boys do," Mitzi knowingly observed, causing Hermie to harrumph and Beth to smile wanly. "Some little boys are easier to train than others. How about you?" she'd cooed to Chuck. "Are you trainable or are you going to grow up to be a wild thing?"

"He already is a wild thing," Hermie had grumbled.

Mitzi gave Hermie her well-practiced pout and lowered Chuck to the floor. "Okay. I guess I shouldn't waste time, since I'm paying you by the hour. Now, where were we?"

With a slight shake of her head, Beth had returned to the contract. Bored by the legal chitchat, Chuck had spent the remainder of the morning roaming restlessly around the conference room, tunneling under Ryan's legs, rolling over and rubbing his back on the rug, whimpering and panting and hovering near the window as if he wanted to go back outside again.

"I think he's thirsty," Mitzi remarked after a while. "Maybe we should get him a drink."

"I'll get him some water just as soon as we finish up," Beth promised, keeping her focus on the contract. Ryan had seen her preoccupied by Chuck before—and by Ryan himself—but when she was doing her lawyer bit, nothing could shake her concentration. No one could accuse her of being a softie today.

Ryan's thoughts roamed restlessly, like Chuck, nosing here, nosing there, trying to get a handle on things. Just as Chuck shuttled back and forth between Mitzi and Beth, bypassing Hermie, so Ryan's thoughts shuttled between the two women.

If anyone was a softie, it was Mitzi, lavishing affection on Chuck as if he were an extraordinary specimen of caninehood. Mitzi was soft in appearance, too, all curves and swerves, her hair loose and luxuriant. If an alien dropped in from another galaxy and asked Ryan to define the term *feminine,* Ryan wouldn't have to do anything more than point to Mitzi.

But to his surprise, he was much more intrigued by Beth's hardheaded approach to the negotiations. For some reason, her single-mindedness turned him on. Ryan had never had a taste for achievement-oriented Yuppies with fancy diplomas. He was a mellow guy. He liked his lady friends mellow, too, and yet...

Maybe it was the way Beth's fingers tapped so purposefully on the keys of her laptop, or the way the narrow bridge of her nose wrinkled when she frowned over a phrase in the contract. Or the way the slender column of her throat vanished into the high neck of her blouse, leaving him to contemplate what he couldn't see, just as her long skirt had enticed him to imagine her legs the first time he'd met her. Maybe it was the fact that, even though she was running this meeting like a skilled pilot flying through a storm, she gave Chuck's belly a rub with her toe every time he wandered close to her shoes. The notion that she could be working her toes in one direction while she worked her mind in another did funny things to Ryan's equilibrium, to say nothing of his libido.

She entered more information into her laptop, then flipped the page on her copy of the original contract. "Just a few more items to review here."

"You know, Beth, this clause here, on the top of page six—" Mitzi tapped a long scarlet fingernail against her copy of the contract "—I think we really ought to leave it as is. It's just about insurance, right?"

"It has to do with liabilities."

"Yes, but it seems to me..." Mitzi's smile sparkled more brilliantly than her diamond-studded earrings. "Well, Ryan has his insurance and I have mine, and I don't really see what difference it makes how much insurance I have. I mean, my insurance is my business. Why should Ryan have anything to do with it?"

"If there's a problem attributable to design changes you imposed on Ryan, your insurance company can hound Ryan's insurance company for reimbursement. Even if your company covers it, Ryan has to protect himself, too. The insurance companies work with each other, hammer out settlements between themselves and then turn around and raise their clients' rates."

"Well, I could fix things with my insurance company so they wouldn't do that, couldn't I?" She blinked innocently at Hermie, who stirred himself to consciousness and perused the clause she was referring to.

Ryan wondered if she was paying Hermie as much as he was paying Beth. Probably more, given the way she liked to throw her money around. As far as Ryan could tell, Hermie wasn't worth a dime unless Mitzi really liked having someone else pour her coffee for her.

Having had his fill of belly-scratching, Chuck sank fully onto Beth's foot, rested his head on his paws and sighed audibly. Ryan suffered a twinge of envy. He wouldn't mind nestling against Beth himself—although her foot wouldn't be the particular part of her anatomy he'd like to cuddle up to.

Why was he obsessing on Beth? Why not Mitzi? It wasn't just brain power—Mitzi was obviously a smart woman, although she wielded her intelligence differently from Beth. And it wasn't beauty, because Mitzi had beauty to spare. So why would Ryan feel drawn to the same woman as Chuck? Why was the prim blond woman at his side making him go quietly insane?

She was a mystery. She kept things hidden behind her conservative apparel and her enigmatic gaze. She was clearly competent, yet awfully easy to rattle. She doted on her dog, yet reigned supreme during a contract negotiation. When she smiled at Ryan, her smile seemed to say *yes* and *no* simultaneously. Sometimes it said *I don't know.* Sometimes *I'm interested.* Sometimes *I'm afraid.*

"I think you can live with this," she was telling him, and he shoved his ruminations to the back of his mind and paid attention to her words, trying not to let the motions of her lips distract him as she explained the warranties. He knew what the clauses said, more or less, but Jeff had never gone into such detail with him. "I've rewritten the heating guarantees to accommodate the solarium addition as well as this section on the possibility of the pipes to the outdoor hot tub freezing."

"I'm going to have to sleep on this," Mitzi announced, folding her copy of the contract. "I never commit to anything unless I've spent a night in bed with it. You can learn so much about your own feelings and instincts from a night in bed, don't you think, Beth?"

Beth sent Mitzi one of her faint smiles. To Ryan's great pleasure, Mitzi's remark had made her blush. Another contradiction to add to his list. Beth was clever and savvy, a city-experienced lawyer, yet sexual innuendoes knocked her out of whack.

Chuck emitted a snore, causing Beth to laugh and slide her foot out from under him. "If he can't stay awake through this, he'll never make a good lawyer," she joked.

"I think he's wonderful," Mitzi said. She leaned over, her jacket barely containing her bosom as she viewed the slumbering puppy under the table. "You're so lucky to have him, Beth. I travel around too much, what with the house in Boca and the lodge on Lake Winnipesaukee and the town house in Louisburg Square.... I suppose I could get one of those silly little lap dogs and carry him around with me, but then people might get the impression that I'm just a ditzy widow." She trilled a laugh.

Ryan wasn't sure whether he was supposed to smile. He glanced at Hermie, who seemed to be suffering from acute indigestion. Then he heard a low, throaty laugh to his left, that same sexy laugh he'd heard from Beth once before. That deep, soul-stirring laugh that turned his imagination into an X-rated drama with Beth Pendleton as its star.

He assessed her with his gaze. Her laughter harmonized with Mitzi's, and her smile reflected the other woman's. It was almost as if they were sharing a private joke, something about the relationship between single women and dogs, and maybe men.

Ryan wished Beth would let him in on the secret, but it was just one more mystery, one more unfathomable clue about who she was and what made her tick. Just one more scrap for him to work over like a dog, sniffling and probing and chewing on it until he could figure out what it was.

Nonmysterious women were easier. They offered simple pleasures and didn't put his stability at risk. They didn't tax his brain or tamper with his heart.

But for some reason, Ryan wanted to solve the mystery.

He wanted Beth.

"I THOUGHT YOU SAID it was like a clothesline on pulleys," she said, watching as Ryan pulled from the bed of his truck a spool of what appeared to be flattened electrical wire. She hovered at the head of the driveway, her hands shoved into the hip pockets of her denim shorts and her mind slipping and tripping in a frantic scramble for confidence.

Yesterday at work, she'd had plenty of confidence. That Mitzi Rumson looked as if she'd arisen fullfledged from the pages of a *Victoria's Secret* catalog hadn't fazed Beth once she'd gotten over the shock of the woman's appearance.

In truth, Beth had liked Mitzi, despite her intimidating pulchritude. Anyone who made a fuss over Chuck was all right with Beth. And Mitzi, for all her flamboyance, was a lot smarter than she seemed. Beth could have been proud of the way she had steamrolled Mitzi's attorney, except that Mitzi had obviously steamrolled the poor man long ago.

But this morning Beth couldn't hide behind her legal acumen. Today wasn't about contracts and warranties; it was about Beth and Ryan alone at her house, and that made her nervous. And excited. And a lot less confident than she'd like to be.

He had on a pair of jeans worn to a soft powder blue, a clean black T-shirt and scuffed leather sneakers. The outfit made him look too young, too frisky—a human version of Chuck, and capable of a great deal more damage than her puppy.

She should have worn long pants, she thought, gazing down at the pallor of her thin, sun-deprived calves. Or else shorter shorts. The knee-length denim shorts she had on looked safe and dull, exactly what a woman who was hot but timid would wear. Her sleeveless cotton blouse was cut high at the neck. She remembered Mitzi's curve-clinging pink jacket and smiled ruefully. Beth would never wear an outfit like that, not in this lifetime.

Chuck erupted in hysterical barking at the sight of Ryan. He stretched and strained at his leash, the loop of which circled her wrist. She had to clench her fist in her pocket to keep him from tugging free and leaping into Ryan's arms.

Not that Ryan would have caught him if he did. "I've got all kinds of goodies," he reported, reaching over the tailgate of his truck and pulling out a skein of clothesline and a couple of aluminum-and-plastic pulleys. "A runner leash, as ordered, and this electric fence. I was thinking about it and I realized this may work out better for you." He lifted a bulky metal tool case from the bed of the truck, then arranged his gear in his arms and sauntered up the gravel driveway.

"An electric fence?"

He tap-danced around the scrambling dog, his gaze trained on her house. "Boy, that's a solid piece of construction, isn't it?"

"I hope so." She smiled tentatively. "I wouldn't like it to fall down around my head."

"Last time I saw this house up close was about five years ago, when an acquaintance of mine was installing the wood stove in the den. I had some extra flashing from a house I was working on at the time, and I sold it to him at cost. It was a good stove he installed. I'll bet it really keeps the den toasty."

"I wouldn't know," she said. "It's June. Cooling the house has been more important than heating it."

"Right." He laughed, a relaxed, genial laugh that rolled soothingly over her. "Anyway, I remember noticing that this place was built like a brick sh—a brick outhouse," he amended, shooting her a smile that was less than apologetic. "There's always a lot of maintenance on an older house, but at least you won't have major overhauls. Stop chomping on my toes," he scolded Chuck, who grinned up at him and then resumed sniffing around his sneakers.

"He's a male," Beth joked. "He doesn't listen."

"Some men listen," Ryan protested.

"Name one." She gave the leash a sharp yank.

"Hermie Beebe."

She couldn't argue that. "Herman Beebe listened to Mitzi Rumson. I imagine most men would listen to her."

"Any man who didn't..." Ryan grinned. "Well, if I know Mitzi, she would probably put a choke chain around his neck and pull hard."

Choke chains. Electric fences. Ropes and pulleys. Beth wished someone had pulled hard on her before she'd fallen in love with Chuck. Learning how to keep him under control seemed more challenging than passing the bar exam. "What exactly is this electric fence, Ryan? I hope it isn't like those fences they use on the cattle ranges out west, to keep the cows from straying."

"Actually, that's the basic idea. I don't know if it's going to work here—"

"It's *not* going to work," she declared, shaking her head for emphasis. "I'm not going to have a big metal fence surrounding my property, Ryan. Especially one with a million volts of electricity running through it."

Ryan was laughing. "The fence is buried. It's just this wire. We'd bury it a couple of inches under the ground, so you wouldn't even see it."

"Then what good would it do? How would it keep Chuck from running away?"

"He would wear a special collar. If he crosses the underground wire, the collar emits a tiny shock."

Aghast, Beth halted. "A shock?"

"It's just a little pinch. Barely that. Just enough to keep him within the perimeter of the fence."

"You want to electrocute my dog," she accused.

"I want to keep your dog from running away and getting himself killed. He'd have a lot more room to move with the electric fence than with a runner leash," Ryan explained, strolling around to the rear of the house. He studied the small back porch for a moment, then surveyed the yard, assessing the scattered trees and the scruffy grass. He returned his gaze to the back porch. "A deck," he murmured.

"What?"

"You need a deck. Something nice and big. That door goes into the kitchen, doesn't it?"

Chuck zigged and zagged in front Ryan, wrenching Beth's wrist every time he stretched the leash. Ryan's visit was supposed to be about him, and his energies seemed fully devoted to making sure the human beings remembered that.

Beth had tried to prepare herself for the possibility that Ryan's visit might also be about her. She recognized that Ryan couldn't mean much by his playful flirting—in a world where women like Mitzi Rumson existed, Beth didn't expect to occupy center stage in Ryan Walker's dreams. But she sensed a friendship developing between them, and she had assumed that his visit this morning might have something to do with that.

She'd never considered the possibility that Ryan was going to get all excited about her house, but he was definitely excited. "Picture it, Beth. A fifteen-by-twenty-foot deck off the back of your kitchen." He sketched his vision in the air with his hands, somehow managing not to drop the assorted tools and equipment he'd unloaded from his truck. "You could put out a picnic table and chairs and eat alfresco."

"I thought we were going to install a runner leash," she said lamely.

"Better yet, a screened porch. Then you could eat outdoors rain or shine."

"I've got a kitchen and a dining room. Why would I want to eat outdoors?"

"Because the air in Devon is clean and it smells good, and outdoors is a great place to be." He glanced at her and laughed. "Sorry. I guess I'm like a sculptor, you know? I see a lump of clay and I want to play with it."

"My house isn't a lump of clay," she protested, although in spite of herself she could visualize the deck he'd described, extending off the rear of her house and overlooking the outlying woods.

Chuck demanded Ryan's attention with a loud bark. "Okay," Ryan acquiesced. "We'll stick to the runner leash for now. Or the electric fence. I still think that's a better bet."

"Will it hurt Chuck?"

"No more than this." Ryan reached out and gave her forearm a gentle pinch. It didn't hurt. In fact, it felt more like a caress than a pinch. She stared at her skin where he'd touched her, surprised that he hadn't left a mark.

"It's just enough to keep a dog safe," Ryan emphasized.

Beth lifted her eyes from her forearm and met his dark, searing gaze. He was less than a foot from her, watching her, tall and strong and absurdly attractive.

I'm not a dog, she almost blurted out. *I don't want to be safe.*

But she did want to be safe. She didn't want to cross any boundaries, electric or otherwise, with Ryan. It wouldn't be worth the risk. Ryan might enjoy flirting with her, but he wouldn't want anything to do with her if he knew the reason she wore high-necked loose-fitting shirts. Beth didn't resent him for that; she simply accepted it. It was the way things were. And she saw no point in crossing the fence deliberately if she was only going to get an electric shock.

"It seems to me," she said brightly, "that it would take an awful lot of wire to fence in my entire property."

Ryan nodded. "I was figuring we'd only fence in an area in the back, maybe half an acre or so. That would still give Chuck more room to run than the runner leash. He'd have shade, he'd have sun, he could chase squirrels and you could leave his water dish under the deck."

"I don't have a deck," she said, then laughed.

"Stick with me, kid, and you could have a great deck," he said. "I'd do a better job building one for you than anyone else. Guaranteed."

Abruptly, it dawned on her that his visit today might not be about friendship, either. It might about business. All her anxiety about his suggestive humor and his seductive smile was unnecessary. He'd come to her house to earn some money on a Saturday morning.

She felt like an idiot. What brainless impulse had led her to think anything personal existed between her and Ryan? "How much is this going to cost?" she asked, ducking her head when she felt her cheeks heat with embarrassment.

"For a good deck? I'd have to take measurements, and I only work with pressure-treated wood, top-grade materials. But—"

"No. I meant for the fence. For putting in the fence."

He tore his gaze from her back porch to look at her. Morning sunlight edged the sharp contours of his face, giving his features a rugged angularity. His brow dipped in a frown. "Don't be silly. I got this stuff—" he waved the spool of wire "—for free. A supplier owed me for a favor, and I collected."

She felt progressively more uncomfortable. "Surely your labor must be worth something."

"Surely my labor is worth the sun and the moon and the stars. But you're not paying for it, Beth."

She wasn't going to accept charity from him. "Why not?"

He dropped his gear onto the grass and clamped his hands on her upper arms. "Hel-*lo?* Are we operating on different planets here? I said I was going to do this for you."

"Why? I'm making you pay for my legal services."

"Walker Construction Company is paying for your legal services, sweetheart. Not me. And Walker Construction would be building your deck—if you come to your senses and hire us to do it. But this—" he gestured toward the spool of wire and the tool box at his feet "—is Ryan Walker doing something nice for Beth Pendleton. Actually," he added when Chuck started sniffing around the toolbox, "I'm doing it for Beth Pendleton's rambunctious puppy. Are we clear on this?"

His words were clear. Even clearer was the way the warmth of his large, hard hands spread up her arms to her shoulders, and from there through her body. What was clearest of all was that even though his touch meant nothing, Beth responded much too powerfully to it, feeling his heat resonate deep inside her.

"Okay," he said, releasing her and bending down to inventory his tools. "We're going high-tech, correct?"

"If you're sure it won't hurt Chuck." The instant he'd removed his hands from her, her arms felt chilled. She wanted to rub her skin, to regenerate the warmth.

"Chuck," he assured her, "is going to be thrilled to death that he can run around outside without getting lost or hit by a car. Trust me, Beth—Chuck is going to love this gizmo. Aren't you, Chuck?" He gave the dog a playful scratch behind the ears. Chuck gave him a sappy smile.

Fine, Beth thought. Let Chuck swoon at Ryan's touch. Beth was going to work on building her resistance to the man.

"What would you like me to do?" she asked, feeling irrelevant as Ryan started to pace the perimeter of the backyard, mentally mapping out the fence.

"Right now?" He didn't even look at her as he kicked the heel of his shoe into the soft earth, marking a path. "Why don't you make a pitcher of iced tea? I intend to get very thirsty."

Perfect. She would go inside and prepare iced tea. She would stay out of his way, as far from him as she could so he wouldn't have any need to imply that they had a personal relationship.

She tied a loop with Chuck's leash around one of the vertical posts of the small back porch and left him outside so he could watch his idol at work. Then she went into the kitchen. Within minutes she was banging the cabinet doors, jerking the sink's faucets, smacking the ice-cube tray against the counter as if she were trying to kill bugs. Several of the ice cubes broke free and skidded down the counter, into the sink.

Calm down, she cautioned herself. *Deep breaths.*

She was not going to let Ryan get to her. She was not going to let him stir feelings in her that might lead her away from safety. Despite her brief, impulsive fantasy of rejecting safety, she wasn't ready to cross the line and risk emotional electrocution.

She had come to Devon to heal, not to hurt. As long as she was nothing more than Ryan's friend, he wouldn't be able to hurt her. She wasn't going to make herself vulnerable to shocks, electric or otherwise.

An hour later, Ryan was sweating.

She watched from the kitchen window as he chiseled a crevice around the backyard and buried the wire in it, one yard at a time. His hair hung damp around his glistening face, and his shirt was pasted to his back, revealing its supple lines. He'd fetched a spade from his truck, and she observed the arch of his spine as he jammed the tip of the shovel into the soil again and again, his biceps bulging as he carved a groove to lay the wire in.

She'd gone outside several times and asked if he needed any help. The first time he'd said no; the second, he'd asked if she could bring him a glass of water. "I made iced tea," she'd told him, and he'd grinned and mopped his dripping brow and mumbled that knowing there was iced tea waiting for him at the end of the job was the only thing that kept him going.

So, he was doing it not for her but for a glass of iced tea. He was perspiring and flexing his muscles and unwittingly putting on quite a show . . . and all he wanted from Beth was a glass of iced tea.

She tried to convince herself that iced tea was all she wanted to give him. But, watching Ryan as he worked— the way his body stretched and arched—was the most erotic thing she'd done in quite some time.

She was on her way to the back door to ask him yet again if she could assist him when her telephone rang. She lifted the receiver from the wall phone and positioned herself so she could continue spying on him from the window above the sink while she spoke. "Hello?"

"Hi," Cindy's voice sang through the wire. "How's it going?"

Beth smiled. She knew what Cindy was really asking. How was Ryan's visit going? Evidently she couldn't wait for Beth to call her with a full report.

"Everything's fine," Beth said noncommittally. "And how are you?"

"Fine, just fine."

"Fine" was stretching the truth a bit. Through the wire, Beth could hear Erica wailing as loudly as a police siren. "What's wrong with the baby?" Beth asked.

"Oh, the usual. Jeff is diapering her. He's diaper-challenged, you know."

"She sounds frantic."

"What you're hearing is the soundtrack of my life. But enough about me. Let's talk about you."

"Let's not."

"Is Ryan still there? Is he making the world safe for Chuck?"

"He's trying. Chuck is gaga about him, you know." Indeed, her puppy had made nothing but happy sounds since Beth had left him to keep Ryan company.

"Then maybe Chuck's a she after all. Or maybe Chuck's gay."

"Chuck is gaga about anyone who strokes his belly."

"Aren't we all." Cindy laughed. "If you haven't got any plans, I was thinking, maybe you and Ryan could come over here for dinner tonight."

"Me and Ryan?" Beth groaned. "Just curious, Cindy—does that invitation apply only if it's the two of us? If I want to come alone, do I get uninvited?"

Cindy sounded affronted. "Of course not! I would never uninvite you. If you want to come alone, come alone." She paused, then added mischievously, "Of course, if Jeff just happens to invite Ryan to come over alone, too, don't blame me."

Beth let out a long breath. Ryan had yanked his shirt completely off, giving her a breathtaking view of his streamlined back, from his broad shoulders to his trim hips. His skin was the color of brandy, gold hued and intoxicating. If Beth had the slightest instinct for self-preservation, she would close her eyes.

Clearly she lacked that particular instinct. Her gaze remained riveted to him as he used the shirt to swab the nape of his neck and under his chin. Then he shook it out and pulled it back on, shoving his hands through the sleeves and letting it hang free of his jeans. It took enormous willpower for her not to hang up on Cindy and race outside to assure him that he didn't need to exercise modesty around *her*.

With a mixture of reluctance and annoyance, she spun away from the window. One tantalizing glimpse of his beautiful torso was enough to remind her that Ryan was out of her class, beyond her reach . . . too flawless. "Don't do me any favors, Cindy," she said into the phone. "Don't play matchmaker, okay?"

"I invited you to come to dinner, not to an orgy."

"You invited *us*. Not me, *us*. That doesn't work for me."

"You're a stick-in-the-mud."

Maybe so, but she just wasn't ready for this. She'd thought she was when she left New York to take up a new address and a new life in New Hampshire. She'd thought she was ready to start over, or to pick up where she'd left off, to stop being a patient and to start being a woman once more.

But not with Ryan. She had healed a lot, but if she was going to begin dating again, it ought to be with someone a little less intimidatingly perfect. "Thanks, anyway," she murmured into the phone. "I think I'll pass on dinner tonight."

"It was just a thought," Cindy said, unrepentant. Erica let out a howl so lusty Beth flinched. "Uh-oh. It sounds as if Jeff is in over his head."

"You'd better go rescue my godchild from his evil clutches."

"Oh, no!" Cindy erupted in laughter. "The box of wet wipes just broke. There are wet wipes all over the floor. I'll be right there, Jeffrey!" she shouted to her husband. "Don't panic!"

Beth heard Jeff's voice, though it was too muffled for her to make out the words, which was probably just as well. "Go help him," she urged Cindy. "He needs you more than I do."

She and Cindy exchanged a quick farewell. By the time she'd settled the receiver back in the cradle, her tension had waned. Cindy meant well. She was only trying to help Beth return to the land of the living—the land of the loving, or at least of mutually acceptable sex. It was a land Beth would like to return to, but she wasn't going to return until she herself felt up to the journey.

Jeff probably wouldn't want guests for dinner, any-way—not if his day didn't improve. She pictured him standing ankle-deep in a pile of wet wipes, with Erica screeching and squirming in his arms. A chuckle es-caped her.

"Share the joke?"

She jumped and spun around. Ryan was standing in the doorway, looking sweaty and weary. And fully clothed, for which Beth ought to have been grateful.

"I just got off the phone with Cindy. Evidently Jeff and Erica..." She drifted off, aware that Ryan wasn't listening. He was surveying the kitchen, studying it inch by square inch, from the wall beside the back door to the cabinets, to the refrigerator, to the doorway lead-ing into the dining room, to the stove, to more cabi-nets, to the sink. The table and chairs. The window. The floor.

"This room needs major work," he said.

Beth didn't take the criticism personally. "Did you ever hear that old saying? If you haven't got something nice to say, you shouldn't say anything at all."

"It's got incredible potential," he said with a grin. "Okay?"

She forgave him. The kitchen *did* need work, and now that he had planted a seed in her mind about a deck off the back door, she was curious to hear what else he would suggest. "Okay. Tell me about this potential."

"Well, you could strip the cabinets, put down a new floor, maybe invest in new appliances if you've got the bucks. It's a huge room, so you could put a butcher-block island in the center. And maybe a stainless-steel double-basin sink instead of that old porcelain fixture. Redo the countertops and you've got yourself something Julia Child would kill for."

She gazed about the room, visualizing it with the renovations Ryan had just described. "Julia Child would kill for it, eh?"

"You ever see her with a fish boner? Sure, she'd kill for it." He moved to the sink, turned on the cold water and splashed a handful onto his face. "Ah, that feels better. I could use some iced tea right about now."

"Did you finish the fence?"

"Yup. You've got an outlet by the back porch. I've tapped into the juice there. I wanted you to come outside before we put the collar on Chuck and untied him—just in case it doesn't work and we have to catch him. But first, I want a glass of iced tea."

"Of course." She crossed to the refrigerator and pulled out the pitcher.

"Hey, is that a crate?" he asked, noticing the large metal cage tucked into the corner near the broom closet.

Beth glanced over her shoulder, then nodded and pulled two tumblers from a cabinet. "Lynne told me it's a way to toilet-train dogs. I don't know if it's going to work, but Lynne knows everything and she told me a crate is the way to go."

"They work," he confirmed. "The theory is, you establish the crate as the dog's sleeping area, and the dog won't mess his own home because he won't want to sleep in the mess. Once he's gotten used to the idea of not messing his sleep area, you expand the sleep area."

"Well, I've only used it one night. But Chuck kept it dry. I pulled him out first thing in the morning and raced outside, and he went to the bathroom in the backyard. This is the second morning in a week that I didn't have to mop the floor!"

"Hey! Congratulations!" Ryan flung a friendly arm around her shoulders and gave her a squeeze. Beth convinced herself his hug implied nothing beyond the cheery words that accompanied it. But her body warmed in his embrace, just as it had warmed when she'd seen him without his shirt. Just as it warmed whenever he touched her, whenever he was near her, whenever she looked at him.

Before she broke from him, he let his arm drop and continued his examination of her kitchen. "You know what would look really good here?" he asked, opening the door to the dining room and peering around it. "A—"

"French door," she completed.

"Exactly! Something nice and light—a blond wood, lots of glass. This room is great, but it's too dark. You need a nice floor, maybe hardwood—"

"Hardwood," she said simultaneously, then laughed. So did he. "Great minds think alike."

She poured the iced tea and carried one of the glasses to him. "I plan to redo the kitchen once I can trust Chuck not to ruin it. I have no idea what all these improvements would cost, though."

She realized, too late, that standing close enough to hand Ryan the glass meant standing too close to him. He gazed down at her, his eyes bright, his hair slicked back and glistening with drops of water, his body heat spreading to her through the narrow space between them. She could smell him—a clean, soapy smell despite his perspiration. She could feel his nearness viscerally.

"I could write you a proposal," he murmured.

It took her a moment to realize that he was referring to her kitchen, not *her*. She wanted to put some distance between him and herself, but she couldn't discreetly flee from him, and she wasn't going to let him know how unnerved she was by him. "You really did come here because you want my business," she accused, maintaining her smile even as her heart rattled in her chest.

"I'd love to get the business from you," he confirmed.

She blushed but bravely held on to her smile. "I don't give my business to anyone without knowing what it's going to cost."

He seemed to be enjoying this double-edged conversation way too much. He leaned against the counter, extending his legs so she wouldn't be able to move away from him without climbing over his feet. "I can do things cheap or I can do them expensive. It all depends on what you want."

"I want..." A faint sigh snagged in her throat, and she swallowed. Why did his eyes have to be so dark and so bright at the same time? Why did his face have to be so open, his mouth so inviting, his body so...*male?* "I want a kitchen Julia Child would kill for," she said.

"You're thinking big," he murmured, his voice just husky enough to carry all sorts of innuendo. "I like that."

"But I won't do it without knowing up front what it's going to cost."

"Oh?" He arched one eyebrow. "I thought you were a risk taker. You adopted Chuck without knowing very much up front."

"I adopted Chuck because I fell in love with him," she pointed out. The back of her neck was tingling. Her hands clutched the slippery glass of iced tea, which Ryan still hadn't taken from her.

"How about if I promise you'll fall in love with your kitchen?"

He was pouring on the charm, and she was drowning in it. Part of her wanted to dissolve in laughter—because Ryan's sense of humor gave nuance to every teasing word he uttered. But another part of her worried—hoped—feared—that he wasn't teasing, that this was for real, that his implications were serious.

If they were, then she was way over her head—in imminent danger of drowning. "Love should be for living creatures," she murmured. "Not for rooms."

"I agree." His voice was barely above a whisper.

Beth's nervous system overloaded. Her breath caught, her pulse seared her veins and her hands went numb. One minute she and Ryan were talking about French doors and hardwood floors, and the next, they were talking about love and risk. Suddenly he was leaning toward her, his eyes questioning, his mouth beckoning.

And then the glass of iced tea slipped out of her fingers and tumbled to the floor.

CHAPTER SIX

"SO WE MOPPED her floor," Ryan told Larry.

His cousin was seated at his desk in Walker Construction's headquarters, which occupied a small warehouse on River Street, down at the southern end of town. The office was part of a suite of rooms that took up about a quarter of the warehouse, the rest of which housed trucks, tractors and tools, as well as a full bathroom, complete with a shower for guys to scrub off the residue of a day's labor before they hit town in search of refreshment.

The office itself was designed with efficiency in mind, rather than aesthetics. The walls were painted an industrial beige and decorated with blueprints and plot maps. The floor was covered with black tile. Steel gray file cabinets lined one wall; the desks were the same gray steel, and there wasn't a single chair in the place that didn't have squeaky hinges.

The air conditioner hummed. The fluorescent ceiling fixtures buzzed. Larry's chair squeaked as he leaned back in it and propped his sneakered feet on his desk. He scratched his head and frowned, miming bewilderment. "Let me get this straight, Ryan. You went over there to get cozy with her and you wound up mopping her floor."

"Well, there was iced tea everywhere. She'd been bragging about how she'd gone a whole two nights without her mutt piddling on the floor, and then she went and spilled iced tea all over the place. Lucky the glass didn't break, or it would have been worse.''

"Far be it from me to criticize your performance with a woman," Larry noted somberly, "but you're usually a little smoother.''

"Tell me about it." Still perplexed by the way things had progressed—or failed to progress—on Saturday, Ryan grinned and shook his head. He'd be the first to admit he'd blown it with Beth Pendleton. One moment, they'd been on the verge of kissing. He'd been sure she was receptive; she'd tilted her face up as he'd angled his downward. She'd stopped breathing when he had. Her eyelids had fluttered. He'd been *that* close....

The next moment, the chance was gone. They'd laughed about the iced tea, cleaned the mess together, and then Chuck had started howling and scratching at the back door, and Beth had let him in after filling a fresh glass for Ryan. But she hadn't seemed terribly interested in kissing him anymore.

He still wasn't sure what—if anything—he'd done wrong. He generally didn't have this sort of trouble when it came to women. If a kiss was supposed to happen, it happened. If a woman wasn't sending out signals, he kept his distance.

Beth had been sending out more signals than a TV satellite. And like a high-definition television set, he'd picked up every signal she'd transmitted. Spilled iced tea shouldn't have been enough to interrupt the broadcast.

"Well, look," Larry said philosophically, "there's always Mitzi Rumson. You told me she's real sweet.''

Ryan groaned and rolled his eyes. Mitzi Rumson wasn't the woman who'd had him tossing and turning all night, horny as hell. Mitzi Rumson wasn't the image that had haunted him through a long, lonely weekend.

"You know, it's not like I'm dying of desperation," he pointed out. "If I were, I'd have Martha Strossen find me someone."

Larry groaned. He'd found himself caught in the town matchmaker's cross hairs on more than one occasion. "No one should ever be that desperate."

"It's no big deal," Ryan said. "I thought I had a chance with the new lady lawyer, and apparently I misread the situation. It's been known to happen."

"To some of us more often than others," Larry muttered with a self-deprecating laugh.

Larry's way with women had always been different from Ryan's. In fact, his way with women had been practically nonexistent. He'd had a few relationships, most recently a long-term affair that would have culminated in marriage if Larry hadn't blinked enough times to clear the fog from his vision and see his girlfriend for what she really was—petulant and immature. He'd more or less recovered from that debacle, but he hadn't yet gotten up the nerve to plunge back into the social scene.

Even when they'd been teenagers, only sons of brothers and as close as brothers themselves, Ryan had always been the one to suggest to the girl he was taking to the movies that she bring along a friend for his cousin. Once women got to know Larry, they liked him just fine. He was nice looking and smart and funny. But he was also kind of timid, kind of reserved ... and woefully lacking in charisma.

For a while during their high school years, Ryan's popularity with the opposite sex had caused friction between him and Larry. But then, when they'd both been seventeen and Larry's father had died, the tragedy had drawn them closer than ever before. Ryan's father had become a surrogate dad to Larry, and once the two boys had finished their schooling, Ryan's father had found places for both of them at the company he and Larry's father had founded.

Besides charisma, Larry also lacked a taste for physical labor. But that, too, hadn't mattered. Once Ryan's father had retired, the cousins had divvied things up to suit their personalities. Larry handled Walker Construction's management, while Ryan oversaw the field work. Together, they'd increased the company's profits by nearly fifty percent in the past few years, and the resentments about who was more popular than whom had passed from memory.

Still, it amused Ryan to think he was turning to his bashful cousin for advice on a woman problem. "I don't know," he opined. "Maybe it's because she's a city woman. You know, or an intellectual. She's a lawyer—she probably went to college forever. Maybe she thinks I'm too lowbrow or something."

"Shake it off, Ryan. If that's the sort of person she is, who needs her?"

Ryan sighed. "I like her, Larry. Need has nothing to do with it."

Larry eyed his cousin speculatively. Perhaps he sensed that Ryan was contending with something almost unheard of in his life—major insecurity about a woman. His smile grew gentle, reassuring. "It's probably nothing. She's interested in you, but she's having second thoughts. That's all."

"How could she possibly have second thoughts about me?" Ryan protested, then laughed. "I put in an electric fence for her dog. She wants me to renovate her kitchen if I can do it for a reasonable cost. She's our new lawyer. You should have seen her on Friday, revamping the contract with Mitzi. She's hot, Larry."

"Except when you want to kiss her. Then she's colder than January."

"I must be losing my touch," Ryan said, unable to shrug off his disappointment. Of all the times for him to lose his touch, why did it have to be now, with Beth?

Why Beth, anyway? How had she managed to get under his skin this way? Was his interest based mainly on her resistance to him? He hated to think he was that shallow...but what if he *had* kissed her Saturday morning? Would he still be pining for her on Monday?

"Give her some breathing room," Larry counseled. "She's just barely settled in town. I don't even know why she's our lawyer, anyway. Jeff was handling everything fine."

"She's better than Jeff," Ryan said sharply.

"Oh, yeah. And you're real objective."

"Thanks for the input." Ryan shoved around the papers cluttering his desk. "I've got a crew scheduled to do interiors at the condos up in Lyndeborough. I'd better truck over there and pretend I'm the boss." He pushed himself out of his chair, which issued a raucous squeak that nearly drowned out the ringing of the phone.

Larry answered it. "Walker Construction." He listened for a minute, then winked at Ryan. "Hang on a second—he's here." He pressed the hold button on his phone and said, "It's the hot lawyer herself."

Doing his best to ignore Larry's simpering grin, Ryan punched the flashing button on his own phone, then lifted the receiver. "Ryan Walker here," he said, reminding himself he was nothing more than a client to her.

"Hello, Ryan." Her voice was soft and cool. Not icy but bracing, like the taste of spearmint on a hot day. "It's Beth."

Beth. Slim and blond, smart and funny and...*damn.* He should have just ignored the iced-tea mess and kissed her anyway. Just to get it over with so he wouldn't be mooning like a lovestruck adolescent.

Sure. He would have pushed for the kiss, and she would have punched him in the nose and sent him on his way.

Keep it simple, he admonished himself. He had to forget about her mouth, and the way she'd gazed up at him, her eyes expectant, her body swaying toward him, waiting, wanting what he wanted....

"How's Chuck?" he asked bluntly, just to get his mind off her.

"I think the fence is working. Chuck's been roaming all over the yard but he hasn't strayed past the perimeter."

She was talking so calmly, he felt himself calm down, too. "Any signs of electrocution?" he teased. "Singed fur? Smoke coming out of his ears?"

Beth laughed. "He hasn't turned into a grilled wiener yet."

"Then I guess you can forget about *Hot Dog Buns of Steel.*" Hearing only Ryan's half of the conversation, Larry gaped at him. Ryan waved him away.

"I really do appreciate what you did, Ryan," Beth went on. "Putting in that fence was a lot of work. I hope I can return the favor someday."

Ryan rolled his eyes. He didn't want Beth's appreciation, and he sure didn't want her doing him a favor.

What he wanted was what he'd almost gotten on Saturday.

"The reason I'm calling," she continued, "is that I've heard from Mitzi Rumson. She phoned from Boston to inform me that she's going to sign the contract as we rewrote it. She's driving up to Devon today—she expects to get into town midafternoon. Will you be available to sign papers then?"

Ryan checked his watch, but there wasn't any point in calculating his day's schedule. He knew that at midafternoon he was going to be working with his crew on the units in Lyndeborough. He also knew the contract didn't require his signature. "I'll be out of town on a work site," he said, "but Larry can sign anything that needs signing. He usually handles the paperwork, anyway."

Her hesitation was so slight he almost didn't notice it. "Okay. Would he like to come to my office, or should I drop the document off for him to sign?"

Was she disappointed that she wouldn't see him? Or relieved? If Ryan kept trying to dissect her every word, he was going to make himself crazy. "Why don't you drop the contract off here?" he suggested. "If you've got some free time, you might take a look at the other contracts Jeff drew up for us. You did such a great job on this one, I'm thinking maybe you ought to double-check what Jeff did on the others."

"Hmm." She lapsed into thought for a moment. "I'm sure we have copies of the contracts on file here. But it might be better if I could go over them with Larry. That way, if I've got any questions, he can answer them for me. I'll have to make it late afternoon, though. Around four, four-thirty."

"Sure."

"Well." She fell silent, as if searching for something more to say. Something about the dog, the fence, the iced tea...the kiss that should have been but never was. Something about how she would like to live that moment all over again, only this time she wouldn't drop the glass. This time her mouth would actually find Ryan's, and they would be completely caught up in each other, and kissing her would be more exciting than either of them could have predicted.

Ryan cursed under his breath. That was what *he* wanted to say. She probably wanted to say nothing more than what she did finally say. "Please tell Larry to expect me there at around four-thirty."

After promising to pass the message along to his cousin, he said goodbye, lowered the phone and laughed at the inanity of his overheated imagination. Either he and Beth would get something on or they wouldn't. One spilled glass of iced tea wasn't going to make any difference in the long run.

And nothing was going to spill today, because Ryan wouldn't even be around to see her. Perhaps, if he kept his distance for the next few days, he would stop thinking about her altogether.

"She's dropping by this afternoon," he announced. "She wants to look at the contracts Jeff did for us."

Larry peered up from the printout he was studying. "Why?"

"Because she does contracts better than Jeff does."

"Great." Larry didn't look pleased. "Our contracts are good enough. What do we need her tinkering with them for?"

"'Good enough' isn't good enough. She's the new contracts expert at Miller and Miller. Jeff hired her to make sure our contracts were better than 'good enough.'"

Larry frowned. "Are you sure this is necessary? You know what they charge per hour."

"She redid the Rumson contract and saved our asses. She's worth what she charges."

"Is that your brain speaking or some other organ?"

Ryan snorted. "I pay for legal advice, Cuz. I don't pay for the entertainment of that other organ. Pull the contracts for her. I'm going to Lyndeborough." He scooped his keys from the top of a pile of message slips on his desk and headed for the door.

Once he was outside in the hot morning sun, he contemplated the uncharacteristic anger he'd felt at Larry's teasing. Ryan was unusually touchy on the subject of Beth Pendleton. She was his company's lawyer, and his brain ought to be the only organ in play when he was discussing her.

But when he thought of her breezy cap of golden blond hair, her wide, expressive eyes and the way her lips had softened into a smile the instant before he'd almost kissed her...

Another organ was definitely involved.

It was probably just as well that he wouldn't be around when she showed up. Until that other organ was under control, he ought to keep his distance from the lawyer whose signals he didn't know how to read.

MITZI'S PRESENCE REMAINED with Beth all afternoon. The flashy young widow had arrived at the office around two-thirty, dressed in a green silk jumpsuit with a generously scooped neckline, her ears, hands and throat adorned with so many dangling pieces of jewelry that she reminded Beth a little of a Christmas tree.

Mitzi's skintight bodice showcased her generous endowments, but after so much time, so much healing, Beth shouldn't let a woman like Mitzi erode her confidence.

In truth, Beth admired her. The woman was gaudy, but she wasn't hypocritical. What she had—money, beauty and guts—she displayed with pride. Beth had always respected women like her in a vaguely amused, vaguely awestruck way. Mitzi would have prompted no uneasiness in Beth if Ryan weren't a part of the situation.

But he was. He was going to build Mitzi's mansion. He was going to see Mitzi on a regular basis—she'd informed Beth that she was planning to rent a room at a nice little bed-and-breakfast in town so she could keep an eye on the construction of her country estate. He was going to be keenly, constantly reminded of everything Mitzi offered, which, at least physically, happened to be a heck of a lot more than Beth could offer. But Beth had made her peace with that. She was simply grateful to be alive, resettled in a lovely new environment, surrounded by friends and clean air and a frisky puppy.

Everything was fine...except for Ryan. Except for the fact that if her hands hadn't gotten slick with nervous perspiration at just the wrong moment Saturday morning, she would have kissed him. And then, God only knew what would have happened, how it would have ended, what Ryan would have done if he'd discovered the truth about her.

At least she wouldn't be seeing him today. She'd survived Saturday's disaster, gone unescorted to the Millers' house for dinner and spent Sunday clearing brush in her backyard while Chuck ran around within the confines of the electrified boundary of her property.

Chuck had seemed thrilled not to be tethered. He'd cantered from one end of the yard to the other, barking and chasing squirrels and anything else that intruded on his territory.

Devon was too small a town to get lost in, and she located the sprawling warehouse building that housed Walker Construction Company without any trouble. She parked in the lot outside the main door, away from the garage doors that carved huge rectangles out of the cinder-block wall of the building. After pulling her briefcase from the back seat, she locked the car and climbed the three concrete steps to the door. It opened into a brightly lit, utilitarian office filled with file cabinets, desks and blueprints. The wall clock was a trite white circle. The shelves held folio-sized books. The calendar tacked to a bulletin board on the far side of the room bore no illustrations.

A man sat at one of the desks, a telephone wedged between his ear and his shoulder as he studied a computer screen. Beth glanced around in search of a secretary or receptionist, but no one else was in the room.

She waited patiently until he hung up the phone, swiveled around in his chair and acknowledged her presence. He blinked, then stood and offered a crooked smile. "You must be the lawyer," he said.

"I must be." She noticed some resemblance between him and Ryan—their hair was the same honeyed shade of brown, although this man's was more neatly groomed. Like Ryan, he stood about six feet tall, and his build was lean and lanky. His eyes were also brown, but not as sparkling as Ryan's, and his expression, an odd, lopsided, I-know-something-you-don't-know grin, put her on her guard.

He shook her hand. "I'm Larry Walker."

"Pleased to meet you."

He regarded her for a moment, his smile failing to reach his eyes. "I'm not real clear on why you're here. Ryan said you wanted to look over the contracts Jeff Miller drew up for us."

"That's right."

"Well, see . . . I'm just not real clear on this. Jeff is your partner, right?"

"Yes, but—"

"And Ryan and I, we've known him forever. We all grew up together. So I'm not real clear on why you want to be checking up on him."

Beth smiled, refusing to let his suspicions rattle her. "As I understand it, Jeff did some work for Walker Construction when your old lawyer retired a few years ago. But Jeff doesn't specialize in contracts, and he's no real estate expert. He knows I'm here to review your contracts. I'm not doing anything behind his back. As a matter of fact, he urged me to double-check the contracts he did for you."

Larry looked less than wholly convinced, but he gestured toward an empty desk. "Here," he said, lifting several thick file folders from his desk and handing them to her. "If you really think this is necessary. . . ."

She didn't want to defend herself again. Keeping her smile rigidly in place, she took the folders from him and crossed to the empty desk. He hovered behind her as she settled herself in the chair, which protested her weight with an ear-shattering squeak, and continued to breathe down her back as she pulled her laptop from her briefcase. If the phone hadn't rung, she suspected he would have remained there for the entire time she perused the contracts.

Sending a silent thank-you to whoever had phoned and summoned Larry back to his own desk, she plugged in her computer and turned it on. When she heard him launching into a conversation on the phone, she allowed herself to study him from the safe distance between their desks. He didn't seem exactly distrustful of *her*, she decided. It was more the idea of someone reviewing the work of his friend that seemed to irritate him. She found his loyalty appealing, even though there was no reason for his concern.

She tried to imagine Larry, Ryan and Jeff, young and full of energy, rampaging through Devon Regional High School like the Three Musketeers—or perhaps the Three Stooges. Jeff would no doubt have been the intellectual of the trio, relying on his wits where Ryan could rely on his physical presence to win a fight. Larry... she wasn't sure what he would rely on. Probably he relied on Ryan and Jeff.

His voice droned into the phone, discussing septic systems. Sighing, she turned her attention to the top folder in the pile. She had faith that Jeff would have done a competent job on the contracts, but in working through Mitzi's contract, Beth had noticed clauses she wanted to improve upon in Walker Construction's boilerplate, particularly the warranties.

She opened a file on her computer and began to take notes. The minutes ticked by without her noticing, so immersed was she in the work. She learned from the contracts that Walker Construction concentrated almost exclusively on residential development and that the company also did an active business in renovations.

She wondered what Ryan would charge her to renovate her kitchen and build a deck off the back door.

Yesterday, while she'd been toiling in the yard, she'd thought about how nice it would be to have a deck big enough for a chaise longue, with a parasol above it and a table beside it to hold a drink. It didn't have to be anything enormous. Just an eight-by-ten extension, big enough for her and Chuck.

If she contracted Walker Construction to build it, would Ryan do the work himself? Would he be outside her kitchen window every day for a month, his shirt off and his back slick with sweat beneath the summer sun?

She shut down that image and opened the next folder.

Larry kept busy on his side of the room. She was aware of him but not terribly bothered by him. He printed documents from his computer, made phone calls, greeted a supplier at the door and ushered him past her and out through a door at the rear of the office. Trucks rumbled into the parking lot. The phone rang again. A package was delivered. Nothing took Beth's focus from the contracts she was reviewing.

Nothing until the door opened, admitting the familiar, husky sound of Ryan Walker's laughter.

Beth flinched, then lifted her hands from the laptop keyboard and took a deep breath. *Don't panic,* she admonished herself, even though the thought of panicking merely because Ryan was about to enter the office was absurd. She'd spoken to him that morning without suffering any qualms, hadn't she? She was his attorney. She could face him without reliving the clumsiness of their last encounter.

Shouting a farewell over his shoulder, he strode inside, his boots clomping on the floor. His face was ruddy, his T-shirt and jeans covered with dust. A red bandanna held his damp hair off his face. He looked big and disreputable and incredibly sexy.

His smile softened as he noticed Beth at her desk. "Well, hello there," he greeted her.

She gazed up at his dirt-smeared face and recalled the way he'd looked last Saturday, leaning toward her, his lips moving closer and closer to hers. A blush threatened, but she fought off her uneasiness with a smile. "Hi," she said, closing the last folder and hitting a key to save what she'd entered into her computer. "I'm just about done here, so—"

"Don't go running off on my account." He was still grinning, his eyes glowing with what appeared to be unalloyed pleasure at seeing her.

An awkward silence ensued. Beth didn't know what to say. She might mention that the contracts were basically in order but that she intended to make some changes in all of Walker Construction's subsequent contracts. She might thank him once more for the wonderful job he'd done installing the electric fence for Chuck. She might make a joke about iced tea.

She might explain to him that seeing him stirred feelings that seemed terribly inappropriate for an attorney to harbor toward a client. Or she might simply say that she'd never before known a man who could look so damned good when he was filthy and sweaty.

She was spared from saying any of those things by Larry, who emerged through the office's back door. "I take it you've met Larry," Ryan said, shifting his gaze to his cousin. "Hey, Cuz. Has she saved us a million dollars yet?"

"Not that I know of. On the other hand, I wonder what her afternoon here is going to cost us."

"You don't have to talk about me in the third person," Beth objected, closing her computer and coiling the power cord. "And I *will* be saving you money down the road, so my fee for this—" she gestured toward the stack of folders "—is a good investment. As I said, I'm finished here, so—"

She started to rise, but Ryan clamped a hand on her shoulder and pushed her back into her chair, gently but firmly. "Larry's a jackass. Don't pay any attention to him."

Beth tried to ignore the inherent strength of Ryan's hand cupped over her shoulder, the warm curve of his palm, the length of his fingers. She discreetly shifted beneath his grip. Her chair squeaked.

"It's a Walker family trait, being a jackass," Larry shot back, then launched into a tirade about a concrete company Walker Construction did business with that had abruptly decided to revamp its schedule for the month.

Shut out of the conversation, Beth busied herself packing her computer into her briefcase. She buckled the case shut and rose from the chair. The creak of its hinges caught Ryan's ear. "Don't go yet," he said, signaling his cousin to wrap up his harangue.

Beth stood by the desk, her patience wearing thin. Ryan and Larry had business to attend to; her presence wasn't required, and she doubted they'd want to hear her explain the subtleties of warranty clauses. The only reason Ryan would want her to remain at the office had to be personal, and Beth would rather avoid that.

Nevertheless, she couldn't very well bolt from the office after he'd asked her to stay. She took deep, slow breaths and sent soothing messages into her nervous system. No matter what provocation Ryan gave her, she was not going to wind up with slippery palms or flaming red cheeks.

Larry finally ran out of things to say on the subject of concrete. His gaze shuttled between Ryan and Beth. "So, we're all set with the Rumson project?"

"Ask Beth." Ryan gestured toward her.

"Not only are you all set, but Ms. Rumson is renting a room in the area while her house is being built."

Larry snorted. Ryan twitched his eyebrows. "Renting a room, is she?"

"By the month. She plans to stay in Devon awhile."

"I guess she likes to keep an eye on me."

"I can't imagine why," Beth said, instantly regretting the tartness in her tone.

"I have yet to have the pleasure of meeting Ms. Rumson," Larry muttered, "but from what Ryan's told me, she's quite a woman."

"Quite," Beth agreed.

"Well," Larry said, with one final look back and forth between Beth and Ryan, "if you don't need me for anything more, I'm out of here." He hesitated, giving them a chance to change his mind. Beth glanced at Ryan, who said nothing. Larry grabbed a Boston Red Sox cap from the top of a file cabinet, planted it on his head, waved and shambled out of the office.

The silence he left in his wake tripped Beth's nerves. "I really should be heading for home, too," she murmured.

"Give me ten minutes to clean myself up, and we can grab a bite to eat."

He said it so casually, she couldn't flat-out refuse. After all, it wasn't as if he'd asked her for a date.

But even though she wanted to be on friendly terms with Ryan, she hadn't forgotten how close they'd come to kissing on Saturday. They could come that close again, and then what would she do? Stop him and an-

nounce, "Before you kiss me, you might want to check
out my chest"?

It was better not to take a chance that kissing would
even become a possibility. "I don't know, Ryan," she
demurred. "I really should check on Chuck."

"Why?"

She frowned. Why, indeed? She had left two bowls of
kibble outside for him, in case one overturned, and two
water dishes. The evening was mild and clear—nary a
rain cloud in sight. And Chuck had plenty of room to
run around in, thanks to the electric fence.

"I'm a mess," Ryan said, then laughed and yanked
the bandanna off his head, freeing his thick brown mop
of hair. "Give me ten minutes to hose myself down and
then we'll grab some sandwiches and a beer. You drink
beer?"

"I—yes, sometimes," she admitted, disarmed by the
question.

"Great. Ten minutes," he said with such finality she
couldn't decline his invitation.

In all honesty, she wanted to go out for a sandwich
and a beer with Ryan. She wanted to have a friend she
could talk to. Talking to Cindy usually meant talking
about diapers and projectile vomiting. Talking to
Chuck meant talking to herself, although he occasionally tossed in a bark to keep things moving along. Last
night she'd telephoned Evelyn from her support group
in New York, eager to hear how everyone was doing—
and talking to Evelyn invariably meant talking about
cancer.

She didn't want to talk about cancer or babies or
whatever it was that she chattered about with Chuck.
She wanted to talk about normal things, adult things,

things two friends would say to each other over a sandwich and a beer.

She returned Ryan's warm, dimpled smile and said, "Okay."

She was still smiling as he bounded out of the office through the back door. She heard his voice drift back out to her in an off-key rendition of "Every Little Thing She Does is Magic," and then heard the watery hiss of a shower being turned on in a remote part of the building. Her smile deepened as she imagined Ryan stripping off his clothes and plunging his body under the hot spray.

She settled back into her chair to wait for him. She pictured the water surging down his work-honed body, soaking his hair, washing away the day's residue of weariness and grime. She thought of how clean he would be when he was done, how refreshed. She thought of the sleek surface of his chest, his flat, hard stomach, his streamlined back and his shoulders.

She felt an unwanted blush invade her cheeks after all, and resorted to the deep-breathing rhythm that kept stress from overwhelming her. Tonight was not about Ryan's perfect body, or her imperfect one. It was about getting a bite to eat, beer and sandwiches.

It was about two friends. Nothing more.

CHAPTER SEVEN

BETH WASN'T SURE why she liked Corky's so much. There were places like it in her old Manhattan neighborhood—clean, dimly lit cafés with intimate tables and friendly waiters. But those watering holes in Manhattan had always been filled with elegant single professionals on the prowl, whereas Corky's seemed to attract a more varied clientele—silver-haired retirees, burly guys in duckbill caps, middle-aged women enjoying a ladies' night out, young couples, old couples...and Ryan and Beth.

Another reason she liked Corky's was that, with so many witnesses lining the bar and occupying the adjacent tables, she could relax and enjoy Ryan's company without having to worry about erotic ideas springing to life between them. The crowd guaranteed her safety, protecting her not only from Ryan's overtures but from her own ambivalent desires.

That wasn't to say she was impervious to him. Showered and shaved, his hair still damp from his shampoo, he looked much more delectable than the overstuffed sandwich the waitress had set before her. His eyes were luminous, showing no signs of fatigue after a long day of work, and his mouth fell naturally into a smile no matter what he was doing—pouring beer into a glass, seasoning his roast beef sandwich with salt, digging into his steak fries. He had a wonderful smile, the sort of smile a woman could discover something new in every time she gazed at it.

Reluctantly she turned her attention to her sandwich. The turkey filling was so thick she couldn't see how to fit it into her mouth without dislocating her jaw. She removed the top slice of rye and speared a piece of turkey with her fork.

"So," Ryan asked, "how did things go with you and Larry?"

She stifled a laugh. It almost sounded as if he were inquiring about the success of a blind date. "I don't think he liked me very much," she admitted.

"Oh?"

"Well, he seemed less than thrilled that I was going over contracts Jeff had handled. It was almost as if he was insulted on Jeff's behalf."

Ryan nodded, as if he'd expected as much. "Was Jeff insulted on his own behalf?"

"Of course not. He *wanted* me to check over the contracts to make sure he didn't miss anything important in them."

"Did he? Miss anything important, I mean."

She glanced up, worried that Ryan would question Jeff's professional skill. But Ryan's eyes were dancing with laughter, and her concern faded. "Minor details," she assured him. "Nothing to lose any sleep over."

"I can't imagine Jeff doing anything that would make me lose sleep," he said. "He's one of the good guys."

"I gather you've known him a long time?"

"Practically forever. He and Larry and I grew up here—and when we were kids, Devon was even smaller than it is now. There were maybe a hundred kids in each grade, half of them boys. The three of us couldn't have avoided each other if we'd wanted to.''

She altered the vision she'd conjured earlier, of the three men as teenagers. Now she pictured them as children, with scuffed knees and ratty sneakers, trading baseball cards and climbing trees. Innocent vistas filled the canvas of her imagination. "And you were all buddies, right from the start?''

"Well, Larry and I couldn't help hanging out together. We were first cousins, our dads worked together, we were the same age. Even though we were really different in personality, we were always pretty close.''

"How are you and Larry different?'' she asked, more interested in Ryan's past than she should have been.

"Larry,'' he explained with affection, "was a quirky kid. He wasn't a great athlete—which wouldn't have mattered to any of us, but he was self-conscious about it, so he always made himself scarce when we were putting together a stickball game or shooting hoops. He used to collect bugs—''

"Bugs?'' She tried not to shudder. She supposed insects had their place in the grand scheme of things, but she preferred their place to be as far from her as possible.

"Beetles, spiders, the occasional firefly. He was really into bugs. For a while, everyone was saying he was going to be an entomologist when he grew up.''

"Why didn't he?''

"Well…'' Ryan drank his beer and shrugged. "When we were seventeen, his dad died in a car accident. When Uncle Bill died, my dad sort of took over as a father to Larry and made sure both he and I had summer jobs in the company. He helped put him through college and all that. It turned out he liked managing a construction company better than studying aphids.''

''So he's the manager and you're the man in the field.''

Ryan nodded. ''He keeps his eye on the details in the office—at least he does in theory.''

''In theory? How about in practice?''

''Larry's great,'' Ryan said, just a touch defensively. ''He can be a little absentminded sometimes—he'll forget what he's doing if a ladybug crosses his path— but he keeps track of the paperwork.''

''And you keep track of everything else?''

Ryan nodded. ''I'm in charge of the field. I see to it that we're using top-quality materials and that everything's put together just right. I'll knock myself out to make sure I've got the exact cabinet hardware a client wants, the exact molding, the exact doorknobs she's chosen. I make sure everything is exactly the way the customer wants it.''

''Is this a sales pitch?'' Beth teased. ''I promise you, if I decide to add a deck off the back door, you'll be the first to know.''

He laughed good-naturedly. ''Your kitchen, too. I could get you some really fine solid oak cabinetry, top-of-the-line counters—''

''I'm seeing dollar signs,'' she muttered, unable to suppress a chuckle. ''Lots of dollar signs. Maybe we should get back to why Larry doesn't like me.''

''I'm sure he likes you just fine.'' Ryan took another sip of beer while he sorted his thoughts. ''The thing about Larry is, he's kind of set in his ways. He's used to things being done a certain way, and if something changes, he gets all hot and bothered about it. When our lawyer down in Manchester retired, Larry fell to pieces until Jeff agreed to handle our contracts. Then he got used to having Jeff as a lawyer, and now suddenly Jeff's turned everything over to you. This sort of stuff rattles Larry. It has nothing to do with you personally."

Beth nibbled on a slice of turkey and nodded. "Change can be frightening."

"You don't seem very frightened."

Surprised, she lowered her fork and watched Ryan, wary about what he was getting at.

His smile was too potent to reassure her. "Let's face it," he observed. "Moving to a small town in New Hampshire from—where were you living?"

"New York City."

"Well, that's a pretty big change. Does it scare you?"

Compared to other changes she'd endured in the past couple of years, moving from New York to Devon had seemed almost anticlimactic. Besides, it had been a change she'd chosen, not one imposed on her. "I'm surprised I've adjusted so quickly," she allowed, her wariness ebbing. "Maybe it's because people here have been so nice to me."

"Don't fall for that small-town warm-and-fuzzy stuff. There are proportionately as many jerks in Devon as there are in New York."

She knew better than to take anything he said seriously when he was wearing that beguiling grin. "Maybe you're right," she played along. "Maybe most people around here *are* jerks. Thank heavens I've got a well-behaved genius of a dog for company."

Ryan guffawed, then took a hearty bite of his sandwich. The din of voices in the background created a pleasant backdrop for their private conversation. No matter how crowded Corky's was, she and Ryan seemed totally secluded at their snug, shadowed table.

"So, what *really* made you decide to move to Devon?" he asked.

She contemplated him across the table, his eyes earnest and determined, his smile daring her to answer. He really wanted to know, and she wanted to tell him—but more than wanting to, she *didn't* want to. What if he reacted badly, withdrawing—or, even worse, pitying her? She liked the comfort level they had established this evening, a mood not quite sensual but shimmering with possibilities. She didn't want to jeopardize it.

She could be evasive without being truly dishonest, she decided. "I've spent my entire life living in large cities," she said. "I grew up in Washington, D.C. I went to college in Philadelphia, law school in Boston and then took a job in Manhattan. I was getting tired of the noise and the crowds. I thought that if I didn't try something new soon, I'd be too old and settled to move."

"Too old?" he scoffed. "You look about sixteen."

"You'll have to double that," she said. "But thanks. You're a very sweet liar." Actually, she thought she looked older than her years. Before the chemo, when her hair was long and her body had a little more meat on it, she'd looked youthful. Not anymore, though. "If I'd stayed at the firm where I was working in New York, I'd have aged about a decade every year. That was another reason I wanted to move. The grind was wearing me down."

"Really? Was it one of those high-power firms?"

"'High-power' was an understatement. I put in eighty-hour weeks until I was offered a partnership, at which point I could cut back to maybe seventy-five-hour weeks. It was crazy. I had no time for a life.''

''I bet Jeff really drives you hard now that you're at the extremely high-power firm of Miller and Miller, Workaholics-at-Law. He's such a slave driver.'' Ryan chuckled. ''And Cindy. Man, she's even worse. When he dragged her home with him after law school, we all thought, wow, those two were going to drive each other to an early grave.'' He leaned forward, as if to confide some great secret. ''I've heard rumors that they sometimes stay in their offices as late as *five o'clock.*''

Beth feigned shock. ''Five? I've never seen them stay that late!''

''It's all Cindy's fault, of course,'' he continued knowledgeably. He popped a fry into his mouth, chewed and swallowed. ''When Jeff was a kid, he was as much a goof-off as I was.''

''At least he didn't collect insects like your cousin did,'' Beth said in defense of Jeff.

''All three of us were known to go AWOL from school on occasion. I don't know how much exploring you've done in the area yet, but if you head north from the town center, oh, say, a couple of miles—it was biking distance for a twelve-year-old boy—anyway, there are these granite cliffs above a river gorge. After the spring thaw, when the river crested, we used to bike up there, climb the cliffs, strip off our clothes and jump in. Well, actually, only Jeff and I jumped. Larry would always chicken out and go looking for spiders.''

''He sounds more sensible than you and Jeff. Jumping off cliffs into a gorge must be dangerous.'' Her voice drifted, her mind distracted by yet another image of Ryan, standing on a rock cliff, stark naked. In her imagination, though, he wasn't twelve years old. He was fully grown, strong and fierce and ruggedly masculine.

He shook his head. "It wasn't that dangerous. The water wasn't rough. But it *was* freezing. It was so cold it made your teeth ache. We made the jump every spring until we were in high school."

"It took you a long time to wise up," Beth chided. But she was still charmed by the annual rite Ryan had described.

"We'd cut school if there was good snow, too. Once we were in high school, we didn't bother cutting school to jump off cliffs. We cut school to go skiing."

"How on earth did Jeff get into law school, I wonder?"

"If he'd spent more time in class instead of running around with me and Larry, he'd probably be better at drawing up contracts today." Ryan picked over the last few fries on his plate and then pushed it away. He emptied what was left of his beer into his glass and leaned back in his chair, stretching his legs under the table.

"Does it snow a lot here?" Beth asked, realizing at once that the question made her appear stupid. The average snowfall of the region was something she ought to have researched before she'd relocated.

Ryan shrugged. "What's a lot? If you're from Washington, D.C., yeah, you'll think it's a lot. If you were from northern Vermont, you'd think it wasn't so much. All told, we get maybe six, seven feet in an average year. Some years we get more, some less. You've got a four-wheel-drive vehicle, don't you?"

"No. Will I need one?"

"On Loring Road? It would be a good idea."

Beth sighed. "Great. I just signed a mortgage, and now I've got to go out and buy a new car?"

"You could buy a used one. Then again, given what you're going to charge us for your services, you could probably afford a whole fleet of Range Rovers."

"Given what I'm going to charge you for my services, I might just barely be able to afford a new deck," she shot back. She enjoyed bantering with Ryan. The sexual undercurrent that flowed between them hadn't disappeared, but she and he were standing safely on the rocks above, and she was in no hurry to strip off her clothing and plunge into the rushing water. Perhaps Cindy thought she ought to get wet with Ryan, but for the time being, the solid, sun-warmed granite beneath her feet felt just about right.

"So." He drained his glass and set it down with a quiet thud. "Tell me the real reason you left New York."

She eyed him nervously. Did he know? If his friendship with Jeff was as close and enduring as he'd just described, maybe Jeff had told him. In which case, she would kill Jeff. It wasn't his business to tell anyone anything about what she'd been through.

"Some guy broke your heart," Ryan guessed, jolting her.

She blinked and collected herself. The sexual undercurrent suddenly rose to flood levels. She had been bristling with indignation at the possibility that Jeff had been gossiping about her health, and instead Ryan was making completely different assumptions. Man-woman assumptions.

"No," she said. "No guy broke my heart."

"Whoever he was," Ryan remarked, as if she hadn't even spoken, "he was obviously a toad. But on behalf of all Devonites, I thank him for sending you our way."

"There wasn't a guy," she said more firmly. Peter's jilting of her had been a trivial irritation compared to everything else she'd been through in the past two years; it hadn't contributed to her decision to leave New York. And even if it had, she didn't consider her romantic history any of Ryan's business.

"You're pretty, you're smart and you're a good sport," he pointed out. "I can't believe you didn't have a million guys falling all over you in New York."

"I dated some," she admitted, "but not very much. I just told you, I was working eighty-hour weeks."

"That still left you, what, eighty-eight hours a week for play."

"Most of which I devoted to such luxuries as sleeping and eating." She smiled. "I hate to disillusion you, Ryan, but I wasn't the belle of the ball."

"I guess those guys in New York really are toads."

How ironic that the one time she was actually telling the truth, Ryan didn't believe her. "All right," she conceded. "I did date a guy for a while before I moved up here, but it wasn't a passionate romance. I think the only reason we stayed together as long as we did was because our schedules meshed." *And because I had two breasts at the time,* she thought wryly.

Ryan scrutinized her, his smile tinged with skepticism. "I just don't get it. Explain to me why a gorgeous lady would bury herself in a town like Devon."

"I'm not gorgeous," she retorted, smiling to mute her impatience. "And I moved to Devon because I've been doing high-pressure things my whole life and I was tired of it. I wanted to simplify my life a little. I wanted to live in a house with a yard. I wanted to walk barefoot in the grass."

"There's no grass in New York City?"

"No grass clean enough for that. Anyway, when I told Cindy I was tired of the grind and wanted a change, she made me an offer I couldn't refuse. She's one of my closest friends. I'm Erica's godmother. And now we're partners. There's nothing more to it than that." *Liar*, she silently accused herself.

Ryan looked unconvinced, but he let the subject drop. "After a winter of blizzards and cabin fever, you may be wishing you did refuse that offer."

"I think I'll like the snow," she said. "And it's not as if New York doesn't have winter. We used to get snow there, too."

"Nothing like what you get here. Devon's going to drive you stir-crazy. Cabin fever is like the plague up here. By mid-February, people turn batty from all the snow. They start talking to themselves and foaming at the mouth. They shoot at dust balls with their hunting rifles. Coming here might have been the biggest mistake you've ever made."

She didn't want to dwell on that possibility, even though she was well aware of it. "I don't think so, Ryan," she joked. "I think the biggest mistake I ever made was adopting Chuck."

"That," Ryan declared, "was the smartest thing you've ever done. Chuck's got the sense to know a good woman when he sees one. It's obvious he's in love with you."

Beth smiled, although hearing Ryan discuss love— even puppy love—made her uneasy. "I really should get home and check on him. I hope that fence worked."

"It worked." Ryan checked his watch and signaled the waitress for the check. "Just be careful he doesn't jump on you the instant he sees you. Dogs in love tend to be very demonstrative."

Beth nodded and fidgeted with her purse. She knew Ryan was talking about Chuck, but still . . . She wished to God she could laugh about this the way she'd laughed about Devon's winters and Larry's fascination with lower life forms. She wished she could relate to Ryan the way she used to relate to men before her life had changed. She wished she could return his salvos without worrying that there was more going on between them than she could handle.

The waitress handed him a check. He pulled a twenty-dollar bill out of his wallet and left it on the table, then stood and offered Beth his hand. It was only to help her out of her chair, she reminded herself. But when she was on her feet he didn't let go.

She had known his grip would be firm and hard. She had known his palm would be warm and leathery, his fingers callused. What she hadn't known was that clasping hands with Ryan would feel so good. When had a man last held her hand like this? Not her father, not the oncologist trying to console her, but a man taking her hand as if they were a couple.

No wonder she was so susceptible to Ryan. He was fun, he was attractive, he was attentive, and the last time she'd been with a man—a man not so attractive or attentive or fun—had been two years ago, in another lifetime.

Ryan didn't release her until they reached his truck. Her fingers tingled in the aftermath of his touch, and she took a few deep breaths to regain her balance. He opened the passenger door for her, and she braced herself before he took her hand once more to help her up into the high seat.

His truck was cleaner inside than out, the vinyl upholstery devoid of construction-site dirt, the floor uncluttered and the cellular phone tucked neatly between the seats. The cab held a pine aroma, which was overtaken by Ryan's freshly showered scent once he climbed into the driver's seat. The engine rattled noisily as he revved it, and then he pointed the truck back toward the Walker Construction Company warehouse on River Street, where Beth had left her car.

Neither of them spoke. Beth stared through the windshield at the pink dusk sky and thought about the man at her side. She thought about what she had told him, what she hadn't told him, what he'd guessed and misguessed. She thought about whether coming to Devon, abandoning her old, high-pressure life and opening herself up to the prospect of a friendship with a man like Ryan Walker was the biggest mistake of her life.

It took less than five minutes to reach the gravel lot outside the sprawling warehouse building. A single spotlight illuminated the parking lot. Except for Beth's car and a dump truck, the lot was empty.

Ryan coasted to a halt next to her car and switched off the engine. He turned to her, and the truck's cab suddenly seemed too small, too crowded. She gazed at the cellular phone and the parking brake. They were mighty feeble barriers, not nearly enough to separate them.

She felt his eyes on her, felt their light and darkness, their laughter, their power. She felt the force of his curiosity, obviously not yet satisfied. She felt that troublesome tide of sensuality eroding the high bluff on which she and Ryan stood, the water splashing against the rocks below them, beckoning.

"Well," she said, relieved to hear the solid sound of her voice, "thanks for the dinner."

"That was a snack, not a dinner."

"It was more than I usually eat."

"Maybe you should eat more." His smile was playful enough to counter the tension filling the car.

Smiling back, Beth tugged on the door latch. Ryan shoved open his door, leapt down from his seat and circled the truck to help her out.

Without letting him take her hand, she climbed down and stepped toward her own car. Smoothing her skirt, she glanced at the matching jacket in the back seat of her own car, where she'd stashed it with her briefcase when she'd left Ryan's office. She dug in her purse for her key and inserted it into the door handle.

Before she could unlock her car Ryan's hand covered hers, immobilizing it. "Next time, let's make it a real dinner," he said.

He wasn't asking. And he wasn't actually discussing the size of a particular evening meal. He was talking about their spending another evening together, about a next time, about the two of them hovering on the edge of a cliff, deciding whether to dive into the gorge.

She ought to correct him, tell him she was all wrong for him, warn him off before he learned the messy truth. But his hand closed around hers, warm and possessive, turning her toward him. His eyes were piercing, his smile inviting, his body sheltering hers in the space between their cars.

She focused on his angular chin, afraid to look at the mouth she wanted to kiss, the eyes she wanted to trust. He lifted his free hand to her cheek and cupped it, his work-roughened fingers scraping gently toward her temple and into her hair. She had nothing in her hands to drop right now, and even if she had been clutching a two-quart pitcher of ice tea, dropping it wouldn't have offered her the escape she'd needed on Saturday.

She needed that escape now. But she didn't want it. She wanted to feel his mouth on hers, if only for a moment. It wasn't as if she were plunging headfirst into a raging river. A kiss was no more dangerous than dipping her toe into the shallowest puddle.

He angled her head slightly, then lowered his mouth to hers. His lips brushed against hers, whisper-soft. It was almost a timid kiss, except that nothing about Ryan was timid. Restrained, she thought. It was a kiss that forced nothing, that allowed her maneuvering room.

Yet her response was anything but restrained. Perhaps it was because so much time had passed since a man had last kissed her, or perhaps it was because the man kissing her now was Ryan. Whichever it was, her entire body felt his kiss. Its quiet heat seeped into her, through her, saturated her with sensation. One sweet, light, closed-mouthed kiss, and her stomach clenched, her thighs ached and her breath caught in her throat before emerging in a small, blissful moan.

She detected a change in him, too. His body grew taut. The hand holding hers tightened perceptibly, and the other hand flexed, plowing deeper into her hair. He stopped breathing and touched his mouth to hers again, a little less tenderly this time.

She sighed. She couldn't help it. Kissing him felt too good. Nerves that had been comatose stirred back to life. Heat swept deep inside her, reminding her of what a man could be like, what a joyous thing passion could be, reminding her of everything that had been lacking in her life for the past two years. Ryan's kiss reawakened the desires she'd ignored for too long, the promise of fulfillment that could make her body whole.

She reached up with her free hand and traced the edge of his jaw. He dipped lower, coaxing her lips apart with his, and she sighed again. The heat inside her was lush and fluid. His skin was warm and dry, his mouth hot and wet. His tongue glided along the ridge of her teeth until she opened fully to him, and when he slid inside they both groaned.

Oh, God. It felt so good, so precious, this closeness, this intimacy that extended only to their mouths, their faces and fingertips and yet flooded through her, thawing every frozen corner of her soul. She nearly sagged from the exhausting pleasure of it, but before she could sink against her car Ryan brought his arm around her. Their hands remained knotted at the small of her back, her knuckles and his digging into her spine, her wrist far too sensitive to the seductive stroke of his thumb. His lips were salty, his tongue ravenous. As her hand moved down to the hollow of his neck, she felt the trembling rasp of his breath in his throat, a low, eager sigh of delight.

This kiss would have to end, because if it didn't, it would lead to only one thing, and she and Ryan weren't about to journey too far in that direction. But just this once, she wanted to drown in the river, to be a woman trapped in a torrent of blind desire for a man.

The minute passed, and reason gave blind desire a slap. Beth removed her hand from his collar, foolishly letting it slide down over his chest until she forced herself to stop touching him. She cleared her throat and he straightened up.

His eyes were darker than before, smoky with unabashed lust. His smile was tentative, not the cocksure grin he usually wore but a hesitant, yearning half smile.

"This won't do," she said, sounding pathetically like a schoolmarm.

"It won't, huh?" Humor sparked his gaze.

"I mean..." She swallowed to erase the quiver in her voice. "I'm your lawyer, Ryan. You're my client."

"I'm also your friend."

"I know, but—"

"And if you told me you didn't know this kiss was coming, I'd call you a bald-faced liar."

She already knew she was a liar. But she wasn't going to lie about the kiss. "I—I guess there's an attraction here, but I'm not sure it's a good idea to act on it. Not while I'm your lawyer."

He chuckled, moving his hand to caress behind her ear. She locked her knees to keep from shuddering and bit her lip to keep from blurting out how exciting his touch felt. "What if I fired you?" he suggested. "You wouldn't be my lawyer then."

"That would please Larry."

"Nah. By tomorrow he'll be used to the idea of you. So if I fired you tonight, he'd probably go into a major funk about it." At last he drew his hand away, releasing her from his seductive spell. "Not that I give a damn about whether he's in a funk, but I like the way you work. I even like your integrity, which, given the situation, is too bad."

"We can still be friends, Ryan. I just think we'll both be a lot happier if we don't let this thing go any further."

He studied her for a long, wistful moment, his smile fading, his gaze intent. "I'll back off for now if that's what you want. But I don't think it's going to make either of us happier."

"It's what I want," she said, telling herself that, happy or not, she'd spoken the truth this time. She wanted to leave Ryan before she got swept away. She wanted to wait until she felt surer of herself, surer of him—or else surer that her instincts were correct, that Ryan couldn't possibly handle the reality she lived with every day. As much as she liked him, as much as she wanted him right now, she wanted even more not to get hurt.

And to be rejected—by the first man she'd dared to open up to—would hurt. It would hurt worse than Peter's betrayal had hurt, worse than the first ghastly shock of viewing her altered body in a mirror, worse than the realization that she had won one of fate's cruelest lotteries when she'd discovered a lump in her left breast one day, a lump that still might come back and kill her someday.

Allowing herself to feel things for a man and then having that man turn and flee once he knew...

She couldn't chance it. Not yet. Not with Ryan.

Maybe she hadn't been lying, after all. Maybe it would make her happier to say good-night and drive away and never let Ryan get this close to her again.

But when she climbed into her car and turned on the engine, peering out her window to see him standing beside her car, watching her, puzzlement and passion clearly etched into his expression, she didn't feel happy. When she backed out of the parking space and turned the car around and glanced at her rearview mirror to find him still watching her, still wanting her, she didn't feel happy at all.

CHAPTER EIGHT

DAMN, but the lady could kiss.

For several long minutes after she'd driven out of the parking lot, Ryan was still staring at the settling dust, still inhaling the sour scent of her car's exhaust, still shaking his head over why a woman who could kiss the way Beth Pendleton kissed—who could set every freaking cell in his body on fire—would abruptly break from him and act like a virginal little girl.

Because he was her client? For crying out loud, who gave a rat's behind that he was her client?

Maybe he hadn't been kidding when he'd said he could fire her. If that was what it would take to get beyond a kiss, he'd consider it. He wanted her that much.

He ran his tongue over his lips, capturing the lingering taste of her, and something twisted tight inside him. Not just hormonal but emotional. He didn't simply want her—he *wanted* her.

He yanked open the door of his truck, climbed in and tried to figure out his response to her. The hormonal part was easily enough explained. But the other part, the emotional part, had him baffled.

Since when had he ever desired a confusing woman? Confusing women were too risky. You had to commit so much time and energy to figuring out what was going on with them that, once you did, you had an investment. Ryan liked Beth, and he'd like to mine that mother-lode of passion he sensed in her. But commitment? Investment? Emotions?

She was a lawyer, for God's sake. What did he want to tangle with a lawyer for?

Especially *his* lawyer.

The smart move would be to back off, just the way she'd asked. Of course, her body had been asking for something a hell of a lot different, but he ought to take a hint and cool it with Beth. He really didn't have to know what it was that made her eyes haunt him, that made her silvery voice thread through him and wrap around his heart, that made her smile whisper all sorts of coded messages to him. He really didn't need this.

Reliving the way her mouth had felt beneath his, the way her hands had moved on him... well, maybe *need* was too strong a word. But *want* wasn't. *Desire* wasn't. *Long for, yearn for, ache for...* And damn, since when did he give up so easily? As a kid, he'd been enough of a daredevil to leap off the cliffs up north of town and into the surging river current. Just because he was an adult didn't mean he'd lost his taste for adventure.

Pursuing Beth Pendleton could be a worthwhile adventure. Hell, kissing her had been one of the most exciting adventures he'd had in a while.

He twisted the key in the ignition, revved the engine and tore out of the lot, reminding himself to keep his attention on the road. But his mind wandered relentlessly back to Beth. He recalled the way her mouth had fit his, the way her tongue had danced with his, the way her hand had felt brushing down his chest...

The light up ahead turned red. Inches from the intersection, he remembered to brake.

She had to be recovering from a broken heart. No other explanation worked for Ryan. Why else, when one little kiss had ignited the world with Roman candles and sparklers, would she have backed off from him?

Some SOB had done her dirt in New York, and she'd fled to the hills of New England to lick her wounds. And now she was afraid to trust a man. She was afraid to let anyone get too close to her. She was afraid of being hurt again.

She'd been awfully adamant in claiming that her decision to move to Devon had nothing to do with a recent failed romance. She had to be lying, cushioning her battered ego, refusing to let Ryan see her wounds.

Either that or something else was going on with her, something he couldn't even begin to guess. And that was where the dangerous investment of time and energy came in. If Ryan kept thinking about her, wondering about her, digging deeper and deeper, he'd wind up in a hole, for sure.

As the sky lost light, the crickets gained volume. Night spilled through the open side window of the truck, cooling his body and clarifying his mind. Maybe—without investing too much—he could pump Jeff Miller for information about Beth. Why not? Jeff had to know what had brought her to Devon besides his offer of a desk in his office. Jeff would know whether she was recovering from a bad affair, and if so, whether Ryan had a chance at speeding along the recovery.

Ryan shook his head and laughed. He didn't often turn to others for guidance in how to succeed with a woman. He didn't have to. But Beth was different. He was so anxious to break through her resistance that he'd gone and spilled his guts to Larry. And now he was going to hit Jeff up for advice. He must be desperate.

This was unusual for Ryan, very unusual. And kind of intriguing.

Veering north off Main Street, he entered the quiet neighborhood where he lived. A few blocks, a left turn and he'd reached his street. The porch light of his modest ranch house glowed in welcome; he'd rigged it to a timer so it would turn on automatically at 6:00 p.m. Dark houses didn't spook him, but he'd wound up with a couple of spare timers after a renovation a few years ago, so he'd figured, why not?

He pushed the button on the automatic garage door opener—another of the improvements he'd made to the house when he'd bought it three years ago—and parked the truck. Emerging from the garage, he filled his lungs with the tangy fragrance of grass and dogwood. The crickets chirped even more loudly, and the night's first star pierced the sky.

Maybe Beth hadn't been lying about her reason for coming to Devon, he acknowledged, taking another deep breath of Mother Nature's evening perfume as he strolled down the driveway to collect his mail from the box. Maybe Beth had honestly decided she was ready to trade in the fast pace of the city for an environment that smelled of dogwood and featured roads without curbs. Ryan had taken a few long swallows of urban living in his life. He'd found it tolerable in small doses, and the male-female action was a lot livelier in Boston than in Devon. But if cities had taught him anything, it was that deep down he was a small-town guy.

How had Beth put it? She wanted to walk barefoot in the grass. Devon was a good place to do that.

Flipping through his mail, he strolled back up the driveway to the garage, hit the button to shut it and entered the house. He tossed the mail onto the kitchen table and beelined to the telephone, determined to call Jeff and get the inside scoop on Beth. But before he reached for the receiver, the flashing light on his answering machine caught his attention. Sighing, he punched the message button.

The tape rewound and clicked into the play position. "Hello, Ryan?" a familiar voice purred on the tape. "It's Mitzi Rumson. I hope you don't mind that I'm calling you at home, but your number is listed in the directory. I'm just calling to tell you how excited I am that we've worked out the contract for my new house. I'm going to be staying right here in Devon, so I can see the house while you're building it." She gave a sultry little laugh. "I've rented a suite of rooms in the most adorable inn—it's called Devon Hill. I'm sure you must know the place. So, Ryan, I'm here, and I expect I'll be here quite a bit now that we'll be working together. I just know we'll be seeing a lot of each other." She recited the telephone number of the inn, murmured something about how ecstatic she was to have a man like him on the job and ended the call, saying, "I can't wait to hear from you."

The answering machine clicked off. Ryan snorted. He knew where Devon Hill was—and it was a lot closer to his home than he would have liked now that Mitzi had taken up temporary residence there.

By the time the machine had reset the tape, Mitzi was fading from his thoughts. She was rich, she was gorgeous, she had commissioned him to build a house for her and that was that. All her coy sensuality didn't do a thing to him. Even if it did, he knew better than to get involved with a client. His lawyer had warned him about that.

An ironic smile curved his mouth as he contemplated his lawyer and her pale blue eyes and her pale blond hair. His smile lost its irony, growing wishful and wistful as he recalled the enchanting sound of her sighs and the cool, slender grace of her hand against his chin, the motions of her tongue against his.

So much for cooling it.

He reached for the phone and punched in Jeff Miller's number. The sooner he found out what was going on with Beth, the sooner he could figure out whether he wanted to be a part of it.

IF SHE'D HAD a deck, she would have been on it. The night had stolen the heat from the air, and the sky stretched above Devon like a royal blue sheet sprayed with stars. Fireflies winked along the edge of the backyard; she could almost pretend their faint flashes were sparks of electricity rising from the fence Ryan had installed.

But she didn't have a deck and she probably wasn't going to have one unless Ryan installed that, too. She supposed other carpenters plied their trade in Devon, but she couldn't imagine hiring anyone but Ryan for the job. Not only because he was her client, not only because he was her partner's childhood friend, but because she couldn't shake the conviction that he would build a better deck than anyone else.

Yet having him construct a deck would be problematic for two reasons. One was that, as long as she and Ryan had a professional relationship, she would feel strange letting their nonprofessional relationship develop. Perhaps that would be for the best, though. She would be better off avoiding anything personal with Ryan.

Which led to the second reason. As long as they weren't going to pursue anything personal, having Ryan at her house, hammering nails and sawing boards right outside her back door, no doubt sweating and removing his shirt and asking her for iced tea... It would drive her crazy.

"Well, I'm probably already crazy, anyway," she said, settling into one of the ladder-back chairs at her kitchen table. "After all, here I am, talking to a dog." She would have been more comfortable in the living room or the den, but she didn't trust Chuck around rugs or upholstered furniture yet, and she didn't want to be alone.

She needed to talk to someone. But Cindy was the only friend she could trust to help her work through her tangled emotions, and when Beth had telephoned Cindy she'd gotten a busy signal. Fortunately, Chuck was a good listener, and he obviously couldn't think of anyplace he'd rather be right now than with Beth.

The moment she'd driven up the gravel driveway he'd gone berserk, barking and panting and drooling all over her as soon as she'd crossed the invisible fence to his side. Together, they'd gone to the back porch, where she'd discovered his food and water dishes empty. This had caused her a twinge of guilt. Should she have left more food for him? An extra water dish? She'd just spent the past hour picking at a sandwich so big it would have taken her an entire week to consume it, and her poor little puppy's food dish hadn't a crumb in it.

Apparently he wasn't hungry, though—at least not for food. When she brought him into the kitchen and refilled his dish, he ignored it for the more immediate satisfaction of running in circles around her and butting her in the shins with his head. What he was hungry for was her company.

She filled a glass with milk for herself, sat at the table and took deep, relaxing breaths, trying to fight off the effects of Ryan's kiss. Chuck could be frenetic if he wanted; his heart wasn't at stake. Hers was, and she needed to calm down so she could think.

"I shouldn't have kissed him, Chuck," she admitted. "That was a big mistake. It's like a dieter taking a bite of fudge. You know you're going to like it more than you should, and it's only going to remind you of what you can't have. Especially if it's the richest, tastiest fudge in the universe. God, Chuck—the man is hazardous. I can't believe what he managed to do to me in less than two minutes. It was more intense than...well..." She felt her cheeks grow steamy, her entire body grow steamy, as she relived her memory of those two minutes of passion.

"Damn it. I really shouldn't have kissed him."

But she *had* kissed him. And like a deprived dieter, she was suffering from the worst sort of craving for more.

"If only I were normal," she muttered, then bit her lip. She didn't like the turn her thoughts were taking. If they continued along that route, she was going to wind up wallowing in self-pity, which was as tempting as fudge. Just one little taste of self-pity, one moment's indulgence, and she wouldn't know how to stop.

Yet there it was, luring her, calling to her—and she hadn't given in to it in so long. Just one small taste, she promised herself. Just one brief nibble and then she'd be strong again. "If only I had all my original equipment, Chuck, I could be living a normal life, with men and sex and...oh, I know, I could have sex now if I wanted, but..."

Chuck wagged his tail and gnawed on the table leg. She hooked her fingers around his collar and pulled him back. "Stop it, Chuck," she pleaded. "Don't eat the table."

Hearing his name, Chuck let out a cheerful bark and rested his head in her lap.

"Good dog." She stroked him behind his ears. His fur was soft and silky, but she found herself remembering a different texture against her fingertips, the warm, slightly scratchy surface of Ryan's jaw.

"If Ryan were perfect," she whispered, still stroking Chuck, "I wouldn't have anything to worry about. He would want me just the way I was. But I don't believe in perfection. I can't. If I did, then I would have to reject myself. Because I'm not perfect. I'm not even close, and I'll never be. I'll never even be normal again."

A sob bubbled up in her throat. She steeled herself against it. If she gave in to the urge—if she let one taste of self-pity lead to another—she would wind up binging on it, and then she would loathe herself afterward. "The hell with being normal. This *is* normal for me, Chuck. This is what I am.

"You love me, anyway, don't you?" She scratched the nape of his neck and smiled as he panted blissfully. "You don't care what I look like, do you?"

He barked his assent.

She kept smiling, but tears burned her eyes.

As a child, she had been raised to believe that if she worked hard enough for something, she could have it. If she wanted a bicycle, she could do extra chores and save her allowance to get one. If she wanted good grades, she could study hard. If she wanted to go to law school, she could take the right courses, cram for the exams, apply her energies toward achieving her goal. If she wanted a good job, a decent income, a partnership offer, those things were hers to earn. Luck was an abstract concept, something she didn't place much stock in. She didn't expect good luck to deliver her heart's desires.

But the thing about not expecting good luck was, she had also grown up never expecting bad luck. And when bad luck had befallen her, she hadn't known how to deal with it.

She had learned. She'd done a good job overcoming her bad luck, coping with what it did to her, denying it the right to ruin her life. She was doing well, she really was.

But she wanted Ryan Walker. She wanted to make love with him. She wanted it to be as easy as their kiss had been. And she couldn't have what she wanted because nothing would ever be that easy for her again.

Much as she hated being weak, right now she needed to cry. Her emotions were too raw, her heart too vulnerable. Holding back her tears required more strength than she possessed at the moment.

She had gone through periods since her diagnosis when she'd been forced to confront everything she'd lost, everything she might lose: her breast; her hair; her health. Possibly her life.

She was still alive. She had regained her health and her hair had grown back. But now she had to acknowledge a new loss: the chance to be a normal woman falling in love with a normal man.

She gave herself permission to grieve over that loss, just as she'd grieved over the others. Chuck wouldn't mind. As long as she kept scratching his neck and cooing to him, he would love her, even if she was weeping.

THE BOTTOMLESS CUP was to morning in Devon what Corky's was to evening—a place of cheap food and

mellow atmosphere. A bit more brightly lit than
Corky's, a bit noisier, a bit less romantic, but then,
Ryan had no romantic designs on his companion that
morning.

He watched as Jeff surveyed the platter before him.
"Omelets and sausage," he said with a contented smile.
"Whatever you do, Ryan, don't tell Cindy. She doesn't
let me eat like this at home."

"My lips are sealed," Ryan promised, surveying his
own indulgence: a towering stack of homemade blue-
berry pancakes dripping with syrup.

"We ought to do this more often," said Jeff, making his meal even more lethal by adding a blizzard of
salt. "As long as Cindy doesn't find out, we could do
it every week. I could come up with a suitable lie for her,
don't you think?"

Ryan smiled. There were obviously disadvantages to
being married—if having a wife who loved you enough
to care about what you ate could be considered a dis-
advantage.

Jeff sliced a thick chunk of sausage, popped it in his
mouth and moaned happily. His tie hung loose around
his neck, and he'd draped his suit jacket over the back
of his chair. He was obviously heading straight to his
office after breakfast.

His and Beth's office.

"Listen, Jeff," Ryan said, cutting into his pancakes.
"I didn't invite you to breakfast so I could watch you
clog your arteries."

"I figured as much." Jeff devoured another chunk of
sausage and peered through his eyeglasses at Ryan.
"What happened? Is Mitzi Rumson suing you?"

"Fat chance. The woman is crazy about me."

"The woman is hot. Be careful she doesn't leave you with third-degree burns."

"I don't want to talk about Mitzi." Ryan sipped some coffee and attempted to keep his tone casual. "Tell me about Beth."

"Beth?" Jeff's smile faded. "Beth Pendleton?"

"Do we both know another Beth?"

Jeff took a bite of his omelet and chewed thoughtfully. "If you're going to tell me she found flaws in the contracts I handled for you, I'll plead nolo. She told me I didn't screw up on your paperwork, but if she told you something different, we can work it out. She's much better at contracts than I am. That's why Cindy and I asked her to join our practice."

"And she's Cindy's good friend," Ryan recited. "And she's Erica's godmother."

Jeff eyed him curiously. "That's right. Is there a problem here?"

"I don't know." Ryan took another drink of coffee and shook his head. "I'd like to get closer to her, if you know what I mean. I was hoping you could help me."

"Close to Beth?" Jeff grimaced.

"Why not? I'm a nice guy," Ryan argued. "Beth and I get along really well. We even kissed last night. It was great!"

"I'm happy for you."

"But then she ran for cover. I don't know if it was me or her, but suddenly she was making a little speech about how lawyers and clients shouldn't kiss each other."

"I suppose ethics is an alien concept to you?"

"Give me a break, Jeff. This has nothing to do with ethics. Beth and I are both adults. And kissing her wasn't just kissing. It was *phenomenal.*"

"Great. It was phenomenal."

"So? What's wrong with her?"

"What makes you think anything's wrong with her?"

"She rejected me." He laughed at his own immodesty, and rationalized it by adding, "After that kiss—which I'm pretty sure was as good for her as it was for me—rejection didn't exactly seem appropriate."

Jeff munched on his breakfast. Ryan studied him, trying to read his mind. Did he think Ryan was way out of line for asking about Beth? Was he playing protective big brother to his wife's good friend? Or was there something more going on?

"My guess," he said, measuring Jeff's reaction, "was that maybe she'd gotten burned by some ex-boyfriend back in New York, so now she's twice shy or something."

"Interesting theory," Jeff conceded.

"Yeah, but is it right?"

Jeff's hesitation in answering with a simple yes or no answer irritated Ryan. "I don't really know much about her social life back in New York," he finally said.

"Jeff. This is *me* you're talking to. What's her big secret? What's she hiding?"

"I didn't say she was hiding anything, did I?" Jeff gave him an innocent stare. "And if she were, why should I tell you? Ask her."

"I *did* ask her, and she gave me a song and dance about quitting the rat race for the quiet life. So I'm asking you because you're supposed to be my friend—although I'm beginning to doubt that."

"Look," Jeff relented, leaning toward Ryan across the Formica-topped table. "Beth is an unusual woman. I've known her a long time. I met her during her first semester in law school, when I was a Three-L. We kept haggling over this one volume in the law library that we both always needed at the same time. My first impression of her was that she was an incredible fighter and I'd never want her to be my opponent in a court case." He dipped the corner of his toast into the melted cheese at the heart of his omelet and bit into it. "My second impression of her was that she was cute, but the chemistry wasn't right. She sensed that, too. After about our fourth blood-letting over that damned volume, she told me she thought I'd like her roommate, and she arranged for me to meet her and the roommate in the student union that evening."

"Her roommate was Cindy."

Jeff nodded. "So right off the top, I'm indebted to Beth. I would never betray her."

"You think helping me to get closer to her would be betraying her? Am I that awful, Jeffrey?"

"I didn't say that." Jeff soaked another corner of toast into the molten cheddar and devoured it. "You aren't awful, but you do tend to wear your brain below your belt sometimes."

"Like hell I do!"

"Remember Sherrianne from Nashua?"

Ryan grinned sheepishly. "All right, well—in that particular instance, maybe. But I'm older and wiser now. And it's not as if all I want from Beth is an easy score. She's a terrific lady. She's incredible. I'm looking for something more with her."

"So? Go for it. What's stopping you?"

"Beth is stopping me. At least, I think she is," he added. After a long night of analysis, he wasn't exactly convinced that Beth was pushing him off for good and forever. The expression "mixed signals" seemed to sum up the situation. "Mixed signals" and a kiss that made

his toes curl and another part of his body become ram-
rod straight every time he reminisced about it.

He fidgeted with his fork for a minute, then lowered
it and reached for his coffee cup. It wasn't like him to
be wound so tight about a woman. Even Sherrianne
from Nashua, bless her cute little buns, hadn't tied him
in knots. No woman he'd ever known had—until now.

"It's obvious Beth is unusual," he said. "*I* think she's
unusual. I'm approaching her with kid gloves. All I'm
asking you is, am I way off base here? Do I have a
prayer with this woman? Am I doing everything wrong?
Does she really prefer caveman types? Should I drag her
back to my cave by her hair? Give me a hint."

"You want a hint?" Jeff polished off his sausage.
"Here's a hint. Pull her hair and I'll kill you."

"Oh, gee, thanks. I'm so glad we've had this talk,"
Ryan said sarcastically.

"Look, Ryan, I don't know what to tell you. I don't
know what her love life was like in New York, and I
don't know what she's up for socially in New Hampshire. All I can say is, if you want to go after her, treat
her nicely."

Ryan spread his hands palms up, the picture of in-
genuousness. "Am I not the nicest guy you know?"

Jeff laughed out loud.

"How about if I swear on a stack of Bibles that I'm
not going to hurt her?"

"Tell *her* that. Don't tell me. She's a grown-up. She
can make her own decisions."

"So, you think I might have half a chance?"

Jeff shrugged. "Ask *her*."

"You know something?" Ryan complained. "You're
really no help at all. In fact, you're so useless I ought to
make you pay for breakfast."

But the truth was, Jeff *had* been a help. He'd told Ryan exactly what Ryan needed to hear—that if Beth had a history she wanted to share with him, it was up to him to ask her about it. If Beth had any desire to let their friendship evolve into intimacy, it was up to him to suggest that to her.

All Jeff could do was state the obvious. The rest was up to Ryan.

"Never mind," Ryan said as Jeff shifted in his seat to pull his wallet from the hip pocket of his trousers. "My treat. You're a pal, Jeff. You really are."

"Whatever you say," Jeff agreed. "I'd just as soon not have Cindy find the receipt and grill me about it. You know, most wives would worry about who I might be taking out to breakfast. Cindy would worry about whether I ate a three-egg omelet."

"That's because she loves you," Ryan said, suddenly feeling like an expert on the subject. He was going to pull this off, after all, he realized. He was going to figure out a way to get to Beth. He was going to make her trust him, make her open up to him, make her realize that kisses like the one they'd shared last night didn't happen every day, to every couple. He was going to prove to her that they could have something special together if only she would give him a chance.

He was going to woo her and he was going to win her, and whatever miserable thing might have happened to her before she'd come to Devon, whatever ghastly experience might have scarred her so terribly, Ryan Walker was going to figure out a way to put it out of her mind.

CHAPTER NINE

BETH WAS NOT in the mood for company.

Even if she'd had a quiet day at the office she would have been exhausted from the previous night's emotional turmoil. But her hours at Miller, Miller and Pendleton had been far from relaxing. She'd landed two new clients, one of whom was a businessman who wanted to sue his previous attorney for malpractice. Beth had spent most of the afternoon reviewing his assorted complaints, and to her great regret, she couldn't avoid the conclusion that he had a legitimate case. The idea of filing suit against a fellow lawyer gave her a headache, but that fellow lawyer had done a lousy job for his client, costing the client a significant amount of money. With great reluctance, Beth agreed to represent him.

Work would have been difficult enough under the best of circumstances. But her circumstances weren't anywhere near the best. She hadn't slept well last night—and when she had drifted off, she'd dreamed of Ryan Walker, dreams that jolted her back to consciousness. Dreams of making love with him. Dreams of stripping naked before him and having him recoil and call her deformed. Dreams of watching him back away from her in horror, crying, "I thought I wanted you, but I don't!"

Reminders of him haunted her while she was awake, too. Whenever her attention flagged, whenever she heard a man's voice, whenever she dared to close her eyes, images of Ryan teased her mind. Sometimes they lapped at her like an ocean at low tide; sometimes they crashed over her, drawing her down in their undertow. They exhausted her as much as the prospect of litigating a malpractice suit did.

By the time she got home, all she wanted to do was vegetate. She stripped off her business dress, took a long, cool shower and threw on a baggy T-shirt and drawstring shorts. She didn't bother with her bra. She didn't bother blow-drying her hair. She wasn't going to see anyone but Chuck, who loved her no matter what she looked like.

Her television was in the den, and she decided, after a few minutes of agonizing, that she would let Chuck join her there, even though the room wasn't dogproof. What was the point in having a pet, after all, if she couldn't have him with her when she wanted his company? Tonight her plan was to turn on the tube, turn off her brain and forget she was a lawyer, or a woman with sexual urges, or a cancer survivor. She wasn't going to be anything but a lump on the sofa. She wasn't going to do anything but talk to Chuck and scratch his back and pray that he didn't chew on the furniture or pee on the rug.

She took him for a walk first, to empty his bladder. Then, with a blend of trepidation and hope, she brought him into the den at the back of the house. The room had obviously been designed for a man's taste. Paneled in knotty pine, it was a small, snug retreat. The windows, which overlooked the woods, were fitted with pine shutters rather than curtains, and the built-in bookshelves were tall enough to accommodate sports trophies. The wood-burning stove sitting on a slab of slate against one wall was cast-iron black, stout and solid.

Ryan Walker had supplied the chimney flashing for the stove, she recalled.

Damn it! She didn't want to think about him. Not only had he been the cause of her insomnia last night, but—worse—he'd been the cause of her tears, her inexcusable wallow in pathos. He'd been the reason she felt incomplete and insecure, and she resented him for it—even though he hadn't done anything to earn that resentment.

Except kiss her, and touch her, and let her know in no uncertain terms that he desired the woman he thought she was.

"No," she said out loud, fending off this new attack of Ryan thoughts.

Chuck peered up at her uncertainly, his tail swishing back and forth. Once he understood that she wasn't going to evict him from the room, he frisked in a circle around the braided rug, yipping and snorting and leaping at imaginary squirrels. Beth pressed the power button on the remote control, and the TV screen flickered to life.

She needed a drink. Not beer—the one bottle she'd had last night had undoubtedly contributed to her maudlin state, and she was still feeling a little hung over from yesterday's riot of self-pity. Tonight she would stick to soft drinks. A nice, cold glass of apple juice would hit the spot.

"Can I trust you alone in here for a minute?" she asked Chuck, who was too busy zooming around the room to acknowledge her.

Of course she couldn't trust him in the room. But she was too weary to snag him and carry him back to the kitchen with her. Hoping for the best, and reminding herself that just minutes ago Chuck had left his mark on every single pebble on Loring Road, she exited the den.

She had just finished filling a tall tumbler with juice when she heard a tapping sound. Turning, she saw a tall, looming silhouette on her back porch, peering in through the window in the door. She screamed and dropped the glass.

Then she realized the silhouette matched Ryan Walker's shape, and her scream mutated into a curse.

She didn't want to see him. He would make her laugh, he would make her think—and he would make her remember what life had been like when she'd had no qualms about her physique. He would turn her on by touching her or kissing her or simply being himself, close to her.

And she wasn't wearing her prosthesis.

Panic rising in her, she backed up a step, as if she could make a dash for the stairs. It bothered her that he could make her feel so self-conscious in her own home. But *everything* about Ryan bothered her at the moment.

She inched back another step and he knocked again, then leaned against the window with his hand cupped above his eyes. Obviously he could see her, and she'd only be inviting unwanted questions if she turned and ran.

Crossing her arms over her chest, she took a deep breath, reminded herself that this was her home and she was entitled to wear whatever she wanted—or *not* to wear whatever she didn't want—and strode to the door to let him in. Maybe he would notice, but maybe he wouldn't. She had always been rather small-bosomed, and her T-shirt hung loose from her shoulders, so if she didn't move her arms...

She opened the door and took a quick step back, out of the spill of light from the ceiling lamp above the table. "What are you doing here?" she asked, instantly regretting her curt tone.

He stepped cautiously over the threshold, carrying a thick folder of papers. "It looks like I'm making you spill your drink," he observed with a tentative smile.

He was dressed in his usual work attire: a pair of jeans, a T-shirt and heavy boots. His hair was mussed, and his jaw bore a faint shadow of beard. Apparently he hadn't showered and shaved before coming here.

Yet he smelled clean, like sunshine and wind. His eyes sparkled and his grin seduced.

Hugging herself more tightly, Beth hurried across the room to the broom closet to get the mop. "You startled me," she explained, terseness replaced by a nervous rush of words. "I wasn't expecting any visitors, and suddenly there was a strange man lurking in my doorway—"

"I'm not so strange," he argued gently, placing his folder on the table and following her to the broom closet. "I guess I should have phoned before stopping by."

"I guess you should have," she snapped, wishing he wouldn't stand so close. When she leaned forward, her T-shirt bloused out, hiding her misshapen chest. But he was only a couple of feet away from her, and if he bumped into her, or viewed her from a certain angle... She needed to think of an excuse to run upstairs and put on her bra. Either that or she needed to inure herself to the fact that he was going to learn the truth about her.

"It's just a spill," he said, evidently thinking her agitation was due to the juice splattered across her floor. "It's not like this is the first time you've ever spilled a drink in my presence." His grin grew even more beguiling as he reminded her of the last time, of the kiss that had almost occurred . . . of the kiss that *had* occurred a few days later.

"You're right," she said, unable to inject any humor into her tone. "This floor has been flooded too many times. I'm tired of mopping it."

"I'll clean it," he said, reaching for the mop.

She leapt back, aware that she was overreacting but unable to stop herself. His frown prompted her to justify her behavior. "It's my floor. I'll clean it."

"Whatever you say." He shrugged, reaching into the puddle of juice to pick up the glass, which fortunately hadn't broken. "Are you okay?"

No, she wasn't okay. She was rattled and strung out and too fatigued to think straight. And Ryan was unwittingly the cause of her frazzled state. "I'm fine," she lied, attacking the puddle with the sponge mop.

"Speaking of your floor, I've brought you some estimates on renovating this kitchen."

Surprised, she straightened and raised her arms in front of her, holding the mop handle as if it could shield her. "I never asked you to write up any estimates."

He studied her speculatively, obviously trying to fathom what was causing her to behave so shrewishly. "All right. It was presumptuous. I didn't think you'd mind."

"Well I do mind." *Don't stare at me,* she prayed silently. But he *was* staring, with bewilderment and curiosity and a dash of annoyance. Surely he must have noticed that something was wrong with her. How could he *not* notice?

"It's not like I cooked this up out of the blue. You told me you wanted to redo the kitchen."

"Yes, well..." *God, just say it. Ask me why I look abnormal. Ask me why my left breast is sitting on my bureau upstairs. Ask me. I'll give you a good excuse to walk out that door. I know you can see, so just ask.*

"And the fact is, I'd do a better job on your renovation than anyone else would. At a good price."

"I don't doubt it." Her voice rasped as tension caused the muscles in her throat to clench. "But you shouldn't have come without calling first."

"Oh," he said slowly, as understanding dawned. He set the empty juice glass in the sink with a thud and turned back to her. "You've got someone else here, don't you?"

"What?" She kept the mop in front of herself, her elbows pressed to her ribs and her hands fisted around the handle.

"You've got a guy here. I'm sorry." He looked mortified.

"No," she murmured, wishing she could erase his embarrassment even though she was more embarrassed than he was. Before she could elaborate, Chuck barreled into the kitchen, barking loudly enough to revive corpses in Maine. "That's the only guy who's here," she said as Chuck hurled himself at Ryan.

Ryan looked relieved—and a bit too pleased to learn that Beth wasn't entertaining a rival. Hunkering down, he gave Chuck a thorough scratching under the chin and behind the ears. "Hey, buddy! How's tricks? Is she treating you well?"

Chuck answered by panting, licking Ryan's palm and then shoving past him to slurp up the spilled juice.

Laughing, Ryan straightened up. "That's one of the great things about having a dog. They take care of the spills. You don't even need a mop."

"Sure," she muttered. Ever since she'd adopted Chuck, her mop had been needed almost exclusively because of him. Watching him consume the juice, she predicted that within another hour she would be mopping that very juice from the kitchen floor—again.

She lifted the bucket into the sink, glad for the opportunity to turn her back to Ryan. The rush of water from the faucet soothed her. As long as Ryan concentrated on Chuck, maybe he wouldn't concentrate on her. Maybe he would forget that she was acting like a harridan, erratic and short-tempered and mildly nuts. She could slip upstairs and put on her bra and act civilly with him.

And then, perhaps, he would be encouraged to kiss her again. And she would be back to the mental wrestling match. To tell him now or later, to give him the chance to be a hero or to discover he was no better than Peter or any other normal man.

Why bother? Why torture herself any longer? She ought to tell him the truth right now. He had probably already figured out something was wrong with her chest; she might as well tell him his eyes weren't deceiving him. It was always possible that he would react better than she expected. He might embrace her and say, "Gee, Beth, isn't that a coincidence! I've been looking for a one-breasted woman all my life!"

Sure. And the sun rose in the west.

She shut off the faucet and turned to find Ryan rifling through the papers in his folder, ignoring Chuck, who was nuzzling his ankles. He must have sensed that Beth was looking at him, because he glanced up from the table. His gaze met hers, solemn and unwavering. "You're really angry with me, aren't you?"

"No." She sighed. She was angry with herself. She was angry with fate. She was angry with God. Ryan just happened to be standing in the line of fire.

"I shouldn't have come. I can see that."

She wanted to refute his statement but she couldn't. He was right. He shouldn't have come.

"If it's because of last night—"

"No." Of course it was because of last night. But she didn't want to get into a lengthy discussion about what last night meant or didn't mean. She didn't want to tell him she'd come home and cried like a baby because she couldn't have everything she wished for. She didn't want to tell him how much she desired him and how afraid she was of being rebuffed by him. She wanted to treasure her illusions for a little while longer.

"The thing is, I put together these ideas for your kitchen and deck. I worked out a bunch of cost estimates for each project, depending on how much you wanted to do. I thought you might be interested."

She *was* interested. But as he himself had admitted, he should have phoned first. He shouldn't have assumed that she would welcome him and his cost estimates with open arms.

"I'll just leave them here, and you can look them over on your own," he said, backing toward the door.

"Fine. Thank you." *Tell him!* her heart cried out. *Better for him to know than to think you're a bitch. Tell him the truth. Give him the chance to say he wants you in spite of everything.*

All she had to do was put down the mop and lift her shirt, and he would see for himself what she was hiding, and why. But what if he recoiled from the sight of her? She couldn't handle his rejection, not tonight. Not yet.

She said nothing.

He gazed at her for a moment longer, and she watched a veil of resignation drop over his face. He didn't beg for an explanation. He didn't even say goodbye. He only stalked to the back door, stepped out onto the porch and slammed the door shut behind him.

The sound of the latch clicking into place, metal against dry metal, echoed in her soul long after his shadow had vanished.

HE DIDN'T STOP until he'd reached his truck. He climbed in, wrenching the door so hard he hurt his wrist, and spewed a string of curses.

What the hell had he done wrong? So he should have called before visiting. Big deal. He'd committed a minor lapse in etiquette, not a crime against nature.

The least she could do was forgive him, considering how he'd knocked himself out for her. He'd been up at the site of Mitzi Rumson's extravaganza today, working with the surveyors and reorienting the foundation. But every time he had a free second, he'd been ringing up call after call on his cellular phone, accumulating estimates on lumber and flooring for Beth's house. Instead of cruising into town to get sandwiches for the crew at lunchtime, he'd sent one of the guys to pick up the food while he trucked over to his favorite supplier of cabinetry to collect samples of various wood stains, veneers and hardware for her kitchen.

He'd arrived back at the site to discover Mitzi waiting for him, all dolled up in a fringed and beaded outfit that displayed more than he wanted to see. He'd had to make happy talk with her while wolfing down his sandwich. He'd had to pretend he was thrilled to have her around. Business was business.

When the crew had called it quits for the day, he'd raced back to the warehouse, not to shower but to write up blueprints and prices for Beth. He'd put everything down on paper, clarifying what a ten-by-fifteen deck would cost her as compared to a fifteen-by-fifteen or a twenty-by-twenty. He'd held the prices low, but they were prices he would honor, not the usual rock-bottom proposals everyone—including the buyer—knew would soar once the project got under way. Then he'd hurried over to her house with his offering.

He wasn't sure what he'd expected. Gratitude at the very least. Friendship. Maybe—if luck had been with him—more than friendship. Maybe an evening with her. Maybe a night.

And what had he gotten for his trouble? A cold shoulder and a glass of spilled juice.

Granted, she hadn't asked him to go to all that trouble for her. If she were anyone else, she might've thought he was giving her the hard sell. But she *wasn't* anyone else. She was his lawyer, Jeff and Cindy Miller's partner. Ryan's friend. She was a woman he'd kissed, a woman he hadn't stopped thinking about since that kiss.

He'd wanted to kiss her tonight, too. He hadn't come to her house explicitly to make love with her—if that had been his purpose, he would have done her the courtesy of showering first—but he sure would have appreciated a warmer greeting. He would have liked at least to hug her.

But she'd been hell-bent on hugging herself. She'd wrapped her arms around her body as if they were a coat of armor, a bulwark against him. When he'd approached her she'd backed off, brandishing that damned mop as if she'd wanted to take a swipe at him. If it weren't for Chuck, the temperature in her kitchen would have approached absolute zero.

Call him an arrogant sonofabitch, but he wasn't used to being treated that way by a woman. He knew he wasn't irresistible to every lady on the planet, but he prided himself on being reasonably able to recognize when a woman was interested in him. If he'd read Beth wrong, so be it. She could have smiled politely and said, "No, thanks." He would have backed off, no hard feelings, no recriminations.

The hell with her. Let someone else build her damned deck—or let her live the rest of her snippy little life in a house without a deck. Let her waste beautiful evenings like this one indoors, protected from the night. Ryan didn't need her.

He twisted the key in the ignition, shifted into reverse and backed down the driveway. Pebbles crunched under his tires; the mild evening breeze wafted into the cab. He felt absurdly lonely.

He could probably cure his loneliness with a quick phone call to a certain young widow in temporary residence at Devon Hill. If he dropped in on Mitzi Rumson, she wouldn't shriek and fling her drink onto the floor and cross her arms in front of herself like a virgin trying to ward off a vampire. More likely she'd fill a second glass—not with apple juice but with something stronger, something a person wouldn't want her pet dog lapping off the floor—and she'd put her scantily clad body into overdrive. If he played his cards right, she'd probably invite him to make some improvements on her bedroom.

And afterward, he admitted dolefully, he would still be lonely. Maybe he would find something in Mitzi Rumson's arms, but he wouldn't find what he was looking for.

What he was looking for was inside the old, deckless house on Loring Road. He still wasn't even sure what it was, but it was more than Mitzi could ever offer him. More than any other woman could.

It was the mystery of Beth, and damned if he was ever going to solve it.

"YOU KNOW WHAT you need?" Cindy opined.

Beth could list about a zillion things she needed, starting with a built-in dishwasher and ending with a warm, male body in her bed. Thinking about warm male bodies only depressed her, so she zeroed in on the safer subject of dirty dishes. "I need a new kitchen," she said.

Cindy eyed her sagely. "That, too. First, however, you ought to build a deck."

Beth groaned. Somehow, unwittingly, Cindy had dragged her back to the subject of a warm, male body in her bed.

It had been several days since Ryan had barged in on her. She still had his folder of samples and estimates in her kitchen. She'd thumbed through the pages he'd produced for her, analyzed the sketches, studied the photographs of various cabinet veneers and floor tiles, and suffered all sorts of angst at the thought of telephoning him and saying she was ready to talk business.

She wasn't. Not with Ryan. But she wouldn't trust anyone else to tamper with her house.

On this mild Saturday morning, she and Cindy sat side by side on the tiny back porch, their hips touching and their feet planted on the ground. Erica was strapped into her stroller, dressed in an adorable yellow sunsuit and a white sun hat, alternately watching Chuck gallop around the yard and tossing bold-colored plastic blocks onto the grass. Cindy and Beth were taking turns scooping up the blocks before Chuck could chew on them.

"If you had a deck," Cindy continued, "you could put furniture on it. And we could sit on the furniture, like grown-ups."

"You sound like an old lady," Beth scolded.

"I'm not old. I just happen to prefer sitting in a chair. Lugging Erica around in utero for nine months destroyed my back."

Beth could have retorted that her body had endured much greater challenges than anything Cindy had experienced in her pregnancy. But she held her tongue. She didn't want Cindy ever to feel she had to watch her words or avoid certain topics to protect Beth's feelings.

"As a matter of fact, I *have* been thinking about building a deck," she admitted.

"Really? Have you gotten any estimates?"

"Yes."

Cindy twisted to face Beth, but the porch was so narrow they knocked knees. Before Cindy could scrunch her body sideways on the steps, Erica flung her rattle onto the ground and let out a howl. "Yes, Your Majesty," Cindy grumbled, lifting the rattle from the ground and wiping off the dirt on the hem of her T-shirt. She handed the rattle back to Erica, then settled back on the porch step. "Are you going to have Ryan do the deck?"

"I don't know."

"Who did you get the estimates from?"

Beth sighed. Cindy already knew the answer—and her question had nothing to do with decks and estimates. "I don't want to talk about it," she muttered.

"Now, now." Cindy brushed a mosquito off Beth's bare arm, then leaned back against the railing post. "I know Ryan. I know he's a scamp, but he's got a good heart. He couldn't have done anything to you that you wouldn't want to talk about."

"He didn't do anything to me," Beth assured her. She scooped a handful of shelled peanuts from the bowl on the top step, and nibbled them one by one. "He's a nice guy, but the chemistry is all wrong between us."

"Ryan's chemistry is the eighth wonder of the world," Cindy argued. "The only antidote to his chemistry—other than marriage to Jeffrey Miller," she added with a quiet smile at Jeff's daughter, who was sucking emphatically on a teething pretzel, "would be if Ryan did something rotten to you." She smiled expectantly, waiting for Beth to supply the rotten details.

Beth sighed again. "He didn't do anything rotten. *I* was the rotten one," she admitted. Her hostility had obviously scared him off. She hadn't heard from him since his visit.

"You? Rotten?"

"Cindy." The word came out as a lament. "I'm just not ready for Ryan yet."

"You're insecure."

"No kidding."

"Why?"

"Why?" A low wail escaped Beth, even though she was smiling. "Look at me. Do I look ready for anything?"

"I'm looking at you, Beth, and what I see is a tired lady in a pair of cutoffs and a camp shirt who ought to be using some sunblock because your cheeks are turning pink from the sun. Other than that, I think you're looking pretty darned good." She continued to ponder Beth intently. Beth braced herself, suspecting that Cindy was going to spout one of her *You need to get wet* speeches. She confounded Beth's expectations, though. "All right, maybe Ryan's too much of a good thing. But Martha Strossen could set you up with someone. She's Devon's resident matchmaker, and I know she could find you someone tamer than Ryan."

"I don't want to have someone found for me," Beth protested. "Don't pressure me, okay? I swear to God, you can be more annoying than Chuck."

Cindy turned to gaze at Chuck, who had planted his front paws on the bark of a red maple and was barking at a squirrel in the branches. "He's gotten awfully big, hasn't he."

"He seems to double in size every day."

"Any regrets?"

"About him?" Beth snorted. "It's too late. I'm in love with him. But I've learned my lesson," she added, smiling wryly. "Leading with your heart is stupid. I fell madly in love with him, and now I'm stuck with all his nonsense. I haven't got the stamina to fall in love more than once a year."

"So Chuck's got you this year. Maybe next year you'll try something with Ryan. Assuming he's still available."

"I'm not going to try anything with Ryan," Beth declared firmly. She'd already tried something with him and it had thrown her nervous system completely out of alignment.

Cindy checked her watch. "It's almost lunchtime. Are you sure I can't talk you into going swimming at the lake with us?"

Beth shook her head. If she was insecure now, it was nothing compared to the way she felt in a swimsuit. "I've got errands to run," she said. "I've got to buy some new throw pillows for the couch in the den. Chuck demolished one the other night. He must be teething, too." She glanced at Erica, who was beginning to whimper, her jaws clamped around her plastic pretzel.

Cindy rose, bent over the stroller and scooped Erica into her arms. "Are your gums sore, love-bunch? I think I've got some ointment for that. Mommy has ointment for everything, doesn't she?" She rummaged in the large tote she'd looped over the back of the stroller. "Look at this, Erica—I've got ointment for your gums and ointment for your scalp, and ointment for your little bottom. Heaven help us all if I use the wrong ointment on the wrong body part." She pulled tube after tube of salve from the tote, searching for the teething analgesic. A clean diaper tumbled out of the bag, and a box of crackers and a pacifier.

Beth came down from the porch to help her. She gathered the diaper and pacifier, then caught a folded newspaper as it tumbled out of the bag. "What's this? Is Erica reading the *Wall Street Journal* already?"

"Oh, that—I meant to give that to you. It's not the *Wall Street Journal,* it's the *Devon Gazette.*"

"The *Devon Gazette?*" Beth unfolded the thin paper. The front page carried a full-color photograph of a Little League team in uniform, standing in front of the hardware store on Main Street. "Oh, wow," she said with a laugh. "I love small-town life."

"You ought to get a subscription to the *Gazette*. It lists every garage sale and craft fair in the area, and it has the best coverage of all the really important news, like whether the Public Works Department should purchase a new snowplow and who won the school district spelling bee."

"This is great," Beth said, flipping through the pages and thinking about how glad she was not to be in Manhattan, where muggings were so common, they weren't even considered newsworthy. What a joy it was to live in a town where Little League teams were considered front-page news.

"Keep it. I've already read it," Cindy said, raising her voice to be heard over Erica's growing crescendo of sobs. She rubbed ointment onto the baby's gums, then cuddled her tight. Erica continued to bawl. "Oh, sweetie, I know it hurts," she murmured, then sighed. "I'll tell you, if there's anything that would make me an atheist, it's teething pain. I can't believe God couldn't have come up with a better way for babies to cut their teeth."

"Poor baby," Beth cooed, stroking Erica's back. Even Chuck trotted over, his brown eyes round with concern for the sobbing child.

"A nap would do her some good. A nap and an afternoon at the lake with Daddy and Mommy." Cindy kissed Erica's cheek. "Yes, Your Majesty. We're going to go home now and get our beach things and go to the lake. Would you like that? Daddy's waiting for us. You know his shoulder comforts you better than mine does."

Even the promise of Jeff's shoulder couldn't console Erica. Beth quickly tossed the tote into the stroller and wheeled it around the house to the driveway while Cindy carried her shrieking daughter. It amazed Beth that a child could be so cheerful one minute and anguished the next.

But life could be like that. One minute a woman could be making partner at a prestigious Manhattan law firm, and the next she could be in an oncologist's office, hearing that the biopsy came back positive.

One minute she could be kissing the sexiest man she'd ever met, and the next minute she could be fleeing a torrent of emotions, racing for higher ground, longing for safety.

Shoving her troubling thoughts to the back of her mind, she strapped Erica into her baby seat in the car while Cindy folded the stroller and slid it into the trunk. Erica's howls subsided. She gazed at Beth through watery eyes, and Beth felt a sharp tug in her soul. Erica was like Chuck, she thought—fussy, demanding, yet overflowing with love.

Of course, Erica would grow up and talk and become a real human being. Erica was all it took to make Cindy a mother. Chuck couldn't make Beth a mother. A woman and a dog did not exactly equal a family. Even with Chuck, Beth was alone.

More troubling thoughts. She tuned them out for as long as it took to hug Cindy and wave her off.

She circled the house to the backyard. Chuck had returned to the red maple, even though the squirrel he'd chased into its branches had gone tree-hopping and was no longer trapped above him. Chuck barked and snuffled. Beth wondered how long he'd lurk beneath the tree before he realized the squirrel was gone.

Coming to terms with reality wasn't easy for anyone, she thought with a sympathetic smile for her puppy.

She lifted the *Devon Gazette* and settled back on the porch steps. After popping a handful of peanuts into her mouth, she leafed through the tabloid, skimming stories about a Brownie troop performing songs at a senior citizen center, a quilter who was donating one of her quilts to the library auction, a member of the Resources Board who was concerned about overfishing in some of the region's rivers. Beth even read the "police blotter"; most of the reports concerned noise complaints, spray-painted mailboxes and dead critters in the road. The worst thing that had happened in Devon in the past week was that someone had hit a deer with his pickup on Route 47—the truck suffered minor damage but the deer survived.

Beth was safer in Devon than she'd ever been in New York. So why didn't she feel safer?

Because New York didn't have Ryan Walker.

Forget him, she ordered herself, flipping another page. She read advertisements, accounts of American Legion projects, house sales in the area. On a back page the town listed all parties in arrears on their quarterly property taxes. She started to fold the newspaper shut when a name on the property tax list caught her eye.

The Walker Construction Company owed the Town of Devon $49,745 in back taxes.

Beth swore under her breath. It didn't matter if she never put a deck on her house or spruced up her kitchen or added ceiling fans and French doors. It didn't matter if she never kissed Ryan again or felt relaxed enough with him to tell him what she'd been through. It didn't matter if she spent the rest of her life without ever finding out if he was a strong enough, loving enough, good enough man to accept her as she was.

All that mattered was that she was Walker Construction's lawyer and her client had gotten himself in trouble. And it was her job, as Ryan's lawyer, to save him.

CHAPTER TEN

RYAN'S DEFINITION of pathetic was when the most exciting thing in your life was watching a flaky millionaire from Boston toddle around a swampy construction site in spike-heeled gold mules.

It had drizzled earlier that morning, leaving the cleared lot muddy and dotted with puddles. Sometime that day, Ryan was expecting a delivery of concrete slabs. By midweek, weather permitting, the foundation would be in. In the meantime, the earthmovers were tracking through the muck, leaving herringbone treadmarks in their wake. A touch of early-morning rain couldn't slow them down.

A touch of early-morning rain couldn't slow Mitzi down, either. She sashayed around the site in an unzipped cherry red slicker that kept flapping open to reveal her short shorts and cropped shirt. She looked like some oversexed sorority girl who had spent last night with her sorority sisters, giggling and painting her toenails gold to match her open-toed shoes.

Ryan knew he was judging her too harshly. She didn't deserve his scorn. All she had done was drive up to the site in her snazzy Mercedes coupe an hour ago, wave cheerily at Ryan's crew and then shadow him, yakking about the imported roseate marble tiles she wanted for the foyer and the customized butcher-block counters of white ash she was ordering for the kitchen. And yakking, as well, about how wonderful Ryan was, how much she trusted him to make her dream—this monstrous mansion—become a reality. She was looking forward to trying out the double-width Jacuzzi he was going to install directly under a skylight in her master bathroom so that she could set lit candles all around the tub and turn it on, steamy with scented water, and strip off all her clothing and lie in the bubbles and gaze up at the stars. There would be plenty of room for someone to join her in that steamy, bubbly, scented Jacuzzi, she'd told him with a pointed stare.

If only he felt the slightest pinch of attraction for her. She was obviously open for business. He could have a grand time with her if he let himself.

But he couldn't pretend an interest that wasn't there. Mitzi was a knockout, she was in-your-face sexy, she was as steamy and bubbly as the Jacuzzi she had described in mouth-watering detail. But Ryan couldn't fake what he didn't feel. And, for Mitzi, he didn't feel anything. To his everlasting regret, an erratic blond lawyer who kissed like no other woman in the world had hijacked his full supply of desire.

Nearly a week had passed since he'd last seen Beth. Nearly a week since that strange, strained evening when he'd brought her his estimates and she'd made him feel about as welcome as food poisoning.

The least she could have done in the intervening days was inform him that she wasn't going to hire Walker Construction to build her deck. One little phone call was all it would take. She wouldn't even have to talk to him. She could tell Larry or leave a message on Ryan's answering machine.

Frequently he had to wait a month to get a thumbs-up or thumbs-down on a bid. But Beth's failure to contact him might have nothing to do with indecision about the project or an interest in collecting more bids before she selected a contractor.

More likely she was avoiding Ryan. For whatever reason, she preferred to pretend there was nothing going on between them, to dismiss the fact that, not only had they managed to set the world on fire with one unforgettable kiss, but they'd had a pretty decent time of it, too, when they weren't kissing. They'd talked and laughed and—idiot that he was—he'd thought they'd enjoyed each other's company.

Either the enjoyment had been one-sided or Beth was the most schizoid woman in New England.

"So, about the towel racks," Mitzi babbled, traipsing with him across the clearing to a pair of ancient pines that stood directly in the path of where the concrete pourer ought to funnel. He'd asked her if those trees could be knocked down, but she'd said absolutely not. This meant the chute would have to be positioned on the north side of the foundation, which would make the entire process more lengthy and costly. It was Mitzi's dollar, though, and thanks to Beth and the wonders she'd worked in revising the contract for this job, he wasn't going to get stuck for the extra cost.

Beth could sure work wonders, he thought glumly. He wished she'd work some wonders on him. He wished...

"If you put electric towel heaters in the bathroom," Mitzi prattled, breaking into his ruminations, "then after we—I mean, me and whoever—climb out of the Jacuzzi, we wouldn't get cold, isn't that right?"

"I told you, Mitzi, all the insulation in the world isn't going to keep that room warm with the blasted skylight overhead. I'll do the best I can, but I can't make any promises if you're going to insist on the skylight."

"It's just that I'd hate for anyone to catch a cold. Winnie—my beloved husband, may he rest in peace—liked a chilly house. He was tough that way. Are you tough, Ryan, or do you like things warm? I'll bet you do.... Say, isn't that your lawyer?"

Ryan spun around, splattering mud across the instep of his boot. Gazing past Mitzi, he spotted a slim blond woman standing on the shoulder of the road, not far from where his crew had parked their cars. She had on a neat beige suit, a shade lighter than her hair, and a blue blouse a shade darker than her eyes. She carried her leather briefcase and held her head high. Her hair fluttered in the dank breeze. Despite the overcast sky, the building site suddenly seemed a whole lot brighter.

The hell with brighter. She hadn't driven all the way to the site to brighten his day. If she'd had anything remotely personal to discuss with him, she wouldn't have tracked him down here. For that matter, if she'd finally made up her mind about the renovations for her house, she would have telephoned. The only reason she would have traveled to the outskirts of town during business hours was to deliver bad news.

The clouds shifted overhead, fifteen variations on gray. They matched his mood perfectly.

Smothering a curse, he excused himself, leaving Mitzi by her precious pines, and tramped across the rutted site to where Beth stood beside his truck. "Fancy meeting you here," he muttered, wishing her face didn't look so smooth and fresh, wishing her eyes weren't so crystalline, so damnably trustworthy.

He didn't trust her. More significantly, he didn't trust himself. Already he was responding to her, his muscles regrouping, his pulse adopting a new tempo, his mouth remembering the shape and texture and taste of hers. His memory was awash with the sound of her laughter, the cool music of her voice when she was negotiating, the love and exasperation she expressed over her dog....

Damn. Seeing her forced him to realize how much he had missed her.

"I'm sorry to bother you like this, but it's important," she said.

Well, he could have figured that much out. She wouldn't have gone this far out of her way for him if it wasn't. "What happened?" he asked sarcastically. "Did Chuck have a run-in with a skunk?"

She lifted her chin as if she thought that would make her look less dainty and out of place at a construction site. Her eyes glinted with an emotion halfway between anger and anxiety. "Is there a place where we can talk without all these people around? It's really important," she said.

He scanned the site, then took her arm and led her around his truck and past an idle bulldozer toward the woods that bordered the lot. Between the trees and the huge yellow tractor, they were shielded from everyone at the site. Enough pine needles had fallen to the ground along the edge of the woods to protect her shoes from the mud.

As soon as he could, Ryan let his hand drop. Touching her did weird things to him. He was too conscious of the silk of her suit, the delicate angle of her elbow. Physical contact with her tested his willpower, and it was a test he wasn't sure he could pass.

The air smelled of evergreens and imminent rain and Beth. It was cool for a mid-June day, but Ryan felt hot. His nerves churned; a muscle ticked in his jaw. He wanted this little one-on-one over with as quickly as possible. The sooner she departed, the sooner he could go back to resenting her.

"Your company is in arrears on its property tax payments," she told him.

That she could state such inconsequential news with such a grave expression caused him to laugh out loud. "What?"

"Walker Construction owes almost fifty thousand dollars in taxes to the Town of Devon."

He laughed harder. "You came all the way out here to tell me that?"

She clearly didn't share his amusement. "I guess you could say I've gone above and beyond the call of duty, but yes, I came all the way out here to tell you that. I wouldn't have bothered, but I had Lynne call Larry to discuss it with him this morning and he refused to talk to her."

"I don't blame him. No one wants to talk to Lynne. When you talk to Lynne, you wind up learning about Stalin's taste in pop music and the mating habits of slugs. *I* sure don't want to talk to her."

"Lynne can be difficult to take, but she's a font of wisdom," Beth retorted. "She gave me excellent advice on how to train Chuck."

"She didn't knock herself out putting in an electric fence for Chuck," he shot back. Alluding to the personal favor he'd done for her was out of line, since she obviously hadn't come to the site with anything but business on her mind, but what the hell. If Beth wasn't going to acknowledge that she and Ryan had a history, that they were friends, that in the not-too-distant past there'd been a chance that they might have become lovers, he would.

She pursed her lips and took a deep breath. "This isn't a social call, Ryan," she said quietly.

"Does that mean I'm paying for this meeting?"

"No." She took another deep breath. He watched her nostrils narrow as she inhaled. He'd never before noticed what a pretty nose she had, how well it balanced the rest of her face. "Ryan..." She sighed, her eyes flitting left and right in an attempt to avoid looking directly at him. "I came here because you have a legal problem. This isn't a good time to talk about...other things."

"When would a good time be?"

At last she met his gaze. Once again her chin jutted out, firm and stubborn. "Do you care about paying the taxes you owe or would you just as soon have the town confiscate your property?"

"Talk to Larry. He's in charge of paying the taxes."

"I talked to him. After Lynne got nowhere with him, I went to the office. He didn't seem to think it was a big deal."

"Neither do I."

"Well, it *is* a big deal. Your company was named on the debtors' list in the *Devon Gazette*."

"For what? Fifty grand?" He shrugged. "I'll bet it's the taxes on a twenty-acre tract of land we bought on spec last year. We haven't developed it yet. We aren't sure what we want to do with it."

"It doesn't matter what you're going to do with it. You still have to pay the property tax."

"Fine. I'll pay the tax."

"Ryan," she scolded, "you're not taking this seriously."

"I said I'd pay it, and I will."

"By the time the town assessor lists you publicly as being in arrears, it's serious. You can't just brush it off as if it were a joke."

She was acting like a headmistress scolding a naughty schoolboy, and he didn't like it. The next thing he knew, she was going to make him write a hundred times on the blackboard, "I will not neglect my property taxes."

"Look," he retorted, not caring if she saw how aggravated he was. "This is Devon. Everyone knows me. They know Larry. They knew our fathers. No one is going to run us out of town on a rail for accidentally missing a tax payment."

"Several tax payments. They don't put you on the list if you're just a month late. You're a *year* late, Ryan."

"So we're a year late. They know we'll pay the tax, and we will. I'm sure Larry thought he paid it. He probably mislaid the bill. He can be a little careless that way. It's no big deal."

"Taxes *are* a big deal. When you're a local business and your local newspaper publishes that you're deadbeats, it's bad. If you refuse to recognize how bad it is, Ryan... You're in denial about this, aren't you?"

"Denial?" He snorted. "Give me a break. Larry isn't a deadbeat and neither am I. Walker Construction is an institution in this town. This isn't your fancy Manhattan law firm. We're in Devon now. People take things a little less intensely here."

"I'm your lawyer. It's my job to take things like this intensely."

"It's your job to represent my company," he snapped. "And I'm telling you to back off." He heard an undertone of rage in his words. She must have heard, too. She had to know that underneath their bickering about his tax debt, he was talking about them, about his frustration with her, his disappointment, his impatience . . . and his disgust with himself for caring. He didn't want to care so much about a woman. But he cared about Beth, way too much. And it infuriated him as much as it bewildered him.

A raindrop shook free from a leaf overhead and landed on her forehead. He couldn't take his eyes off the clear bead against her flawless skin. She seemed oblivious to the raindrop as it shimmered above the graceful arch of her eyebrow. "I'm not trying to give you a hard time, Ryan. I'm just a competent attorney doing my darnedest to keep you out of legal hot water. I want you to explain to Larry how important this tax mess is. I know he doesn't like me, but—"

"He likes you fine." Ryan's voice emerged in a hoarse growl. Every nerve in his body was poised, every sensory organ focused on that trembling raindrop.

"Ryan." Her voice sounded suddenly strained, too. She must have realized he was no longer listening to her tirade, no longer seeing a lawyer. All he saw was a woman he desired.

The raindrop was driving him crazy. Whatever happened next—and he knew damned well what was going to happen next—he would blame it on temporary insanity, brought on by a single drop of precipitation.

He bowed toward her and brushed his lips against her brow. The droplet was chilly, her skin warm. Her shoulders flinched, her head jerked slightly, but she didn't shrink from him. She held her ground, her sensible leather pumps planted on the carpet of pine needles, her arms stiff at her sides.

Her hands, he noted, were not curled into fists. Things were not about to degenerate into violence.

Allowing himself a small grin, he grazed her forehead with his mouth once more, kissed the bridge of her nose, then the tip. "You are so beautiful," he whispered.

"No, I'm not," she whispered back, sounding surprisingly resolute. She wasn't fishing for compliments or itching for an argument. She was simply stating a fact.

A nonfact, he amended. An erroneous fact. With her slender, fine-boned figure, her exquisite features, her fair coloring, her creamy skin and long-lashed eyes and her mouth, less than an inch from his, less than half an inch...

His lips found hers, locked onto hers, reveled in the familiar taste of her. He slid his hands under her jacket, clamped them on her narrow waist and pulled her against him. She tasted good. She tasted electrifyingly, galvanizingly, splendiferously good. She tasted like honey and melon, like bittersweet chocolate and mint. She tasted like passion.

He deepened the kiss, probing her mouth with his tongue, entering, conquering. His body responded and he urged her more snugly to himself, letting her know what he was feeling, what he was wanting. She shuddered and lifted her hands to his upper arms. Her fingers arched around his hard biceps, and he imagined them curling around another, harder part of him, squeezing, stroking.

He felt a raindrop strike his face from an overhanging tree branch. He was so hot, he almost heard the cool water sizzle as it slid down his cheek. Beth was hot, too, her body molding to his, moving with his. She dug into his arms with her fingertips and whimpered as he brought his hands down to her hips and pressed her to himself.

"Ryan, stop," she whispered. She was shivering, but he knew she couldn't be cold. She had practically buried herself in his embrace; her body was nestled so tightly against his, he could feel the burning heat of her skin through the layers of clothing that separated them. She hid her face against his shoulder and sighed brokenly.

"I'm stopping," he murmured, but the only thing he stopped doing was kissing her. His hands remained on her bottom, molded to the sweet roundness of her, guiding her against his erection.

"I don't want this," she said.

"Yes, you do. We both do."

"It's wrong."

"I swear to God, if you hit me with that lawyer-client crap again, I'll fire you. Even if I wind up in jail for failure to pay my property taxes."

Her muffled laugh vibrated against his neck. Slowly she extricated herself from his arms, and he saw that in spite of her laughter she wasn't really smiling. "Ryan, I just—I can't do this."

"Do what?" he asked, watching her closely. He *knew* she wanted him as much as he wanted her. He *knew*. He could taste it in her. He could feel it. He was on fire with it.

So what couldn't she do? Why?

"I can't get involved with you."

He slid his hands back up to her waist but refused to let go of her. Peering down into her upturned face, he saw that she looked glass-eyed and damp-lipped and troubled. "Why not?"

"I'm not..." She took a deep breath but refused to look away from him. "I'm not what you think I am."

"What do I think you are?"

She held his gaze for a long moment, then lowered her eyes to his chin. "I...I don't want to talk about it, Ryan, okay? Not now. I came here to get it through your thick skull that property taxes are important."

As far as Ryan was concerned, the most important thing right now was the unrelenting tension in his groin and, surprisingly, the even greater tension in his heart. The woman who could ease both those tensions, the woman who could make him laugh and make him smile and make him hard, the woman who could invade his thoughts and his dreams without any apparent effort. The woman who claimed to be not what he thought.

Property taxes were way down on his list of priorities. "Can I see you tonight?" he asked.

"No."

"Tomorrow night?"

She bit her lip and shook her head.

"How about if I promise to cut a check for the Town of Devon and hand-deliver it to the assessor's office this afternoon?"

A faint smile teased her lips. "Ryan... It's not that I don't like you. I do."

"Whoa. That's a relief. I was beginning to think, the way you just kissed me, you hated my guts."

"Okay," she conceded. "When we kiss, you—you sort of make me lose my mind a little."

"It's a start," he teased, wishing she would give him a bigger, more genuine smile. "How can I get you to lose your mind a lot?"

He got another smile from her. "I don't want to lose my mind, Ryan. I just . . . I don't think I can handle anything more right now."

"What am I asking you to handle? We're on the same wavelength here, Beth. We're both heading in the same direction. We want the same thing."

She shook her head, her smile so sad, he had to restrain himself from gathering her in his arms again.

"Life isn't so simple, Ryan," she said. "Nothing about this is simple."

"Nothing about this is complicated, either," he argued, although he had the distinct feeling the conversation had left him behind. He'd suspected for a while that something was going on with her, something strange and secret, something she couldn't seem to share with him. Whatever it was, he was certain that he could make it go away if only she would let him—and if only he didn't scare her away by pushing too hard, too fast. "I'm not looking to do a number on you, Beth. I'm sure we could work it all out if you'd let me in on whatever the heck is going on with you."

"I can't discuss it now," she said abruptly. "It's the middle of the morning, we're standing next to a huge piece of earth-moving machinery and I've got to go back to my office. I'm handling a closing at noon."

"Oh. Well, we sure wouldn't want you to be late for a closing," he scoffed. So what if he sounded impatient? Here they were, on the brink of something incredible, a passion that could move the earth far more profoundly than any machinery at the site, and she wanted to handle a closing.

"I'm sorry, Ryan," she murmured. He saw tears in her eyes, unshed but glistening. If anything she'd said in the past five minutes came from her heart, it was this.

But why did she have to be sorry? Why couldn't they just figure out what was hanging her up and take care of it? Why did he feel her retreating from him when he was absolutely certain that they ought to be moving forward together?

Why in God's name was she on the verge of crying?

Lots of questions, but he wasn't going to get any answers. She was already walking away, ducking under the massive arm of the bulldozer and moving in swift, desperate strides across the muddy site to her car.

YOU ARE NOT OKAY, she told herself, gunning the engine and tearing away from the construction site. *You did not do a single thing right. You botched everything.*

She couldn't believe she'd lapsed into medical jargon, of all things, when she had reproached Ryan for his lackadaisical attitude regarding property taxes. His refusal to believe anything was wrong reminded her of her own refusal to believe that the disease she'd been diagnosed with actually killed people. No, the lump couldn't really be a malignancy; no, the malignancy couldn't really be that terrible; no, she really wasn't going to lose her breast.

Admittedly, refusing to believe that a failure to pay property taxes had serious repercussions wasn't the same as refusing to believe that she really, truly had cancer. But Ryan had been in denial.

And what had Beth been in?

Not love. Not rapture. Just a strange, inexplicable state of madness. Maybe it was chemistry, as Cindy had suggested. Maybe magnetism. The inexorable force of gravity. Planetary forces drawing her and Ryan together. Hormonal spasms.

Yet none of it seemed particularly scientific or logical. Ryan was a gorgeous hunk, but Beth had never before responded so emotionally to a man just because he was a gorgeous hunk. Perhaps it was his wit that drew her to him, his dexterity, his ability to build things. Perhaps it was his mesmerizing brown eyes or his thick, strong hands or the way his tongue stole inside her mouth and claimed it. Maybe it was the way his body had sought hers, his hardness moving against her.

Logical or not, she was responding to him all over again, even though she'd reached Main Street.

Her response to him made sense. But his to her? How could he call her beautiful when a woman with Mitzi Rumson's outstanding physical attributes had been lurking at the other end of the clearing? Why wasn't Ryan kissing Mitzi, holding her, rocking her body with his? Why Beth?

Because he didn't know the truth, that was why. Because when she argued that she wasn't beautiful, he didn't have a clue what she was talking about.

She arrived at the converted Victorian off Main Street with enough spare time before the closing to devour a cup of yogurt and pack her memories of her confrontation with Ryan into a neat little compartment at the back of her mind. She entered the conference room determined that not for one minute would the buyer, the seller, the two Realtors and the bank mortgage officer assembled around the long table in the erstwhile dining room suspect that her emotions were in turmoil.

The closing went smoothly. By three o'clock, the last *i* had been dotted, the last *t* crossed. The principals had shaken hands, the banker had presented a check to the seller, and the seller had presented a check to Beth. She kept a smile pasted on her face until everyone was done congratulating one another and wishing each other well, then rushed back to her office and collapsed into her chair like a punctured blow-up doll. Although the windows were open and the low-lying clouds had kept the temperature down, she was sweating. She felt limp and drained from the effort of not thinking about Ryan.

And she was going to keep up that effort, she insisted, hauling herself out of her chair and crossing the hall to what had once been the kitchen. A large portion of the original kitchen was now Cindy's office, but the remaining nook contained a sink, a small refrigerator, a stove and a microwave. One of Erica's pacifiers lay on the counter.

Beth pulled a pint bottle of orange juice from the refrigerator, wrenched off the top and carried it into her office. She took a swig of juice and pulled out her folders for the malpractice case she'd agreed to take. The challenges it presented were so complicated and convoluted, reviewing it might keep thoughts of Ryan from running amok in her mind.

She pored over the file for two hours, unearthing numerous grounds for a suit. By five o'clock the orange juice was gone and she was seeing double from too much reading. If she were at her old firm in New York, she would be ordering out for Chinese food right now and planning to spend another two or three hours finetooth combing the file. But she wasn't in New York, and Chuck had been outdoors in the damp, dreary weather all day, and she was going to go home.

She closed the file and locked it inside her desk, then shut down her laptop and slid it into her briefcase. Tossing the empty juice bottle into the recycle bin, she stood, stretched and promised herself to go home and hug Chuck in gratitude because the only problems he caused her related to his teeth, his bladder and his bowels. Those were problems she could handle without losing a piece of her soul in the process.

Briefcase in hand, she left her office and headed down the hall. Lynne sat at her desk in the reception area, chatting with Jeff. His tie hung loose, and his eyeglasses were misted from the humidity. He had been in court all afternoon, and he looked as if he'd completed quite a workout. "How'd it go?" she asked.

"Great." Despite his exhaustion, Jeff seemed invigorated. "I got three of their witnesses to admit it was too dark to see my client's face. I think we've got a shot at reasonable doubt."

"Your client is guilty as sin," Beth remarked.

"How do you know? It was too dark to see his face." Jeff grinned smugly.

"Reasonable doubt is a tricky concept," Lynne pontificated, leaning back in her chair and looking alarmingly knowledgeable. "According to the Constitution—"

The front door swung open. With the heavy thud of his boots against the rug, Ryan Walker announced his arrival at Miller, Miller and Pendleton, Attorneys-at-Law.

"Ryan!" Jeff greeted him heartily. "Hey, pal, what brings you here?"

Ryan ignored him. He ignored Lynne, who seemed upset that his entrance had interrupted her analysis of the Constitution. His gaze zeroed in on Beth.

His hair was damp, his cheeks glistening slightly from the late-afternoon drizzle. His T-shirt clung to his torso; mud clung to the hems of his jeans. His eyes were the color of espresso, dark and strong and dangerous.

"We have to talk," he announced.

Beth swallowed. Her hands felt cold, but the nape of her neck felt warm. So did her belly. So did her cheeks, her thighs, the hollow between her hips. Memories of his kisses inundated her, memories of his callused fingertips stroking her skin, memories of the possessive sweep of his tongue into her mouth, memories of his body seeking hers.

Memories of the accusation in his gaze.

He had the right to know the truth. Before anything further happened between them, he had the right to know. She couldn't put off telling him any longer.

"Yes," she said, seeing only him. "We have to talk."

HER OFFICE HAD CHANGED considerably since he'd last seen it. The floor was now covered with a burgundy patterned rug, the pictures had been hung, and the shelves were full of leather-bound books lined up like soldiers in uniform. Curtains graced the windows, and the desktop was polished to a mirror gloss.

He took it all in with a quick glance, then narrowed his focus on her. He had come to her office steaming with anger, ready to pick a fight, ready to shake an explanation out of her—or shake some sense into her. But now that they were alone in her office at the end of the hall, having left Jeff and Lynne gaping after them in bemusement, all Ryan wanted to do was remove her neatly tailored jacket, her blue shell blouse and every other scrap of clothing she had on. He wanted to kiss her all over. He wanted to suckle her breasts and slide his tongue between her legs. He wanted to hear her groan when she climaxed.

And then he wanted his turn at groaning.

And then, afterward, if they ever came back down to earth, they could talk.

She kept her jacket on, her blouse neatly tucked in, her hands folded primly before her as she moved to the far side of her desk. Her eyes were a bit too bright as she studied him, her lips thin with tension.

"What I was thinking," he began, "was maybe if we went to bed once, we'd get over it."

Her cheeks darkened with rosy color. "Get over what?"

"This—infatuation. This obsession. This lust."

She gazed toward the window as if contemplating a quick escape over the sill. Then she sighed and turned back to him. "Ryan..."

"All right, look." He had to keep this light, non-threatening. He had to assure her that he meant her no harm. He had come to win her over. "I talked to Larry. I told him that if he didn't pay the property tax tomorrow, I would personally tar and feather him. He's going to take care of it. Consider it done, okay?"

"Ryan."

"I'm just telling you I'm being a good boy. I heard everything you said this morning—"

"No, you didn't."

He itched to touch her, to take her in his arms and hold her tight. "I did," he murmured, circling the desk. To her credit, she didn't back away as he closed in on her—although she really couldn't, not without banging into a bookshelf. "I heard every single word you said. All the stuff about how life isn't simple and you're not what I think. I also heard the part where you said you liked me and I make you lose your mind. You make me lose mine, Beth. I think we ought to lose our minds together."

"You said you came here to talk," she murmured when he was less than an inch from her.

He *had* come to talk. But now he was with her, enclosed in her office, all alone with the most frustrating, tantalizing, enigmatic woman he'd ever known, and he wanted more than her words.

She turned as he reached for her, but he looped his arms around her waist and drew her back against him. He felt the angles of her shoulder blades through her jacket, the curve of her bottom through her skirt. Her hair smelled of a citrus shampoo; he nuzzled it with his chin.

"Ryan." Her voice emerged throaty, breathless. "I need to tell you something."

"Okay," he said, using his chin to nudge aside her hair so he could kiss her ear. She gasped as he nibbled the lobe, as he pressed his lips to her jaw. She shivered and wilted against him. "Are you losing your mind yet?" he whispered.

"Yes." It was half a sigh, half a snarl. "And I don't want to. We have to talk."

"We'll talk later," he suggested, flattening his palms over her taut belly. He felt the ridge of her lower ribs and glided his hands upward. If he could just cup his fingers around her breasts, if he could caress her, if he could turn her on half as much as she turned him on—

She clamped her hands over his and peeled them away. "Ryan."

He waited for the heat in his groin to subside. He didn't trust his voice, but if talk was truly what she wanted, he would tell her what was on his mind. "Let me make love to you," he whispered.

She didn't immediately respond. Her fingers curled around his wrists. "You might not want to."

Not want to? She had to be crazy to think that, even crazier than he was from the need to love her. "Why wouldn't I want to?"

"I have one breast."

CHAPTER ELEVEN

IT WAS AS IF a tiny shock had jolted him, not enough to kill him or even hurt him, but enough to bring him to a full stop. She imagined it was like what Chuck would feel if he tried to cross the electric fence at her house. Ryan's hands stiffened almost imperceptibly in hers. His breath caught for a fraction of an instant. His body twitched, and when the twitch passed there was a space between her back and his chest that hadn't been there before.

She closed her eyes. The room was so quiet, she could hear the ticking of her wristwatch.

This wasn't going to go well. She knew it as soon as she sensed the new space between Ryan and herself, a protective buffer he suddenly considered necessary. Her flesh was still warm from his embrace; her heartbeat still raced from his kiss. But now he knew about her and he was going to behave the way Peter had when she'd broken the news to him. Ryan was going to sail off, stranding her alone on the shore, high and dry.

"You have one breast," he said. His voice sounded altered. The undertone of humor that always lurked in it, even when he was angry, had somehow disappeared.

"Yes."

His arms were still looped around her waist, but the moment she loosened her grip on his hands he released her and stepped back. He didn't want to touch her; she understood. He couldn't bear to be close to her.

She was wrong about that, actually. He placed his hands on her shoulders and rotated her until she was facing him. Mustering her courage, she gazed up into his face. He looked utterly bewildered. "What are you talking about?"

"I found a lump in my breast two years ago. It turned out to be malignant, and I had a mastectomy."

"You had cancer?" Horror mixed with his bewilderment, and grief. God help her, if she detected even a trace of pity in him, she would scream.

"Yes," she said carefully, monitoring his expression. She would rather he rejected her than pitied her. She would rather just about anything than pity. "I had breast cancer."

He scrutinized her, thoughtful, intent, his eyes glinting with what might have been panic but definitely wasn't pity. She realized with some small relief that telling Ryan hadn't been as difficult as she'd expected. It had been harder to telephone her parents when she'd gotten the results of the biopsy. It had been harder to share her appalling news with Cindy. Perhaps she had told enough people enough times that she no longer choked on the words. Or perhaps she'd dreaded this particular conversation with Ryan so much that the reality of it was anticlimactic.

"God." His hands remained on her shoulders, solid and consoling. He wasn't afraid to touch her, after all. Maybe she'd been unduly pessimistic. Maybe he would rise to the occasion. "How are you now?"

"The doctors say I'm in remission," she answered, then allowed herself a tiny smile. "I prefer to think of myself as cured."

He nodded. His face was close enough to hers that, if she rose on tiptoe, she could kiss him. But a new emotion was filtering into his eyes, now. Not pity, thank heavens, but something almost as bad—wariness.

Slowly he let his hands fall from her. He continued to stare at her, curious, bemused, clearly apprehensive. "I thought—I thought only older women got that."

"It's more common in older women than younger ones," she confirmed, content to keep the conversation on a scientific level. "I was thirty when I was diagnosed."

"And then—you came here? To Devon, I mean. I knew you'd left New York for a reason. Is this it?"

She nodded. "I did a lot of thinking while I was undergoing treatment. I thought about how I'd been living such a high-pressure existence. I thought about how I wanted to spend the rest of my life, and I decided it wasn't as a lawyer for big-city developers. I know it's a cliché, but I wanted to stop and smell the flowers."

"You wanted to walk barefoot in the grass," he recalled.

"Yes. And Cindy said, 'Come to Devon.' So I came."

He abruptly broke from her and prowled in a restless path around her small office. She stayed out of his way, letting him brood, letting him burn off his nervous energy.

After a few circuits, he halted near the window. "Why didn't you tell me this earlier?"

Don't read the worst into it, she cautioned herself. Ryan wasn't saying what she'd hoped he would say— some variation of, "Who gives a damn about a silly old breast? You're perfect just the way you are." But he hadn't run away yet. He hadn't gagged and grimaced and fled. She could forgive him for being disconcerted.

''What should I have said?'' she asked, attempting a smile. 'Hi, I'm Beth Pendleton and I've got one breast'?''

He rested a hand against the windowsill. She noticed a faint scar near his thumb, a line paler than the sundarkened skin around it. She thought of her own scar and tried to imagine his thick, tan, trivially scarred hand stroking her skin. The picture wouldn't come into focus. The notion of Ryan caressing her simply didn't seem possible.

It dawned on her that he was no longer studying her face. His gaze angled down to her chest. ''It looks—I mean, you look normal.''

''I'm wearing a prosthesis,'' she explained. ''It's molded into the shape of a breast and it slips into a pouch in my bra.''

A tendon stood out in his neck. The hand that at first glance had seemed relaxed on the windowsill was in fact white knuckled. He was fighting his tension, but Beth wasn't willing to lay odds who'd win the bout.

''I thought…I thought women got…cripes, I don't know about this stuff. You know, an implant or something.''

''Reconstructive surgery,'' she said, feeling his tension seep through the air like bacteria, infecting her. She maintained as calm a facade as his, but her throat seemed to constrict, rebelling against the medical terms. She didn't want to discuss her treatment choices with him. She wanted to cross the room to him and have him open his arms to her. She wanted him to hug her and murmur, ''You took me by surprise, that's all. I honestly don't mind, Beth. I still think you're a desirable woman.''

But if Beth had learned anything during the past two years, it was to play the hand she was dealt, not to wish for what she couldn't have. Ryan wasn't going to open his arms to her. And since he wasn't, she wasn't going to cross the room.

"I considered reconstructive surgery," she told him, forcing out the words. "But I decided against it. I talked to other women who'd had the surgery, and not all of them were satisfied with the results. It was a major procedure, and there was a chance it would make future mammograms harder to read, and given that I'm young and have a lot of screening ahead of me..." *And I didn't want to disguise the truth,* she added silently. *I wanted to remember what I'd been through so I would appreciate everything I still have. I wanted to know who I was and where I'd been. I didn't want to hide from myself.*

Those were her own private reasons, reasons Ryan would never understand. He didn't really seem all that interested in the whys, anyway. What he cared about was exactly what she'd expected, what she'd dreaded—she had only one breast. She was physically imperfect. She was missing something men tended to think was terribly important. Ryan couldn't desire a woman who didn't have two nice, big breasts.

If she had let the surgeons reconstruct her left breast, she would have looked like a real woman, and then he would have assumed that her medical history was irrelevant. That she'd been sick, that she'd confronted her own mortality, that she'd ridden one of the most ghastly roller-coaster rides fate had ever designed wouldn't have mattered to him as long as when it was done she emerged with a matching pair of knockers.

"When...when you take this...*prosthesis* off—"

"There's nothing," she said bluntly. "Just a scar. A healthy right breast and a scar."

He turned to stare out the window and collect himself. When he turned back, he asked, "What have other men said?"

"What other men?"

"Other lovers."

She took a deep breath, afraid her voice would waver. If she hadn't already scared him off, this answer was bound to. "There haven't been any."

"But—you said this happened two years ago," he reminded her unnecessarily.

"I know how long ago it happened," she snapped, mortified by his implication. No, there hadn't been any other lovers. It had taken her two years to build up the strength to get through a conversation like the one Ryan was putting her through right now. "I was dating a man when I was diagnosed. And if you're wondering what he said when I told him, it was goodbye."

Ryan turned back to the window. He didn't seem able to look at her.

"You can say goodbye, too," she said brusquely. She didn't want to make this easy for him, but watching him torture himself to come up with the right words only made her feel more awkward. Her hopes weren't going to be realized. Ryan wasn't going to accept her, knowing what he now knew. They were both dancing around a foregone conclusion. They might as well just get it over with.

"Look, Beth, I—" He inhaled and turned from the window, giving her a sheepish smile. "It's just, you really took me by surprise with this."

"I'm sorry I didn't do a better job of breaking the news." Like hell. She wasn't sorry at all. She was too bitter to be sorry, too disappointed that Ryan hadn't reacted the way she would have dreamed.

"Look." He raked his hand through his hair. Just like his tension, his discomfort was contagious. The more perturbed he looked, the more perturbed she felt. "I guess I—I wasn't figuring on this, Beth. I mean, I don't know what to think."

You know what to think, she almost said aloud. *What to think is that you don't want to make love to me anymore.* "Why don't you go think about it on your own?" she muttered instead, praying for him to leave before she fell apart. Not that she intended to fall apart—she had endured worse things in her life than having the most virile, sensual man she'd ever met reject her. But just in case... She didn't want him to see her cry.

He couldn't help but sense her bristling hostility. "I know I'm not handling this right, Beth," he said, his eyes dark with apology. "I'm sorry about that, but this one falls a little out of my range of experience."

"I'm sure it does." His experience no doubt comprised countless lovely women, all of them endowed with their full complement of mammaries.

"I'm trying to be honest. Would you rather I lied?"

Yes. "Honesty works for me."

"I just didn't bargain for this."

"Ryan. I'm making it easy for you." She strode to the door and opened it. "No explanations necessary."

He started toward the door, but when he was within a few feet of it—a few feet of her—he paused. "You hate me, don't you?"

"No." She opted for honesty, too, and was amazed to discover that, at bottom, she didn't hate Ryan. She couldn't hate him for being normal, for expecting her to be normal. "I'm a bit more of a challenge than you're looking for. I can't blame you for that."

"I wish..."

He sighed, reached out and traced a line with his index finger along her cheekbone. She felt the heat of his touch spread through her face, into her mind, into her soul, and it threatened to thaw her icy self-protectiveness into tears. She blinked and struggled for control.

"You were right," he admitted. "It's not so simple."

"I know." She willed him to lower his hand. After an interminable minute he did. His eyes were wistful, his mouth twisted into a wry, sad smile that made her soul grow even warmer, melting the grit inside her until it was as soft and thick as quicksand. He looked as if he were about to kiss her, but he thought better of it and stalked out of her office. And then she sank to the floor, closed the door and let the quagmire of her misery swallow her up.

LYNNE AND JEFF were gone from the front room, thank God. If either of them had stopped to make small talk with Ryan, he might have slugged them.

He slammed out of the building, down the steps of the quaint front porch with its gingerbread trim and across the sidewalk to where he'd parked his truck. He got in, slumped behind the wheel and let out a doleful breath.

Well, he thought, he was some kind of bastard, wasn't he?

A few ripe curses tripped over his tongue. They were directed at the world in general and himself in particular, but not at Beth. Never at Beth.

His heart was breaking for her, yet he'd never intended for his heart to be involved. He'd thought they were friends, good friends, rapidly becoming intimate friends. But his heart?

It hurt. His head hurt. His gut. His soul. Not just because of what she'd been through but because of himself, his knowledge that he wasn't strong enough to deal with it.

If he tried to make love with her, he might wind up feeling sorry for her. Or guilty. Or shamed in some way. He would have her harrowing medical history staring him in the face the moment she took off her clothes. He wouldn't be able to escape it. It would be like going to bed with a patient, not a woman.

God forbid, looking at her might affect him in the worst sort of way. He might see her and go limp. A man's body sometimes had its own will in these matters. If his behavior just now had been insulting, imagine how insulted she would be if they wound up in bed and he couldn't perform.

It's not so simple, he thought, hearing the warning in her voice. It wasn't simple and, damn it, he'd wanted it to be. He'd wanted things smooth with him and Beth, easy and happy and joyously erotic. But the instant things stopped being simple, he was out the door.

He wasn't good enough for Beth. Not given what she'd been through. Not given how inept he was at dealing with it. She was brave, she was indomitable— and he was a stupid, selfish sonofabitch who would rather make a quick exit than admit that he couldn't possibly love a woman who was missing a breast.

The hell with love. Beth had never asked him to fall in love with her. She had never indicated that she wanted to exchange vows with him. As far as he could tell, taking a vacation trip to X-rated heaven with him might have been all she'd ever wanted.

He couldn't do it. He was immature, he was shallow and he liked things simple. And when it came to Beth, the only simple answer was to say goodbye.

He cranked up the truck's engine and steered away from the curb, wondering how much self-loathing he was good for. Expletives tumbled from his lips—spicy oaths, nasty blasphemies, foreign-language obscenities—but they barely began to express what he was feeling.

He drove directly to Corky's. Tonight was a night to sit alone in a crowd, downing beers and calling himself names. He wouldn't be able to drink enough to alleviate his pain—self-inflicted, he reminded himself, although he aimed a few more profanities in the direction of the world at large—because if he consumed that much liquor he wouldn't be able to drive home, the bartender would call a cab and the humiliation would make him hate himself even more. But a few beers, to take the edge off...

It didn't matter. He was dirt. Lower than low. And he had a feeling the edge was going to cut him to ribbons.

THE HANGOVER he lugged with him to work the next morning wasn't from consuming too much beer. He'd been drunk on remorse last night, inebriated from anger. Every time he'd tried to pick apart his mood to see what it was made of, he'd discovered a different element, and the effort had left him as sick as if he'd downed a few gallon-size jugs of rotgut.

He was incensed because Beth had been sick. He was ashamed because he was a jerk. He was appalled because when he'd first met her, he had been enchanted by her appearance, and now he couldn't think about the way she looked without thinking about the way she would look without her clothing on. Thinking about that made something inside him shrivel up—yet he couldn't stop thinking about her. He was still obsessed with Beth Pendleton—and it infuriated him.

He despised the doctor who'd treated her, even though that doctor might well have saved her life. He despised the medical establishment for not having come up with a cure for breast cancer that didn't include hacking up a woman's body. Most of all, he despised the strange reflexes programmed into Y chromosomes that made men think breasts were so vital to a woman's sex appeal.

And he despised Larry for being awake and alert when Ryan entered Walker Construction's office.

"Good morning!" Larry called to him from his desk, where he was using an X-Acto knife to slice open a shipping carton.

"What's good about it?" Ryan grunted, trudging to his own desk and trying to recollect how many aspirin he'd taken before he'd left home that morning. If it was as many as he remembered, he wouldn't be able to take any more until lunch, not without burning a hole in his stomach.

"One thing that's good about it," Larry said as he pried back the flaps of the carton, "is that the new printing company up in Concord came through with our stationery order in less time, for less money, than the old outfit we were using. This is great," he declared, lifting a sheet of letter paper and holding it up to the light to study the watermark.

"Swell. We've got stationery. My day is made." Ryan scanned the schedule pinned on the wall to see who was slated to be up at the work site. "Are we getting the concrete today?"

"I don't know. It's impossible to pin those guys down. I left several messages on their machine yesterday."

"Then we're not getting it. They would have called back if they were coming." He rubbed his temples with his fingertips. He felt as if a kettle-drum symphony was being performed in his skull. "Did you pay the property tax?"

"That Town of Devon thing?" Larry toted the carton to the supply cabinet at the back of the room. "I'll get to it."

"Do it today," Ryan commanded. The symphony had gotten louder, adding crashing cymbals to the cacophony.

Larry shuffled back to his desk, his deck shoes whispering against the linoleum. "I said I'd get to it, Ryan. Don't be a nag."

Two long strides brought Ryan to his cousin's desk. He planted his fists on the blotter and bore down on Larry. "This is *important*," he fumed, echoing Beth's words to him yesterday. "We've been placed on the public deadbeat list."

"Hey, come on." Larry sat in his chair, his expression pugnacious even though he seemed to be squirming. "I couldn't find the tax bill, okay? I must have put it somewhere, but I can't for the life of me remember where."

"We probably got four tax bills. You don't get put on the deadbeat list until you're a year overdue. They send the bills quarterly, don't they?"

"Yeah, but—okay, look—"

"Don't tell me *look*," Ryan retorted. "*You* look. Find the damned tax bill and pay it. Today."

"Hey, Ryan. What's bugging you?"

"Nothing." Nothing he was willing to discuss with Larry, anyway. "All I'm saying is, this is important. You've got to pay the tax bill. What was the amount?"

Larry rummaged through the papers on his desk. "I wrote it down somewhere," he mumbled, scattering scraps, reading a few and frowning. "Oh, here it is," he announced, locating a torn envelope. "Forty-nine thousand, seven hundred forty-five."

Ryan cursed—it was becoming a habit with him—and reached for the spiral-bound company checkbook. He took the envelope from Larry, plucked a pen from Larry's shirt pocket and wrote the damned check himself. "Is this going to bounce?"

"Probably."

"Transfer the funds to cover it," he demanded, tearing the check out and shoving it at Larry. "And then hand-deliver this to the town clerk. Do you think you can handle that?"

"I don't like your attitude," Larry commented.

"I don't like my attitude, either. Just do it. I've got to track down the concrete guys."

"Don't snap their heads off the way you just snapped mine off," Larry commented blandly, folding the check in half and tucking it, along with his pen, into his shirt pocket. "They aren't family. They don't have to take it."

"If you weren't so goddamn careless about our taxes, you wouldn't have to take it, either." With that, Ryan stormed out of the office. It wasn't fair for him to vent his rage on Larry. He hated himself for inflicting himself on his cousin, but what the hell. He already hated himself for everything else—he might as well hate himself for this, too.

"So, HOW'S THAT malpractice case coming along?" Cindy asked Beth.

Beth groaned. The malpractice case was coming along better than anything else in her life at the moment.

Not true. Chuck was coming along well. He hadn't had an accident in the house in the past two days, and at bedtime he happily romped into his crate and slept there. She was feeling well, and the past few days of drizzle had revived her withering lawn.

Other than that, life stank.

"I think we'll be able to serve the other side with papers soon," she told Cindy, who stood in the doorway of Beth's office, with Erica propped on her shoulder. Erica's baby-sitter had broken a tooth biting into a stale bagel that morning and had raced to the dentist, leaving the baby with Cindy, who had a white cloth diaper spread over her shoulder to protect her blouse if Erica spit up. Beth tried not to feel smug about the fact that Chuck was now neater than her own goddaughter.

"Jeff thinks you're crazy," Cindy reported. "He believes suing a brother attorney is bad form."

"This attorney—" Beth waved at the file open on her desk "—is no brother of mine. He ripped my client off. He misrepresented him. He cost him a ton of money. Frankly, he deserves to get shot between the eyes. He should be grateful I'm just demanding recompense."

"Touchy, touchy." Cindy eased a lock of her hair out of Erica's clenched fist and lifted the baby higher on her shoulder. "Are we premenstrual or is something wrong?"

"Neither." Beth managed a smile for Cindy. "To tell you the truth, I'm feeling good about this case. It's going to raise our profile in southern New Hampshire."

"Jeff and I are satisfied with the profile we have, Beth." Cindy ventured a step into the office. She studied Beth, concerned. "This isn't New York. We aren't looking to make a big splash. We just like to serve our clients and earn our money."

"It's not going to hurt Miller, Miller and Pendleton for people to know that we aren't afraid to take on the tough cases."

"I know. And unlike Jeff, I think you're absolutely right in working on this malpractice case. I'm just saying, relax. You know how an exercise wheel works—the faster you run, the faster the wheel spins, and the faster it spins, the faster you have to run. You didn't come to Devon to be a hamster caught on an exercise wheel. You came to slow down and get your life back in balance."

Beth's life was never going to be in balance. But that wasn't Cindy's fault, and Beth wasn't going to take out her frustration on her best friend. "You're right," she conceded, biting her lip to keep from mouthing off.

"I'm not criticizing you, Beth. I'm just lending you a different perspective."

She wished Cindy and her beatific baby would go away. "Fine. I appreciate what you're saying."

"Because I'd hate to see you get into the workaholic routine again."

"Okay. Fine." It took all her self-control not to clamp her hands over her ears and scream.

Luckily her intercom buzzed, ending the discussion. She pressed the button on the intercom. "Beth,"

Lynne's voice called through the speaker, "Larry Walker is on the line."

Her heart bumped against her ribs when she heard the name Walker. It wasn't the Walker she'd been hoping to hear from—and *no,* she wasn't hoping to hear from Ryan. He was too normal, too ordinary, too typically male. By now he had probably found his way into some other woman's bed—Mitzi Rumson's, maybe, or someone like her, someone with two beautiful breasts.

She took a deep breath and silently recited her soothing chant about how she was all right and everything was going to be fine. But nothing was going to be fine. She wasn't all right, and telling herself she was didn't make it so.

"Thanks, Lynne," she said, shooting Cindy a look of dismissal before she lifted the receiver and pressed the flashing button. "This is Beth Pendleton." Another sharp look caused Cindy to roll her eyes and shrug one shoulder, the other immobilized by Erica. With obvious reluctance, she left the office, giving Beth privacy for the call.

"Beth?" Larry sounded uncertain. "This is Larry Walker from Walker Construction."

"Yes, what can I do for you?"

"Um...well." He sighed heavily. "I'm having a problem with this tax thing, you know? The overdue property tax?"

"Right." Despite her churning nerves, her voice betrayed no impatience.

"Well, see, according to my notes, I sent the town a check six months ago."

"Do you have the canceled check? That would prove you'd made the payment."

"No. It's like—I think the check got lost or something. And I forgot about it. But I talked to the town clerk and she's hitting us up for all this extra money—not just interest, but a fine. And the records are kind of fouled up. I can't figure out how much I'm supposed to pay. They're asking us for way too much money. I've seen the assessment on that tract of land. None of this makes sense."

"Have you talked to your accountant?" she asked.

"We don't have an accountant. I've always taken care of the books."

No wonder everything was fouled up, she thought with a grim smile. "What do you want me to do?" she asked. Calling in a lawyer to straighten out a tax bill was like calling in a brain surgeon to remove a splinter from a finger. Beth could do it, but it seemed like overkill.

"Well, I was sort of thinking maybe you could come in and help me get the files straightened out."

"Perhaps you could come to my office." She assured herself that the suggestion had nothing to do with her desire to avoid Ryan. She was thinking only of sparing Larry the expense of having to pay for her travel time to and from Walker Construction.

"The thing is, everything is in my computer. So I was hoping you could come here."

It was her turn to sigh. She didn't want to go there to review his files or for any other reason. She didn't want to run into Ryan when her feelings were still so raw, her disappointment so keen. She doubted he would want to run into her, either.

Unless... He had never seemed like a Machiavellian schemer to her, but what if he'd contrived to have Larry lure her to Walker Construction? What if he wanted to meet with her on his own turf and he'd assumed she wouldn't take his calls, so he'd told Larry to figure out a way to get her out of her office?

If that was his plan, it was a stupid one. There was nothing Beth would say to him at Walker Construction that she wouldn't say in her own office or at her home or anywhere else. Of course she would take his calls, of course she would talk to him—as a lawyer. If she absolutely had to.

Still, she wouldn't discount the possibility that Larry's request carried a hidden agenda. "Did Ryan ask you to call me?" she asked, keeping her tone devoid of emotion.

"No!" Larry replied heatedly. "No, he didn't. All he said was that if I didn't straighten out our problems with Town Hall I was dead meat. He never mentioned you at all."

So much for Machiavellian schemes. Ryan clearly wanted nothing to do with her.

"I've got to tell you, Beth," Larry continued, "Ryan's been a real bear lately. When he told me I was dead meat, I actually considered upping my life insurance. I don't know what's bothering him. It's not like him to be so grouchy. And frankly, I don't want to cross him, you know? I just want to straighten this thing out so I can get him off my back."

Ryan's grouchiness was not Beth's problem. However, she sympathized with Larry. As easygoing as Ryan usually was, she wouldn't want to be the object of his wrath.

"All right," she agreed, glancing at her appointment calendar. "How about if I come over at three o'clock this afternoon?" She would have preferred a later time, but she estimated that Ryan would return to

the office from the construction site at around five and
she preferred not to see him.

She wasn't afraid of him. She wasn't even afraid of
her own response if she were to run into him. She just
wanted to avoid any unpleasantness, that was all.

"Three would be great," Larry said.

"I'll see you then," she promised, then hung up and
prayed that at three o'clock Ryan would be somewhere
else.

CHAPTER TWELVE

"KNOCK, KNOCK, anybody home?" a lilting voice sang out.

Beth glanced up from the monitor of Larry's computer to see a vision in silver and gold waltz into the warehouse office. It took a moment for her eyes to adjust to the metallic glare. Inside the skintight silver Lycra shorts and matching tank top, behind the yards of gold circling her throat and wrists and dangling from her ears, stood Mitzi Rumson.

Beth tried to smile, but she was weary and bleary from struggling to make sense of Larry's convoluted files. His manner of record-keeping bore an uncanny resemblance to a crazy quilt. Entries in one column belonged in another. Payments due and payments received hadn't been properly logged in. But once she had analyzed the company's budget thoroughly, she'd determined that Walker Construction had never received one of its quarterly property tax bills from Devon. She'd used that as grounds to reduce the fine the town had levied against Ryan and Larry.

For the hour she'd been wrestling with the company's records, Larry had hovered over her, attempting with less than stellar success to explain what his odd notations meant. Every now and then, he'd raced off to bring her files or glasses of water. At the moment, he was in a storage room, searching for the company's last three years of budget files so she could make sure he wasn't in default on anything else.

Mitzi's vivacity made Beth even more conscious of her own fatigue. The woman had on so much jewelry, she clanked when she walked, reminding Beth a little of the way Chuck's license and identification tags clanked on his collar. One of Mitzi's necklaces was, in fact, a collar—hammered out of gold.

"Well, hello there, Beth!" Mitzi bounced across the room. She was wearing ultrachic platform sneakers, white with silver racing stripes. "I didn't know you were going to be here. What are you doing? It looks awfully complicated. I'm all thumbs when it comes to computers."

Beth managed a limp smile. Of course Mitzi hadn't known Beth would be at Walker Construction. Chances were, Mitzi had come in search of Ryan.

Which meant he might be on his way over now. Which meant Beth had better pack up and exit as soon as she could.

"I'm helping Larry straighten out his records," she explained, reaching under the desk for her briefcase.

"Oh, right. Larry's the desk jockey. He doesn't get dirty like Ryan." Mitzi propped one voluptuously curved hip on the edge of Larry's desk. "Ryan gets dirty enough for both of them, doesn't he? I'll tell you, it's a zoo up at my house today. They're pouring concrete. Oooh." She wrinkled her pert little nose in disgust. "It's amazing to think that building an architectural masterpiece can be such dirty work."

"Is Ryan at the site?" Beth asked nonchalantly.

"Directing the concrete pouring and getting dirty. It's not a pretty sight—although even when he's a mess, Ryan is *always* a pretty sight."

And so are you, Beth thought without a trace of jealousy. How could she be jealous of someone so unremittingly good-natured?

She saved the revised payment schedule she'd worked out on Larry's computer and hit a button to copy it onto a disk for herself. Given how disorganized Larry was, she had a feeling he would be calling her again, pleading for help. With her own copy of his files, she would be able to navigate him through his debt schedule without having to drive to the warehouse.

"Well, I just stopped by to drop off these pictures I found in a magazine," Mitzi went on, pulling several many-times-folded clippings from a silver vinyl fanny pack and smoothing them out. "See this solarium? Isn't it spectacular?"

"Spectacular" was an understatement, Beth thought as she studied the glossy photo spread of what appeared to be a four-story-high glass-enclosed atrium. "This isn't what your solarium is going to look like," she pointed out, well aware of the specs in the revised contract Mitzi had signed with Walker Construction.

"Oh, I know, but isn't it divine? It's the *idea* I want my solarium to convey, that feeling of celestial airiness. Do you think Ryan could change it to make it a little taller? I know the plan calls for a nine-foot ceiling, but maybe we could bring it up a little. I'd pay the extra cost, naturally," she added when Beth frowned.

"It's more than just a matter of extra cost," she warned. "You have the challenge of keeping the house warm in the winter."

"Well, there are plenty of ways to generate heat," Mitzi purred.

Her attention shifted abruptly as Larry entered through a back door. "Beth? Here's what I found," he said, one slim file lying flat on his palm like a waiter's tray. The instant he noticed Mitzi, he stopped cold. His eyes widened, his mouth fell open and the file slid off his hand and onto the floor. The folder opened, scattering dozens of receipts around his feet.

Beth's gaze shuttled back and forth between Mitzi, who pushed away from the desk and stood, and Larry, who appeared for the moment to have been literally struck dumb by the sight of her. Mitzi beamed him a luminous smile and extended her hand. "Hi, there! You must be Cousin Larry!"

"I must be," he rasped. Beth had always considered him a slightly gawky version of Ryan in appearance. Now he was truly gawky—gaping at Mitzi as if he'd found himself unexpectedly in the presence of a goddess. His mouth still hung open, and he didn't even acknowledge the spilled file.

"I'm Mitzi Rumson," she said, meeting him at the center of the room and closing her hand around his. "I've heard so much about you."

"I've heard a lot about you, too." His eyes remained fixed on her face.

"Ryan plays in the mud all day while you do the real work." She was as charming and bubbly as a hostess at a high-society gala. "I think he's envious of you. You really ought to let him sit at your desk sometimes and push those computer buttons. It would be so good for his ego."

Larry blinked. Mitzi had apparently put him in a trance.

"I'm really sorry you weren't there when we worked the contract out. I'll bet you would have had some wonderful input. You seem like the type of man whose input would really make a lady's day."

He gulped. "I'd like to think so."

Beth understood she'd become a fifth wheel in the room. She quietly slid her disk into her briefcase and stood. The clock on the wall read a few minutes past four. If she left now, not only wouldn't she have to witness Larry stumbling over himself under the impact of Mitzi's transcendent beauty, but she would also be able to avoid an encounter with Ryan.

"I think everything is a bit more organized now, Larry," she called over, but he was too spellbound by Mitzi to hear her. She tiptoed out of the office, letting the door close quietly behind her.

After several days of drizzle, the clouds had finally broken apart, uncovering patches of sky bluer than any she'd ever seen in New York or Boston or Washington, D.C. Cities simply didn't have skies like New England's. Their air didn't smell as good. Nor did Cupid aim his arrow as well in crowded metropolitan areas as he did in a warehouse office in Devon, New Hampshire. The little imp had bull's-eyed Larry's heart, and the notion lifted Beth's spirits, even if Larry seemed rather outclassed by Mitzi Rumson. For all Mitzi's razzle-dazzle, Beth believed the woman had a good soul. She didn't think Mitzi would ever be gratuitously cruel to Larry. He could enjoy being smitten without serious peril.

Smiling, Beth started down the few steps to the lot, then halted when she heard the rumble of an approaching truck. A gray pickup slowed and veered onto the gravel, kicking up dust. Beth's spirits plummeted.

If she made a quick retreat to her car, Ryan would know how eager she was to avoid him. She wasn't going to be cowardly, even if the sight of him, vague and washed out through the glare of the late-afternoon sun on his windshield, caused her stomach to churn and her mouth to go dry. She tightened her fingers around the handle of her briefcase and stood perfectly still, determined not to act as if the mere sight of him short-circuited her nervous system.

His truck rolled to a stop. She heard a metallic whine as he yanked on the parking brake, and then silence as he shut off the engine. He didn't immediately climb out. Perhaps he wanted to give her time to escape.

Ridiculous. She was his company's lawyer. Their brief attempt at a romance was history, best forgotten. She and Ryan were going to have to deal with each other professionally, and now was as good a time as any to start.

So she stood her ground. And after a long minute, Ryan emerged from the truck.

Mitzi hadn't been exaggerating when she'd said Ryan had gotten dirty at the construction site. A beige residue smudged his jeans, caked his boots, dusted his bare, sinewy forearms. His face was smeared with grime; his hair was stringy with sweat. If anything reflected what a handsome man he was, it was the fact that he could look good even when he was wearing a day's worth of dirt.

He pulled a red bandanna from the back pocket of his jeans and wiped his face. His eyes were opaque, unwavering on her.

She discreetly clenched her briefcase, hoping it wouldn't slip from her sweat-slick hand. "I think Larry and I have straightened out the property tax problem," she said, cringing inwardly. Shouldn't she have said hello first? Shouldn't she have greeted him a bit more courteously?

"Is it paid up?" he asked, apparently happy to leave things on an impersonal level.

"Yes. I managed to reduce the penalty five thousand dollars."

"You did?" He shoved the bandanna back in his hip pocket. Beth noticed the way perspiration glued his shirt to his chest, revealing its athletic musculature. She noticed the way his fingers flexed, the way his jeans hugged his thighs. She noticed far too much about Ryan.

One thing she noticed was that even though she'd just saved his company five thousand dollars, he wasn't smiling.

"That should more than cover my fee," she pointed out.

He still didn't smile. He took a step closer to her, his gaze locked onto her face. He didn't glance at her neat navy blue suit, her pistachio green blouse, her stack-heeled blue leather pumps. He stared only at her face, which grew hot from the relentless sun—and from his relentless attention.

"How's Chuck?" he asked.

She exerted herself not to flinch, or laugh. Surely Ryan didn't give a hoot how her dog was. "He's fine."

"Did you get a choke chain?"

"Not yet. It doesn't seem necessary. Chuck is remarkably smart and sensitive. I say no, and he listens."

"Of course he's smart and sensitive. He's crazy about you, right?"

She again had to suppress the urge to flinch. Laughter was no longer teasing her throat, though. Whether Ryan was merely commenting on Chuck's perceptiveness or else buttering Beth up for some hidden purpose, she didn't know.

She *did* know that, for all her mental pep talks, she wasn't prepared to get personal in any way with Ryan. She inhaled, held her breath and exhaled. Inhaled, exhaled—and kept silent.

"We have to talk," he said bluntly.

"About what?" Her voice sounded steadier than she felt. She studied the stains marking his shirt, the smear of dirt on his chin.

His jaw flexed as if he were literally chewing over his words. He was close enough to touch her, but he didn't. He was also close enough for her to see that his eyes weren't opaque at all. They swarmed with shadows; they looked tired and sad and troubled. Eyes were supposed to be the mirrors of one's soul, but Ryan's eyes seemed to be mirroring Beth's soul, not his own.

"Can we talk?" he persisted.

"Now?"

At last he looked away from her, only to glance down at his disreputable appearance. "I've got to wash up."

If he asked her to hang around at his office while he showered, she would refuse. The last time she did that, they'd wound up sharing their first kiss. She wasn't going to travel that route again.

"I've got to go home and take care of Chuck," she said. "He's smart and sensitive enough to start barking for his supper about this time every day."

Ryan ran his hand through his hair, lifting it away from his brow, which was streaked with sweat. "Why don't I swing by your house in a half hour, and we can go grab a bite to eat? Then we'll talk."

Ever the lawyer, she tossed various arguments onto her mental scales and weighed them. If she declined his invitation, he would take her for a coward—which would be an accurate reading of her feelings. But she was too proud to let him know that.

On the other hand, if she agreed to have a bite with him, he would be the one doing the talking, since she had nothing to say to him that she hadn't already said.

She had no idea what he wanted to talk to her about, unless it was to apologize. She supposed an apology wouldn't be bad. "All right," she said. "We'll talk."

She turned and headed for her car, refusing him a farewell glance. She would grab a bite with him and let him speak his piece, and that would be the end of it. There would be no good-night kiss this time. She would never let him kiss her again.

THE INSTANT HE SAW HER, he knew he would have to act.

If only he knew what action to take.

Anything to ease his mind, anything to salvage his soul. Anything to make him feel better about walking out on her.

The days since his last, fateful encounter with her had been utter torture. He had thought his self-loathing would fade, but it hadn't. It had evolved into something more complex, something that resembled loneliness, and yearning, and genuine regret.

He missed her laughter, her intelligence, her pretty blue eyes. He missed swapping jokes with her. He missed bouncing ideas off her. He missed watching her dominate a contract negotiation with her quiet expertise. He missed her dog.

He missed the possibility that they could have worked on her house together, improving it, making it more of a home. He missed the way she'd smiled and asked him about his childhood, absorbing his words as if she were truly interested in what life was like in Devon.

He missed her courage. He missed her spirit. He missed the promise that something more could have developed between them, something he'd never known with another woman, something he'd never wanted until he'd met Beth.

Well, that promise was shot to hell because he was a jerk and he'd blown his chances with her, deliberately.

He entered the office to drop off the work charts and make sure Larry had the paychecks all set for the crew, who would be stopping in to get pick them up as soon as they finished closing down the site. To his surprise, Larry was huddled with Mitzi Rumson, of all people. From where Ryan stood, it looked as if Larry were demonstrating the different screen savers on his computer. Mitzi, who resembled a misplaced medieval knight in her formfitting silver outfit, seemed enthralled by Larry's flying toasters.

The two of them barely glanced up at Ryan's entrance. He felt like an intruder.

"Um—don't forget the paychecks," he mumbled.

"Not a problem," Larry said without turning. Then he proceeded to explain another screen saver to Mitzi, who gazed at him raptly. She was a savvy lady, more intelligent than she let on. Ryan was positive she must have seen a screen saver before. But she absorbed every word Larry said as if he were explaining the meaning of life.

One thing Ryan didn't want to hear was Larry's take on the meaning of life—or, for that matter, his take on screen savers. Without another word, Ryan sauntered out of the office.

He drove home, let himself into the house and headed straight for the shower. His reflection in the mirror above the sink brought him up short. He looked as if he'd just spent the past seven hours rolling in cement. The foundation had been finished today, and all the excess concrete had apparently wound up on his face. He supposed he was lucky Beth hadn't run from him, shrieking in disgust.

It took a while to scrub the day's filth from his body. He needed that time; he needed the warm water pounding down on him, the soapsuds sliding over his skin, the humid bathroom atmosphere filling his lungs and cleansing him from the inside out. He needed to clear everything from his mind and body so he could think about what to say when he saw Beth.

You're looking good.

It was the truth—she *did* look good. But she had her clothes on. God only knew what she would look like undressed.

And he was a bastard for wondering about that.

I've been thinking about you.

He hadn't *stopped* thinking about her since last Monday, when she'd told him about herself. He thought about her as he wanted her to be—perfect in every way—and he thought about her as she actually was. He thought about how his own fears and failures were keeping him from her. He thought about what she must have gone through two years ago, about what it would be like to be told, at the ripe old age of thirty, that you had cancer. He thought about the last bastard in her life, the one who'd said goodbye.

I've handled this all wrong.

Well, golly. She didn't need him telling her that. She could reach that conclusion all by herself.

He rinsed the last of the shampoo from his hair and twisted the faucet, shutting off the spray. He stood dripping in the glass-enclosed stall, his hair cool and heavy against the nape of his neck, his skin beaded with water. He still had no idea what to say to her.

He toweled off, blow-dried his hair and put on some nice clothes. Not the usual T-shirt and jeans, but a pair of khakis and a button-front shirt. His choice of clothing didn't bode well. If he'd felt confident that this evening would go swimmingly, he wouldn't have worried about how he looked.

Did Beth worry about how she looked? Did she fuss with that—that thing in her bra to make sure her appearance was normal? Did she smooth her blouses just so over her chest and tighten the bra straps so the thing—*the prosthesis*—wouldn't slide out of position? Did she gaze into her mirror, all spruced up in one of her well-tailored suits, and see not a beautiful woman but a lady with a fake breast stuffed into her blouse?

Wasn't that what Ryan saw when he gazed at her?

Was he beneath contempt for admitting it? Or just honest?

Sighing, he shoved his wallet into his hip pocket, grabbed his keys and stalked out to the garage, determined to hang on to his honesty when he was with her. She probably didn't want to listen to him beat himself up over what an ass he was. But he had to explain—to himself, if not to her—why he was unable to pursue a romance with her. He had to, because if he didn't he would keep on tormenting himself until he was no longer a functional human being.

The lights flanking her front door were on when he drove up her gravel driveway. Using her front door seemed too formal, though. No matter what else happened tonight, he wanted to find his way back into a friendship with Beth. Friends used back doors.

He was relieved to see the back porch light was on, as well. So was the light in the kitchen. He climbed the porch steps and rapped sharply on the door.

Through the window above the sink he heard Chuck barking exuberantly. At least one resident of the house on Loring Road was happy about his visit.

The door swung open, and he came face-to-face with Beth. If she had looked in her mirror, she couldn't possibly have seen anything except a beautiful woman. A beautiful woman with golden hair and topaz eyes and delicate pink lips, a beautiful woman who glowed with health and hope and inner strength. The most beautiful woman Ryan had ever met.

She had changed out of her business suit and into one of her swirling flowered skirts and a cotton blouse. He realized for the first time that she always wore loose blouses with high necks, even in the summer. He would never have noticed if he hadn't known about her.

She looked not quite forbidding, but not exactly welcoming, either. In her hand she held a glass of tomato juice.

"Can I come in?" he asked. He'd meant to invite her out, to take her to Corky's or some other neutral territory. But seeing her standing before him, so slim and delicate and vulnerable, made him want to remain right where they were until he could figure out what to do about her—and about his own tangled feelings for her.

She mulled over his question for a moment, then stepped aside and let him enter the kitchen.

Chuck sprinted through the dining room doorway and hurled himself at Ryan. Unfortunately, Beth stood in his path and Chuck was running too fast to detour around her. He rammed into her legs and she stumbled, splattering tomato juice onto Ryan's shirt.

"Oh, no! Bad, Chuck!" She set down the glass and hunkered down in front of her dog. Clasping his snout in one hand, she wagged her other hand at him and scolded, "No pushing! No running like a maniac! No, no, no!"

Chuck eyed her anxiously, then turned to Ryan and whimpered, obviously hoping to find an ally in him.

Ryan directed his gaze from the woebegone puppy to Beth, still wagging a punitive finger at him. "It looks like he understands the word *no.*"

"At least he understands when I'm angry with him. But he's got to learn not to charge at people all the time."

"Does he charge at people a lot?"

"If he does it once, it's one time too many."

"It's a reflex, Beth. Lots of dogs like to protect their own against intruders."

"You're not an intruder," she said, then caught her lower lip in her teeth, as if she wasn't quite sure that was true. Straightening up, she regarded him with dismay. "Look at your shirt."

He glanced down. A few spatters of red dotted the area above the pocket.

"This is awful." Beth groaned, crossing to the sink. "Bad dog, Chuck. Get in your crate."

After one final, plaintive whimper that won him no reprieve, Chuck slouched toward his cage.

"It's no big deal," Ryan assured her, ignoring his shirt to watch as Chuck crawled into the cage and rested his head atop his paws. She'd really done a fine job of training the dog. She didn't need Ryan. He must have been kidding himself to think she could possibly need his help with her dog.

"I've got him trained to go in his crate when he's naughty. I haven't got him trained not to jump on people every time someone walks in the door. I feel terrible about this, Ryan. Every time you show up, something gets spilled. I can't be trusted with a glass when you're around." She glanced at his shirt, then sighed forlornly and reached for a clean dish towel. "It's my fault as much as Chuck's. I'm so clumsy."

"It's all right."

"It's not all right. Those stains will set if you don't rinse them out right away." After soaking the towel beneath the faucet, she carried it across the room to him, catching the drips of water in her free hand. "You've got to rinse tomato juice out right away or it will stain permanently," she explained, dabbing at the spots with the towel.

He barely felt the cold water soaking through his shirt. What he felt were Beth's hands, wiping, blotting, rubbing, drying. Moving against his chest. Groping. Stroking. Arousing him.

Don't respond, he ordered himself. *You know her story. You know you can't make love to her. Don't let yourself feel anything . . .*

Abruptly she seemed aware of what she was doing to his shirt—and to him. Her hands fell still and she peered anxiously up at him. "I'm sorry," she murmured, her cheeks pink with embarrassment.

He covered her hands with his—only to keep the towel from dripping onto his shoes, he told himself. He pried it from her tense fingers and tossed it onto the table. "What are you sorry about?"

"Everything."

"I came here to apologize to you," he said, although he was not at all sure about that. When she gazed up at him, her eyes so troubled, so unbearably lovely, he wasn't sure of anything.

"I don't want your apology," she said.

"What do you want?"

She stared at him for a moment longer, then lowered her eyes. He knew what she wanted, because he wanted it, too. In spite of his fear. In spite of his dread. In spite of every ounce of common sense in him, every clanging alarm bell reminding him that a man couldn't sleep with a woman who'd been through what Beth had been through without bearing the weight of her tragedies on his own back.

He wanted what she wanted.

SHE WANTED TO HATE HIM, but she couldn't. Not when his arms closed around her, when his body felt so right against hers, when his mouth found hers, covered it, nibbled and stroked and conquered hers. There were things she wanted far more than she wanted to hate him.

That she could desire a man who didn't love her, who wouldn't love her, was frightening. That she could desire him as much as she did was even more frightening. Yet he touched his mouth to hers again, warm and slow and tantalizing, and other feelings, needs and hungers tempered her fear. No matter what she'd been through and what shape she'd emerged in, she was a woman.

"Ryan," she whispered against his lips.

His hands flattened against her waist, broad and strong. He leaned back so he could view her face. "I didn't come here for this," he confessed.

"I know."

His fingers moved in quiet circles against her back. Heat from his body shimmered in the air between them. "Do you want me to leave?"

"No." She swallowed, steeling herself for his answer before she asked, "Do you want to leave?"

"I wish I did. It would make my life a hell of a lot easier."

That was honest. His eyes were honest, too, as dark as the corner of the night where dreams were kept, as dark as the passion that drew her to him. His honesty told her that he was as afraid as she was.

If he could match her fear, she would match his honesty. "If it—if it doesn't work out—" *if you see me naked and change your mind* "—it's all right. I would understand."

"I don't know what's going to work out here, Beth," he admitted. "I just know I can't keep going the way I've been going. I can't sleep. I can't smile. I can't do anything but think about you. People hate being around me. *I* hate being around me. I don't know what's supposed to work out, or how."

"Ryan—"

"All I know is, something's got to happen with us, one way or another. You understand what I'm saying, don't you?"

Not quite, but she didn't want to analyze it. She just wanted him to kiss her again. She looped her arms around his neck and pulled him down to her, and his kiss told her he was beyond analyzing the situation, too.

She didn't remember bringing him upstairs, turning the lamp on her dresser to a low setting, folding back the covers on her wide brass bed. But suddenly there they were, and she knew she would remember everything from here on in. She would remember his lips on hers, his hands gliding over her shoulders, along her back, down to her hips and up into her hair. She would remember the feel of his tongue against her teeth, his callused fingertips against her cheek. She would remember every moment of this, either because it would be so good or because it would be devastatingly bad.

Panic nipped at her. It *would* be bad. It would be dreadful. Maybe he would ask her to keep her blouse on so he wouldn't be forced to see her. Maybe he would just lift her skirt. Maybe he would keep his eyes closed and pretend she was someone else, someone normal.

He kissed the crown of her head. "You're nervous," he guessed aloud.

"Yes."

A low laugh escaped him. "So am I." He used his thumbs against her jaw to tilt her head back. "Do you have protection?"

"Yes. In the night table drawer." God, this was so unromantic. Like a clinical exercise. Getting wet with him was going to be like swimming laps against the clock. She shut her own eyes so she wouldn't have to see the tension in his face—and so he wouldn't see the tears gathering along her lashes.

He raised one of her hands to his mouth and kissed her palm. She felt something new, something burning through the chilly layers of anxiety and apprehension, something warm and bright and yearning. It grew even warmer, even brighter as he pressed her hand to his chest. Behind the dampness of his shirt she felt the beat of his heart, strong and steady. He couldn't possibly be as nervous as she was.

She forced herself to move forward, to keep going before she chickened out forever. It took an incredible effort to unbutton his shirt. Each button brought her closer to the moment of truth, the moment they were both too honest to escape. But she persevered, sliding the last button through its slit and tugging his shirt free of his trousers.

She had seen his chest before. She'd known it was a magnificent expanse of muscle and sinew and taut, sunbronzed skin. He was so beautiful. She envied him his perfection.

He watched her as she sketched random, feathery lines across his skin. It had been so long since she'd touched a man this way, since she'd felt a man respond to her touch. She was sharply attuned to the pattern of his breath, the flat surface of his abdomen, the stiffening of his nipples as she scraped her fingernails gently over them. He shrugged off his shirt, allowing her to explore his shoulders. They were ridged with bone and tendon, lean yet powerful. His torso had everything it was supposed to have but nothing extra. No thick pelt of hair, no inflated muscles. Just sleek grace. Just Ryan.

He continued to breathe slowly and regularly as he brought his hands to her blouse. She suppressed the urge to shiver, to scream, to lock herself in the bathroom. This was it; everything was going to come to a crashing halt in the next minute. She had to prepare herself for disaster. She had to promise herself not to blame him, not to blame herself, not to dissolve in tears.

She stood stoically as he plucked open the buttons and slid the blouse down her arms. He laid it on the dresser behind him, then studied her bra. No lacy lingerie, nothing seductive, nothing remotely pretty about it.

She concentrated on the steady rise and fall of his chest as he breathed.

He reached around her and popped open the fastening. The bra went slack, and she eased the straps down her arms.

He stared at her. She dared to peek at his face. His expression was inscrutable as his gaze moved from her right breast, round and firm, to the scar that marked the left half of her body, underlining what was no longer there.

A minute passed. More than a minute. The silence wailed at her until she could no longer bear it.

Crossing her arms defensively to hide her nakedness, she spun away and swallowed her tears. She had expected this. She'd known it would happen. She was going to be all right. She had been primed for failure from the start.

"It's okay, Ryan." She had to force the words around the sob that filled her throat.

"What's okay?" His voice was a soft rasp behind her.

"You're turned off. I understand. It's okay."

He reached around her, eased her right arm away from her chest and brought it behind her. He pressed her hand to the thick bulge beneath his fly. "Does it feel like I'm turned off?"

No, but if she turned around, if she forced him to look at her again . . .

Oh, hell—it had nothing to do with him. *She* was the one who was demoralized, the one ashamed of her body. She was the one who didn't like how she looked. He was handling it just fine.

She traced him through his slacks, arching her palm around the thick, hard swell, trailing her fingers up and down until he groaned and covered her hand with his own to keep her still. "Look at me, Beth," he demanded, taking her by the shoulders and rotating her to face him. "I want you. Okay? I want you."

A tear skittered down her cheek, but she ignored it. She brought her other hand to him, and he wrenched open the fly and shoved down his slacks and shorts. She continued to stroke him as if he were not just a man but a miracle, his arousal a gift just for her. She cupped him, fondled him, ran the length of him, reveled in his warmth, his size. She was scarcely aware of him opening the button of her skirt, letting it slide down her legs to pool on the floor around her feet. He wedged his hands inside her panties and eased them down, and then kissed her hard, dizzyingly hard, so hard her knees threatened to buckle.

Without breaking the kiss, he lifted her, ringing her legs around his waist, and carried her to her bed. She felt the linens cool against her back as he lowered her to the mattress and then followed her down. He kissed her again, a deep, greedy kiss, a kiss that told her there would be no stopping, no turning back. No revulsion. No rejection. No shame.

He let his hand drift from her chin to her throat, to her collarbone, to her breast. He circled it, then moved on, skimming down across her belly and lower.

She was moist. Hot. Her body lurched when he found her, when he parted the folds of skin and slid one finger inside. "Are you okay?" he whispered, gliding in and out, brushing his knuckles against her thigh.

"Yes . . ." It was less than a sigh.

"I know, you said it's been—"

"Don't stop."

"A long time—"

"Ryan . . ." Pressure was building inside her, threatening to tear her apart.

"We should slow down..."

"No. Please...I want you."

He turned from her and rummaged in her dresser. She heard the rattle of a box being tattered, the hiss of foil being ripped, and then he was back, rising onto her, settling between her thighs, sinking into her, slowly, completely.

Her body strained against the almost-painful invasion. He was right—it *had* been a long time. Too long since she'd been with a man. Too long since she'd been loved like this.

Another tear slid down her cheek. He moved within her. "Relax," he murmured, grinding his hips, withdrawing and then plunging into her again. "Relax, Beth. Let it come."

She clung to him. It didn't matter if she felt nothing more. She had this. She had him. He hadn't fled in horror. It was enough.

"Stay with me." He propped himself up on one arm and lowered his other hand to her hips, angling her more snugly to him, helping her to find his rhythm. "You're so beautiful, Beth, so beautiful. I want you with me all the way. Just come with me...." His voice was a husky lullaby, a sensuous litany. He brushed his lips against her temple, against her cheekbone, her ear. He kneaded the soft flesh of her bottom. "Yes. Like that. Stay with me now, Beth. I'm not going to leave you. Stay with me."

The tension returned, the heat, the fierce coil of sensation twisting tighter and tighter inside her. He thrust harder, quicker, deeper. She felt sweat slicking his back, felt the harsh rasp of his breath against her cheek, his whispered pleas in her soul. She felt her own body rising with his, taking him, letting him take her. *You're so beautiful,* he had said, and she was a woman, his woman, complete, lacking nothing. She was perfect. This was perfect.

The tension broke, shattering inside her, hurling her down into the pulsing splendor of it. Ryan groaned and grew still, buried inside her, so deep she wanted him never to break from her. So deep he was a part of her.

She had held back nothing with Ryan, and she would hold back nothing now, not even her tears, sweet, salty tears of relief, of joy. Of love.

CHAPTER THIRTEEN

HE HAD NEVER before considered sex so...*emotional*.

He lay next to Beth, her slender body nestling into his, her legs intertwined with his and her hair brushing against his chin, and contemplated how much he'd thought and felt while they'd been making love. He was used to sex being fun, spectacular, arguably the most pleasant physical experience a person could enjoy. But this...

This had been different.

From the moment she'd removed her bra and he'd seen the flicker of pain in her eyes, pain that in a blink transformed to resignation, his soul had become completely ensnared, caught up in the current flowing between them. Beyond lust, beyond the usual male hunger for that most pleasant physical experience, he'd suddenly felt he needed more.

He needed her not to be resigned. Beth Pendleton was not going to have to settle for less than everything he could give her—and everything he could give her included a hell of a lot more than just his body.

He hadn't known what to expect when she'd bared herself to him. He had assumed there would be a scar, a flatness where she should have had a breast—and there was. But much to his amazement, what he'd seen had been not the scar but a woman who had endured something awful and gotten through it. He'd stared at her and thought, *Thank God it isn't worse. Thank God she's all right.*

From that moment on, he'd understood that whatever occurred between Beth Pendleton and himself wasn't going to be just a pleasant physical experience.

He had never before talked so much during the act. That was another odd thing. Usually he was content to let his body do the talking. But Beth had looked so unsure, so insecure. He'd had to coax her along, had to let her know how attractive she was, how lovely, how vital, how much she turned him on, how much he needed to turn her on. If she hadn't come . . . he didn't think he could have stood it.

It all seemed so new to him, this seething, simmering knot of tender emotion. Of all the things that had scared him about getting involved with Beth, this—the emotion—was the scariest. Yet accepting it made him believe he was courageous, too. Beth wasn't the only brave person in her bed.

"Are you done crying?" he asked her.

Lifting her head from his shoulder, she sniffled and gave him a bashful smile. "I'm sorry."

"I'm the one who should be sorry. Usually the woman has a smile on her face at the end."

"Those were happy tears," she told him, then attempted an unconvincing scowl. "What woman has a smile on her face?"

"Some woman in my past whom I will never again in my entire life think about," he vowed with fake solemnity. Beth grinned and subsided against his shoulder.

His joke might have made her smile, but thinking about his past made him think about hers. He didn't have the right to ask, but he couldn't seem to stop himself. "That other guy, the one who walked out on you . . . ?"

Beth shifted against his shoulder but didn't withdraw. "What about him?"

What about him? Ryan could have been as big a fool as his predecessor. He'd come mighty close to making the same mistake. "Maybe . . . maybe it wasn't . . ." He groped for a tactful way to say it, then gave up. "Maybe it wasn't your body that freaked him out. Maybe it was your mind."

"My mind?" She started, but he had his arm wrapped tightly around her so she couldn't escape.

"I don't know if you're aware of how strong you are, Beth. A guy . . ." He sighed, acknowledging the inadequacy of his words. "Most guys are intimidated when a woman is tougher than they are. They find it threatening. So they run away."

She pressed against his arm, and he loosened his hold enough that she could lift her head and gaze down at him. "You didn't run away."

"Like hell I didn't. I'd still be running right now, except . . ."

"Except you stopped running."

"Except I wanted you even more than I feared you."

She scrutinized his face, her eyes still damp, her smile so poignant, it caused his heart to ache. Slowly she lowered herself back into his embrace. "You're tougher than you realize, Ryan."

"No," he argued. "I'm not tough. I'm just crazy about you, that's all." He rose then, rolling her onto her back and himself onto his side. Even with that sad slash across her chest, she had a sexy body. Her waist was so narrow he couldn't begin to guess how all her organs fit inside her skin. Her ribs were delicate, her pelvis a gentle cradle for the mound of pale curls between her legs. Her breast was beautiful, round and sweet, her nipple as red as a berry.

He cupped his hand around the warm, firm flesh and watched the nipple tighten. He glanced at her, all of a sudden feeling uncertain. Was he supposed to touch her there? Would it make her painfully aware of what she was missing? He just didn't know.

"That feels nice," she murmured.

"I just..." He should have spent more time arousing her this way. He usually lavished plenty of attention on a woman's breasts. But in Beth's case, the term *breasts* didn't apply. And he'd been so afraid of doing the wrong thing, making her feel uncomfortable, accidentally brushing up against scars he couldn't see but knew she had.

"You can touch me anywhere," she told him.

"It won't hurt?"

Her eyes were like gems, multifaceted and sparkling. "It won't hurt."

She seemed to understand that he was asking her not about physical pain but psychic pain. "Are you sure?"

"It's my body, Ryan. I live with it every day. I'm sure."

Nervous, yet sensing that this was some sort of test, he moved his hand from the feminine curve of her breast across her sternum to the other side. It felt like a part of her, just one of many parts of her that made her different from all the other women he'd ever known.

He was getting turned on again, not from her body but from her strength, her trust and from his memory of how she'd felt climaxing around him, how *he'd* felt, how he wanted to feel again. Given the way she gasped, the way her hips arched and her unbearably blue eyes misted over, he suspected she was getting turned on again, too.

"I want you," he confessed. "Even more than before." The want was lodged not only in his groin but somewhere deeper, in that dangerous place where thoughts and dreams and hopes and fears lived inside him. That part of him was more aroused than his body. That part of him wanted Beth to accept him the way he had learned to accept her.

If he'd been scared before, he was even more scared now. But he couldn't stop, he couldn't run away, not anymore. Not from her.

"HOW CAN YOU SAY it isn't love?" Cindy asked.

Beth adjusted the laces on her sneakers and leaned back until the porch step above the one she was sitting on dug into her spine. "There's a huge difference between love and—and what's going on between Ryan and me," she explained, rummaging in her purse for her sunglasses.

Cindy remained unconvinced. "Kindly explain. What's the huge difference?"

Beth sighed. Dressed in a pair of khaki shorts, a cotton T-shirt, ribbed white socks and her sneakers, she was ready for the bicycle outing Mitzi Rumson had organized. Mitzi had invited Beth, Ryan and Larry to meet her at Devon Hill. From there they would bike to a park about three miles away, where Mitzi was planning to have a basket of fruits, cheeses, cold beverages and pastries waiting for them. God only knew how much she'd paid the caterer to drive this basket to the park. But Mitzi seemed determined to become Devon's newest—actually, its *only*—creative hostess.

"If you want to talk about love," Beth suggested, "let's talk about Mitzi and Larry."

"They're totally wrong for each other," Cindy declared. Erica seconded her remark with a squeal. She was seated in her walker in the backyard, watching Chuck, who was gleefully strutting his stuff for her, chasing butterflies and chipmunks and occasionally his own shadow. Cindy and Beth had finished a light lunch—which would have tasted much better if they'd been able to eat al fresco, Beth reminded herself, imagining her tiny porch expanded into a full-size deck. She really would have to review the proposals Ryan had written out for her. As soon as she had a free minute. . . .

She might not have a free minute until October, she thought with a private smile. Her days were filled with real-estate closings and negotiations on the malpractice suit she'd brought against the inept attorney, and nearly all her evenings were filled with Ryan. Sometimes they went to Corky's for dinner, sometimes to her house, once to his—although he'd revealed that his culinary prowess extended only to dialing a pizza place that delivered.

After dinner, they would sometimes make love—and sometimes not. One night, after she and Ryan had both had exhausting days, they'd simply snuggled up in bed and fallen asleep. And two nights in the past week they hadn't seen each other at all. Neither of them had specifically requested a night alone, but both of them had seemed to need it.

Beth supposed Ryan wanted an occasional night off from her because if they spent too many nights together, their relationship would start to seem like a commitment. She had a strong suspicion that Ryan wasn't the sort to embrace a commitment with a woman. If he was, he'd have gotten married long ago.

Beth's reason for choosing to spend a night apart from him now and then wasn't all that different from Ryan's: she didn't want to become dependent on him. She didn't want to lose her heart to him. If she saw him every night, made love to him every night, exposed herself body and soul to him every night, the commitment, recognized or not, would already be made.

She didn't want to fall in love with Ryan. He was good for her right now, almost too good. He made her feel better than she'd ever felt before. He made her laugh, made her smile, made her believe in herself. Surely that was enough to satisfy her.

And since Beth refused to consider herself in love with Ryan, she was getting her romance fix vicariously, by observing the blossoming of love between Larry and Mitzi. They seemed intent on proving the cliché about opposites attracting. Larry, shy and chronically befuddled, seemed infatuated with the jazzy, snazzy, wealthy widow from Boston. That was less surprising than the fact that Mitzi appeared equally infatuated with Larry. After all those weeks of flirting with Ryan, she had found herself a man who didn't have a flirtatious impulse in him. The day he gave Mitzi an ant farm, she'd been so thrilled she'd floated into Beth's office and gushed for nearly an hour about what a guy he was.

What a guy, indeed. If Ryan gave Beth an ant farm, she might refuse to see him again.

But Larry's peculiar magic seemed to work on Mitzi. And today, on a beautiful, mild Saturday afternoon, that magic was going to work on Beth, too. She was going to unwind and have fun and not think about love or commitment or anything but the crisp blue of the sky, the sweet scent of the air and the fact that she was alive and healthy and happier than she'd been in a long, long time.

"I don't care what you say," Cindy remarked. "You're in love."

"I'm not in love," Beth retorted. "Ryan and I are only getting wet together. It's nothing more than that."

"I've known you a long time, Beth. I've seen you when you were with Peter, and that guy in law school— what was his name? Richard. And that fellow you were dating for a while in New York, the divorced guy."

"That was never anything serious," Beth scoffed. "We only went out a few times."

"None of them was ever anything serious," Cindy said. "Even Peter wasn't anything serious. Your face didn't glow with him the way it's glowing now."

"It's glowing," Beth argued, "because I'm looking forward to this outing. I haven't gone biking in the country in years. This is going to be a real treat."

Cindy ignored her explanation. "And you've got this aura of contentment about you, too. Like everything's coming together, everything's falling into place."

"Everything *is* falling into place. I have a home, I'm feeling good, my dog no longer piddles all over the house—"

"And you're in love with Ryan Walker." Cindy studied her friend intently. "What's the matter? Does it bother you that he's in construction and you're a hotsy-totsy lawyer?"

"God, no!" Beth laughed at the absurdity of Cindy's suggestion. "I've never cared about status, Cindy—you know that. Besides, law isn't exactly a highly esteemed profession these days."

"Then what's the problem? Are you afraid he doesn't love you back?"

Beth hesitated. There was a hefty portion of truth in Cindy's guess, but if Beth conceded the point to her friend, she would no longer be able to pretend otherwise to herself.

"I know he doesn't love me," she admitted. "That certainly puts the kibosh on anything developing between us."

"How do you know he doesn't love you?"

Again Beth hesitated, tossing thoughts around in her mind, viewing them from different angles, unwilling to give voice to any of them before she understood the implications. She *did* know Ryan wasn't in love with her. It wasn't as if he'd stood up and announced that he wasn't, but...

She knew from the way he smiled at her, always holding something in reserve. She knew from the way a shadow passed across his eyes whenever he gazed at her flawed body. Sex was always serious between them—intense, glorious, yet somber, almost sacramental.

Before she and Ryan had become intimate, his smile had been freer. But then it had changed. Everything had changed between them once he'd seen her. She wasn't like other women. Loving her demanded more from a man than she had a right to expect from Devon's most eligible bachelor.

"I just know," she said tersely.

The rattle of Ryan's truck cruising up the driveway prevented Cindy from probing further. "Well, I guess it's pedal time," she announced, rising to her feet and crossing the yard to fetch Erica. "I don't know...I used to think biking was fun until I became the mother of a baby who stays up half the night in teething pain. Now my idea of fun is taking a nap."

"She won't be teething forever," Beth said, trying to convince herself that the quiet surge of joy she felt was because Cindy could no longer interrogate her about Ryan, rather than because he had arrived.

"Sure," Cindy complained, gathering Erica's things and cramming them into her tote. "A few years from now, she'll be keeping me up all night breaking her curfew."

"Not my goddaughter," Beth promised. "I won't let her." Another surge of joy swept through her at the sound of Ryan's truck door slamming shut, at the crunch of his sneakers on the gravel. She forced herself to walk slowly around the house to greet him, squelching the urge to race into his arms.

She couldn't suppress the sudden giddiness, the burst of sunshine at the center of her soul, radiating outward to kiss every cell in her body the instant her eyes met Ryan's. The grin that took over her mouth, the shimmering pleasure of knowing she would spend an entire afternoon with him. The awareness that there would be nothing overly emotional about today, nothing to challenge them, nothing to force them to define who they were or where they were heading in their relationship...

She was allowed to be happy in Ryan Walker's company. She was allowed to go just a little fuzzy inside when he kissed her hello. She was allowed to feel her hips grow heavy and her pulse flutter in her throat just because he was with her. It had nothing to do with love.

"Mitzi said she rented us bikes," he told her once Cindy had taken her leave and they'd locked up the house. "I've got an old bike somewhere but it's pretty rusted, and I didn't know whether you had one, so I let her go ahead and rent bikes for both of us.''

''If we brought our own bikes,'' Beth assured him, ''Mitzi wouldn't feel like the hostess. She wants to provide the afternoon's entertainment—and that starts with providing the afternoon's bikes.''

''You're right.'' Ryan opened the passenger-side door for her and helped her up into the truck. He let his hand linger on hers for a moment and sent her a quick, private smile that ignited a low heat in her belly.

It wasn't love, she told herself. It wasn't love that made her insides quiver whenever she gazed into his eyes. It wasn't love that made her skin tingle in the wake of his touch. It wasn't love that made her as happy to sleep with him as to make love with him, as happy to sit quietly with him as to talk and laugh. It wasn't love that made the world around her seem just a bit more vivid when he was with her, that made the future seem more worth fighting for.

It wasn't love. It couldn't be. Beth refused to acknowledge it.

Maybe she was just in denial.

MOST OF THE TIME, Ryan loved being with her.

He loved looking at her, loved teasing a smile out of her, loved watching her eat, loved feeling her lithe, slender body wrapped around his at night. On those nights when they weren't together, he loved knowing she was across town, just a phone call away. He loved lying in bed when he was too tired to think, and dialing her number and hearing her voice before he fell asleep.

But then there were other times. Times like right now, when her eyes seemed almost too bright with hope, and her hair was more golden than the sun and the air seemed to vibrate with her presence. Times like this scared him.

He wanted what he and Beth had—but he wanted it simple. And she had warned him all along that things could never be simple between them.

Like when they were making love. He had never really thought much about the phrase "casual sex" before—how could anything that felt so bone-deep good be casual? But with Beth, sex was different. Sex was viewing her ravaged body and seeing her entire history, and wishing he could throttle the guy who'd walked out on her when she'd been diagnosed. If he'd been with her then, he wanted to believe would have stayed with her, fought alongside her, been her partner in the battle.

That word—*partner*—scared him most of all.

He had always imagined himself married someday, fathering a few kids, settling into the family-man role. But when he'd imagined it...damn, but he felt guilty to have to admit that the woman in his fantasy hadn't been touched by disease.

He was vermin, holding back from Beth because of something completely beyond her control. He was scum for wanting her to be something she could never be, wanting her to give him the assurances that weren't hers to give. But he was entitled to a few points for honesty, wasn't he?

He was going to have to deal with his ambivalence soon. It wasn't fair to string Beth along, letting her think he could give one-hundred percent when he hadn't yet convinced himself of that. But to tell her the truth would mean losing her, and he couldn't bear that.

He was definitely vermin and scum...but for now, he was just going to put it all out of his mind and enjoy a glorious afternoon with Beth.

Devon Hill stood on a small rise on the western end of town. White clapboard with black shutters, a broad front porch and a screened side porch, the three-story house looked like a Hollywood movie's idea of a New England inn. Geraniums blossomed in window boxes on the upper floors; the flower beds bordering the porches bloomed with rhododendrons and azaleas. Four shiny new bicycles stood near the front walk.

Mitzi and Larry rose from the porch's sloping Adirondack chairs as Beth and Ryan strode up the front walk. Mitzi waved enthusiastically, and when she jogged down the porch steps her bosom heaved. It dawned on Ryan that maybe there was too much of her—too much hair, too much curving flesh, too much leg exposed beneath her shorts, which barely covered her butt. Ryan preferred the discreet allure of Beth, her legs long and tan but the tops of her thighs hidden from him, visible only in his memory.

"Look what I got!" Mitzi chirped, digging into the large tote bag Larry was lugging down the steps behind her. She pulled out four bike helmets. "The pink one's for you," she said, handing Beth a pastel-pink helmet, "and this one's for you," she said, passing a black helmet with yellow lightning streaks on it to Ryan.

"Lightning?"

"Check out mine," Larry said cheerfully, displaying a white helmet with what appeared to be a fly's wings painted on either side.

"Ugh. What's is that?"

"A hornet," Larry said proudly. "Mitzi's getting into bugs."

Ryan's laughter washed away the last of his uneasiness about Beth. "Poor Mitzi. I thought she had taste."

"If I had any taste," she conceded, "I wouldn't have fallen in love with Larry. The bikes are rented, but the helmets are to keep." She strapped on her own, which, not surprisingly, was a metallic gold to match her miscellaneous jewelry.

"These look so nice," Beth said, examining one of the two women's-style bikes. "I've never seen so many gears on a bike. It's been years since I rode."

"Riding a bike is just like sex," Mitzi said breezily. "Once you know how to do it, you never forget."

Beth smiled. Ryan didn't know whether she'd deliberately looked at him—or, for that matter, whether he'd deliberately looked at her. But somehow their gazes intersected above the bicycles. The piercing blue of hers penetrated him, impaling his soul. He would *never* forget sex with her. He would never forget the way she could make his emotions climax along with his body. He would never forget the way she energized him, drained him, made him feel strong and weak at the same time. Once a man made love to Beth nothing would ever be the same again.

Scary thoughts. He shoved them away, ordering himself not to think about anything but the mild weather and the exercise, the exhilaration of a long bike ride with food and drink and the company of good friends as his reward.

They mounted their bikes, strapped on their personalized helmets and started along the winding country road. The air was spicy with the scents of evergreen forests and fresh-cut grass. Robins darted among the branches of leafy oak and sycamore trees. Even with his helmet on, Ryan could feel the wind slapping his cheeks.

Mitzi and Larry led the way. Beth and Ryan rode behind them, side by side on the two-lane asphalt. When a car came along, Ryan slowed and fell into line behind Beth, but once the car had passed them, he pulled out next to her again. He liked looking at her neat little rear end perched on the bike seat and her calf muscles flexing as she pedaled. But more than that, he liked being able to talk to her.

"She's really crazy about him, isn't she?" he said, motioning with his chin toward Mitzi and Larry, who were far enough ahead not to be able to hear him.

"Is it reciprocated?"

"Are you kidding? Larry has lost the ability to speak in complete sentences. He's gone bonkers over her."

"That's so sweet." Beth smiled—a smile as sweet as Larry's and Mitzi's new love. "Did you hear about the ant farm he gave her?"

Ryan rolled his eyes. "I couldn't believe he did that. A woman like Mitzi Rumson... You give someone like her diamonds and gold, don't you?"

"I think she's got enough jewelry. I'll bet—" Beth steered slightly closer to him "—her dear, departed husband, Winnie, never gave her an ant farm."

"Well, true love is a strange beast."

"It's an endangered species," Beth contended. "It's people like Mitzi and Larry who help keep it from becoming extinct."

Ryan reflected on her words. He doubted she'd intended for him to mine any deep philosophical meaning from them, yet he couldn't help himself. When he was with her, when he thought about her, when he kissed her and slid his body inside hers, the strange beast—true love—growled at him and bared its teeth. He knew it was rare—frightening yet beautiful, like a tiger or a panther, some sleek, fanged jungle cat ready to sink its teeth into him.

He pedaled harder into the road's incline.

"These gears," Beth muttered, falling behind him. "Ryan? Are your gears sticking?"

"Try the left-side lever."

"That's for the large gears, isn't it? I want to down-shift on the small gears, but it keeps sticking."

He slowed to her speed. "You'd better use the large gears, then."

She coasted, shifted and started pedaling again. "The last bike I had, back in New York City, had ten speeds. Ten was more than enough."

"New York City is flat. New Hampshire is hilly. Besides, anyone who would demand her own personal Palace of Versailles on the outskirts of Devon would never be satisfied renting ten-speed bikes. Mitzi likes things elaborate, in case you haven't noticed."

"I noticed." Beth smiled at him. The gentle pink hue of her helmet matched the color the sun had raised in her cheeks. She looked so fresh, so exquisitely female, so downright sexy....

Ryan felt the beast's fangs nip at him once more.

They reached the top of the hill. Ryan shifted gears and headed down, listening to the gears chatter as his bike zipped along. From the time he was a kid, he had always loved downhill biking. It was almost as thrilling as jumping into the gorge after the spring thaw—that sense of indestructibility, that soaring freedom. The wind tugged at his shirt and roughed his ears. The bike's wheels hummed. Mitzi's high-pitched laughter blew back into his face.

He almost didn't hear the sound behind him—a click, a squeak and then silence. Squeezing his handlebar brakes a few times to avoid skidding, he glanced over his shoulder. Beth's bike was lying on its side on the grassy shoulder. Beth was lying on her side next to it.

A curse lodged in his throat. He stopped, U-turned and worked the pedals hard, ascending the hill to her. By the time he had leapt off his bike she was sitting up—slowly—and shaking her head.

He tossed down his bike and sprinted over to her. "Are you okay? What happened?"

"I don't know." She shook her head again, hugging her arms to herself. "I shifted gears and it bucked me off. I'm sure I did something wrong—"

"No, no. Don't move," he ordered her, yanking off his helmet and then easing hers off. He checked her bare knees—no blood, no bruises—and then her face. Her eyes looked as clear as always, evenly focused. "Does it hurt anywhere?"

"Just my shoulder. I sort of landed on it. The grass is so soft here, I'm sure I—"

"Which shoulder?" Her right hand was cupping her left elbow. "Your left?"

"It's okay, Ryan. Just a little sore."

He touched it and she winced. "It's not okay," he argued.

Her eyes flashed with tears of anger and chagrin. "I can't believe this. I'm so clumsy, I—"

"You're not clumsy. You said the gears jammed."

"I've ruined everything. This was supposed to be a nice outing, and—"

"Stop. It's not your fault." He moved his hand gently along her upper arm, but she didn't flinch or jerk away. "That doesn't hurt?"

"No. Just my shoulder. Oh, Ryan, I'm sorry."

By this time Larry and Mitzi had arrived, panting from having scaled the steep hill. "What happened?"

"Her gears jammed and the bike threw her," Ryan said before she could start apologizing again. "She was having trouble shifting gears earlier."

Mitzi erupted with a few ripe, well-chosen expletives. "That damned rental place. They'd better be insured for this. Maybe we should sue them. Does anyone here know a good lawyer?" She grinned at Beth, and Ryan came as close as he ever had to adoring her, just because she was trying so hard to make Beth feel better.

"Beth's a lawyer," Larry said, missing Mitzi's joke. Love had obviously made him a bit dense.

"She hurt her shoulder," Ryan reported. "I think she should get it looked at right away."

"No!" Beth argued. "I'm not going to ruin this picnic."

"You don't get a vote, lady." He straightened up and scooped his helmet from the grass. "You guys wait here with her. I'm going to bike back to the inn and get my truck. I'll take her to a doctor."

"We'll all go," Mitzi decided.

"No," Beth said, more calmly this time. "If you want to keep me company until Ryan gets back, okay— but then you two can go on. There's no need for everyone to come to the doctor with me. I don't even need a doctor," she added, although the color had drained from her cheeks, giving her complexion a waxy pallor. She was obviously in pain.

"Don't let her move her arm, okay?" Ryan told Mitzi and Larry as he righted his bike and mounted it. "I'll be back in ten minutes." He gave her one final, quelling look, then headed down the hill toward the inn.

BECAUSE IT WAS A SATURDAY and no doctors in town had office hours, Ryan drove her to a hospital in Manchester. He insisted on making a sling for her arm with his belt so it wouldn't jostle around during the drive. It didn't hurt, really—just a deep ache throbbing from the base of her neck to her shoulder.

She hated herself for falling. This was supposed to be a carefree afternoon, a chance to bask in the glow of Larry and Mitzi's blossoming love. And instead, she was going to spend the afternoon in an emergency room, getting her arm X-rayed.

Ryan seemed to be taking the mishap in stride. "I'm really sorry," she said as he pulled into the parking lot outside the emergency room entrance.

"I'm sorry you got a bum bike."

She blinked away the tears gathering along her lashes. "I hate hospitals."

He shot her a quick look, but she knew he couldn't understand the fury seething beneath her surface calm—indeed, he probably couldn't even sense it. She had developed her ability to fight the negative, to refuse it a chance to take her over. Like a military reservist always on call, she knew how to don her armor in a hurry. But she didn't have to be happy about being called up.

"This time," he pointed out, his voice low but firm, "you have me. It won't be so bad."

The anger burning like a flame inside her dimmed, as if he'd poured cool water on it. This time she had Ryan. It was as close to an avowal of love as she'd ever heard from a man.

She had Ryan. She would dance through this trivial ordeal, because she had him. There would be no battles to wage, no tragedies to overcome. A doctor would tell her she'd suffered a deep muscle bruise, or a sprain, or a pulled tendon, and then she would go home. With Ryan.

They entered the emergency room together. In contrast to the raucous city hospitals in New York, this emergency room was blessedly empty. A nurse recorded Beth's insurance information and took her directly to an X-ray room. Ryan couldn't accompany her down the corridor, but she still felt him with her. His nearness gave her strength.

A technician X-rayed her arm and shoulder in a few positions, then sent her back out to the waiting room. Ryan had been leafing through a magazine, but the moment she entered, he dropped it and smiled at her. "What's the word?" he asked.

"They have to develop the X rays."

He nodded. "You know, since we're down here in Manchester, we ought to do something urban. This day doesn't have to be a total wash."

"Okay." If she let herself love him, this would be one reason. He could take a disaster and turn it into an adventure. He could show her a way to feel good about something lousy.

"We can take in a movie, then maybe find ourselves a restaurant a little classier than Corky's."

"Dressed like this?" She gestured at her rumpled shorts and T-shirt.

"We can go shopping and buy some clothes. Hey, lady, we're in the big city."

She chuckled. "What a date. Shopping in Manchester."

He wiggled his eyebrows lecherously. "Maybe I could sneak into the fitting room with you."

"You wouldn't see anything you haven't already seen."

"But I'd see it in a new setting. The curtain, the mirror, the narrow space, that little bench.... We could get creative." He winked, making her laugh and blush at the same time.

"Ms. Pendleton?"

Beth turned to see a man in a doctor's white jacket standing near the reception desk. "Yes?"

He approached her, smiling benignly. He couldn't have been much older than her; no doubt he was an unlucky resident who'd drawn the Saturday shift. "I'm Dr. Matthew Rose," he said. "Let's go to my office and talk."

She didn't ask Ryan to come with them but she was glad when he fell into step beside her, his hand resting lightly against the small of her back. They walked along the corridor, passing the X-ray room and entering Dr. Rose's small, square office. It looked like so many doctors' offices Beth had visited—the nondescript carpet, the wall-bracketed shelves holding books and family photos, the walls decorated with posters provided by pharmaceutical companies, touting their products. A fluorescent panel on one wall was illuminated, and Beth recognized the X rays clipped to them as photos of a shoulder.

"The good news," Dr. Rose said, gesturing toward the two visitors' chairs that faced his desk, "is that you fractured your collarbone."

"That's good news?" Ryan blurted out.

"A clavicle is an easy bone to knit—especially a simple fracture like this. We'll have to immobilize the arm for a short while. We'll put you in a removable sling, so you'll be able to bathe and so on. An over-the-counter pain-killer should get you through the next day or so. It's really not a major injury.''

Beth heard a subtext in Dr. Rose's tone, something Ryan would never have detected because he'd never had to listen for it. But she had heard it before. It made her stomach tense up, her eyes sting, her breath tear through her lungs. ''What's the bad news?'' she asked, her voice as hard and cold as stone.

Ryan sent her a look of surprise. Dr. Rose, unfortunately, didn't. He crossed to the X-ray panel. ''You've had breast cancer, Ms. Pendleton.''

Tell me something I don't know. ''That's right.''

Dr. Rose's expression transformed from benign to sympathetic. Beth shuddered inwardly. She knew that expression as well as she knew the colorations of his voice. She knew. This was going to be bad.

''I'm sure you're aware that one of the grave dangers is that sometimes breast cancer cells can migrate into the bones.''

No. She didn't want to hear this. She couldn't stand it. She didn't deserve it. It wasn't fair.

''Of course, these are just some preliminary X rays I'm looking at, Ms. Pendleton, but there's a dark spot here, a thickness—'' he pointed to it and she closed her eyes so she wouldn't have to see ''—that looks suspicious. It could be nothing, but right here...'' She forced her eyes open, but refused to gaze at the dark spot he was pointing out. ''This isn't a second fracture. I'm not sure what it is. You'll have to have your oncologist investigate it. I would suggest you get it checked as soon as possible.''

No. This wasn't supposed to happen. She had been through enough already. She had gotten her life back on track, she was happy, she was—dear God, she was in love. *This wasn't supposed to happen.*

"All right," she said quietly, calmly, reasonably. She wasn't really in love. Maybe that was why this was happening—because she wasn't in love with Ryan, because she had promised herself she wasn't going to fall in love with him. A suspicious thickness in her bone was a way to keep her unruly heart in line.

"I'm sorry, Ms. Pendleton." Dr. Rose said nothing for a minute, then smiled, one of those ghastly, pitying smiles that medical professionals gave cancer patients when they ran out of other options. "If you'd like a few minutes alone...?"

"Yes, thank you."

He tiptoed out of the office, closing the door behind him. Beth shut her eyes once more, unable to look at the illuminated X rays, at the bland room, at Ryan.

She felt a hand on her right arm. Ryan's hand, warm and solid and powerful. "Are you okay?" he whispered.

No. She was not okay. She had just been issued a ticket for another ride on the roller coaster from hell. And she couldn't ask anyone to take the trip with her. Certainly not Ryan. She loved him too much to ask him to go through this with her. She did love him, damn it. She did.

She loved him enough to spare him this, to give him the opportunity to escape it. She loved him enough not to force her bad luck on him. She loved him enough to set him free, because he couldn't possibly love her enough to stay.

And then she would be alone, for much longer than

the few minutes Dr. Rose had granted her. However much time this new chapter of her life was going to take, she was going to endure it alone.

CHAPTER FOURTEEN

"I'M ALL RIGHT," Beth said briskly. "Really. I'm okay."

"If you say that one more time," Ryan warned, "I'm going to know you're lying."

She gave him a crooked smile, one that shouted loud and clear that she wasn't even remotely all right. A small suitcase lay open on her bed, and she was spending an awfully long time arranging the few garments she had to pack for her trip to New York. Her left arm was in a sling, but her left hand still worked well enough, collaborating with her right hand as she fussed with each article of clothing, folding and unfolding and refolding it until he wanted to scream.

If he dared, he would have charged across the room, pushed her out of the way and crammed her things into the bag, neatness be damned. But this—the packing, the trip to New York, the whole thing—was her show. So he held back, lounging in her doorway and watching, wondering, as he'd been wondering since yesterday afternoon, what in God's name he was supposed to do.

He had told her, way back when she'd tried to warn him off and he'd been wise enough to pay attention, that this was a new experience for him. Nowhere in the Ryan Walker wiring was there a circuit for trips down to New York City for bone scans.

He had lacked a circuit for mastectomies, too, yet he'd somehow managed to hook one up. But that hadn't been anywhere near as difficult as he'd expected, because even missing a breast, Beth was the sexiest woman he'd ever met.

This other part, though, this bone scan... This was different. This was present tense, and it was major. This was the sort of situation he'd prefer not even to have to think about, let alone deal with. But it had to be harder on Beth than it was on him, and if she was going to deal with it, why shouldn't he? He could be just as tough as her.

"I know you've already turned me down," he murmured, "but it's no big deal for me to drive you to New York." It *would* be a big deal to drive her to New York, not because of the time or the miles, but because of her reason for going. There were certainly enough doctors in Manchester or Nashua—or Boston if she wanted to see a big-name oncologist at a big-name hospital. But she'd insisted on returning to her doctor in New York, the one she believed saved her life.

Personally, Ryan believed Beth had saved her own life. She was too much of a dynamo to let anyone else do that for her. Her New York doctor had probably only helped a little.

"I appreciate the offer," she said now, just as she'd said every other time he'd offered to drive her down— at least a dozen times in the past twenty-four hours. "But no, thank you."

"It's only a five-hour trip," he persisted. "I wouldn't mind."

She peered up from the sweater she had been meticulously folding. Her eyes were sharp, almost crackling with electricity. "The commuter flight will get me down there in no time flat," she said, then shook the sweater out and folded it all over again. Her slim fingers worked with the mechanical finesse of a concert pianist's, but without the grace. Her back was rigid, her lips nearly white with tension.

He had never seen a woman so frightened in his life—or so determined to hide her fear. Maybe he could put everything out of her mind for a few minutes with a good, hard kiss. Or something else equally good and hard. He could knock the suitcase onto the floor, throw her onto the bed and make her come so many times she'd forget her own name. And then she'd miss her flight and he could drive her down to New York and be with her.

And once there, he could listen to all the specialists toss around their jargon, and he could gawk at the huge, daunting diagnostic machines, and he could watch Beth get jabbed with needles and zapped with laser beams and whatever the hell else the doctors were going to do to her in their search for an explanation for the mysterious smudge on her X ray.

Oh, God. He didn't want to think about it.

Well, it didn't matter what he did or didn't want. She wasn't even giving him a choice. She had dropped a shield over herself, locking Ryan out of her crisis. Since yesterday afternoon, when Dr. Rose at the emergency room had scared the spit out of her, Ryan had been able to read her signals. He'd tried to respect her decision, backing off and leaving her all the room she needed.

Having run out of items to fidget with, she lowered the lid of her suitcase and clicked the latches shut. "Chuck likes to take a long walk first thing in the morning," she said, staring at a spot two inches to Ryan's left so she wouldn't have to meet his gaze. "And he'll only sleep in his crate. You don't have to take him back to your house. He'll be okay here, I think, as long as you let him out first thing in the morning. He likes a dog biscuit at the end of his walk, and fresh water—''

"Beth, I know dogs. And I know Chuck. We're guys. We understand each other.''

Her face, angled away from the bedside lamp, was washed by gray shadows. "He likes lots of petting,'' she continued. "And he likes to be talked to.''

"No problem.''

"He doesn't need a choke chain. I know you thought he would, but he doesn't. Promise me you won't put one on him.''

"Relax.'' Ryan couldn't stand the distance anymore. He stormed across the room, took her in his arms and hugged her close. She felt too thin, even though Ryan knew she couldn't have lost any weight since yesterday. She felt frail, breakable, as if she were losing substance. "Let me come with you,'' he whispered, trying not to plead. "I'll stay out of your way, Beth. I just think this might be a little easier on you if—''

"If I have to worry about you along with everything else?'' she snapped.

He cringed. Her rejection hurt. He shouldn't take it personally, but he couldn't help himself. He wanted to be her hero, and she was cutting him down, cutting him off.

"You don't have to worry about me,'' he retorted, trying not to sound angry. "This is about you.''

"Yes.'' She pulled back and glared at him. He saw fear mixed in with the anger lighting her eyes. Fear and remorse. And grit in her voice as she said, "It's about *me*, Ryan. You don't know what you'd be signing on for if you came to New York with me. If you did know, you wouldn't want to be part of it. And I'm not going to let you tag along for the ride and then come to your senses and leave me. I'm not going to let you do that."

"Why are you so sure I'm going to leave you? I'm not that other guy, okay?"

"This isn't about my breast," she railed. "It isn't about physical beauty. It isn't about sex. This is my life."

"I know," he said, still not sure what she was getting at.

She seemed to realize that. "You can't begin to know. You can't begin to understand what it's like to be always expecting some doctor to find a smudge on your X ray. You've never had to live with a sword dangling over your head. I live every day of my life with that sword. And if you get too close to me, Ryan, the sword is going to be dangling over your head, too."

Her words buffeted him, staggered him. What was she saying? That he couldn't be with her unless he was prepared for her to die? That he couldn't love her unless he could experience her constant fear of death?

Maybe she *was* saying that. And if she was, if that was what it took to be Beth's lover...

She was right. He couldn't begin to know, and he wasn't sure he wanted to be a part of it. Even if she let him, even if she welcomed him...he wasn't sure.

She watched him, evidently reading his thoughts as they played across his face. Slowly she unwound, her bitterness draining from her, leaving behind a stony calm.

"So you'll take care of Chuck for me?" she said quietly.

"Chuck and I will do just fine without you," he promised.

"Okay." Her eyes flickered with a bleak light. It reminded him of the resignation he'd seen in them the first time they'd made love. This time, he didn't know how to make things right for her. This time he couldn't.

"I've given you Evelyn's phone number," she reminded him, all business now. "I'll be staying with her tonight, and tomorrow I'll be at the hospital."

"I know."

"I'm not sure what day I'll be flying back. It's going to depend."

It was going to depend on what the doctors told her, what they learned about the dark spot on her collarbone. "When you get home, you get home," he said.

"So don't let Chuck worry if I'm not back right away."

Chuck? Hell, what about *him?*

He wasn't going to worry about her. She didn't want him to—and if she didn't want him to, well, he didn't want to, either.

Never had he imagined that Beth would be the one to run away. He'd thought she was tougher than he was but he'd been wrong. She was running, fleeing from him, not giving him a chance.

Obviously, she didn't think he could be the man she needed. She didn't have enough faith in him.

So he was going to drive her to the Manchester Municipal Airport, and he was going to drive back to Devon, and he was going to take care of Chuck. And he was going to convince himself that her decision to cut him out of her life at this crucial moment was the kindest thing she could have done.

CHUCK AND I WILL DO just fine without you.

The engine of the turboprop droned in her ears like a

mosquito magnified a thousand times. The plane flew
close enough to the earth that she could see the profiles
of towns and rivers and hills below, the contours of
western Massachusetts. In less than an hour she would
be at La Guardia Airport; in less than ninety minutes,
at Evelyn's comfortable East Seventy-fifth Street
apartment. In less than a day, she would be done with
this nightmare.

No. She would never be done with it. There would
always be bone scans, always tests and extra tests, always the scars of a woman who had walked through fire
and wore her memories on her chest, in her heart. There
would always be a kernel of dread that, somehow, she
wouldn't win the next battle.

Chuck and I will do just fine without you.

Ryan couldn't have meant those words the way they
came out—but once he'd said them, she hadn't been
able to stop playing with them, lifting them to the light,
peering through them. They implied that someday—
someday within Chuck's lifetime, perhaps—the world
would do fine without her.

That was too morbid a thought, and she shut her eyes
against it, closing herself off from the panorama of
treetops and silver threads of river below the airplane.
An entire universe existed down there, without her.

She wasn't going to think about death. She was going to think about Ryan. That was as depressing a concept as she could handle.

That they were going to break up was a foregone
conclusion. It would be her doing, her decision. Her
fear of losing him when she needed him most.

It made some kind of cockeyed sense to her that
sending Ryan over the side of the ship in a lifeboat was
more humane than waiting until the ship had gone un-

der completely and he had to swim for his life or else risk getting sucked under with her. She loved him, and because she loved him she'd had to give him the freedom to walk away before she went down.

She forced her eyes open again. Below her stretched the ragged outline of Connecticut's southern shore, the waters of Long Island Sound curling and frothing against the rocks, wearing them to sand. Beth felt worndown, too, her stone-hard courage eroded to a fine powder that the waves could carry back into the Sound. There was nothing to anchor her to earth now. Not Ryan. Not Chuck. They would do fine without her.

She had only meant to get wet with Ryan, to rediscover the pleasures of her body. She hadn't meant to fall in love with him.

But she had. And now she was going down. Alone.

FRIENDSHIP WAS OFTEN defined by what two people had gone through together. Beth had gone through law school with Cindy. They'd lived together in those hectic, formative years of their early twenties, years when Cindy had met Jeff Miller, thanks to Beth.

What Beth had shared with Evelyn was medical. They were both survivors, foxhole comrades, and there were certain things they both knew that someone who hadn't been in the trenches could never possibly understand. When Beth had phoned Evelyn to say she was coming down to New York, Evelyn had insisted that Beth stay in her guest room. It hadn't been an invitation. It had been an edict.

She spent the evening with Evelyn, whose husband discreetly vanished into the bedroom to watch television, leaving the two women in the living room to catch up on old news. Evelyn reported on the other women in

Beth's support group. Then she asked Beth to describe everything about her life in Devon.

Beth told her about the tranquility of Miller, Miller and Pendleton as compared to her former law firm. She told Evelyn about her partners, her godchild, her house, her dog. She told Evelyn about the starlit evenings and the song of the crickets in her yard and the everpresent scent of pine.

"Who would have guessed?" Evelyn chuckled. "The consummate city girl has fallen in love with rural New England! So, have you made new friends up there?"

"Some," Beth hedged.

"Anyone special? Anyone of the male persuasion?"

Beth rolled her eyes and felt color scorch her cheeks. "I've been dating a little," she said.

"Oh, Beth." Jumping to the right conclusion, Evelyn squeezed Beth's hand. "Don't tell me. He hasn't been able to take it."

"I haven't given him a chance," Beth admitted. "I didn't want to have to learn the worst about him."

"That's not really fair, is it?"

"Nothing is fair," Beth argued, not bitterly but with quiet resolve. "I thought he might be looking for a way out, so I left the door open."

The two women sat in silence for a few minutes. Then Evelyn said, "Remember what the social worker at the hospital said at one of our support-group meetings? She said that when something like this happens to you—" she gestured vaguely at Beth's chest and then her own "—it's a good time to think about what you've been doing, to consider your life with the understanding that you might die tomorrow. And you're supposed to ask yourself, would I die feeling bad about what I did?

Would I wish I'd done something else? Or would I die without regrets?"

Beth remembered. She remembered thinking at the time that if she died right then, she would regret having spent so much of her life at her office, working instead of playing. She would regret never having owned a house with a yard, with grass and flowers and an ocean of sky above her. She would regret never having owned a pet. She would regret never having fallen in love.

She might die tomorrow—just like anyone else. And if she did die tomorrow, she realized that she would no longer have regrets. She'd taken the social worker's advice to heart and changed her life. She'd quit the demanding job, bought her house with a yard, gotten herself a dog. Fallen in love.

She hoped with all her heart that her tomorrow was many, many years off. But if it came upon her all of a sudden...

She would have no regrets. Not even about Ryan. Certainly not about Ryan.

SHE REQUESTED a sedative. The procedure wasn't painful, or even particularly uncomfortable, but she hated having to lie motionless inside the MRI scanner, isolated and closed in, hearing nothing but strange metallic echoes. It made her feel as if she were in a coffin, and that was a feeling she wanted to avoid.

She had no reason to be anxious. Her doctor had talked with her for a long while, asking how she was feeling, how she was faring up in New Hampshire, whether she'd experienced any particular pain in her back, her hips, her ribs or shoulders. He'd reviewed the X-rays from her fractured collarbone. He had told her not to worry.

She worried anyway. She lay inside the metal tunnel of the scanner, closing her eyes, feeling the sedative make her blood thicken and her brain turn cottony. She hadn't slept well last night, and weariness combined with the drug to lull her into a dream state. She thought about her legal malpractice case, about how a case that ought to be stressful seemed remarkably mild, how everything seemed mild in Devon. She pictured the blue, blue sky up there, and her creaky old house on Loring Road. She could almost hear Chuck barking, welcoming her home.

She sank deeper into a trance. The scanner's rays moved along her body, and she pretended they were Ryan's hands, touching her, fearless, loving.

Ryan.

Why had she fallen in love with him? It couldn't be just because he was sharp and funny, or because he was so damned attractive. It couldn't be because he was comfortable in his own skin, easy and graceful even in stained work clothes and heavy boots. It couldn't be because he was a skillful lover.

Skill wasn't what made her feel so good in his arms. He was trustworthy—that was it. Trustworthy and honest. So honest, he didn't bother to hide his doubts. So honest he never used the word *love*, because to use it would have been false.

The machine emitted an eerie, echoing hum, sending a shiver down her spine. She wished she could have Ryan for just a few minutes more, to hold her while she went through this, the way he'd held her last night. She had been so distraught, and he'd taken her into his arms and tried to impart his strength to her. If only she could be as strong as he was, as carefree, bold enough to stand on a cliff above a gorge and jump in. If only she could be whole, like Ryan. If only...

No if only's. No regrets. She had done what she was meant to do in this life, and if the test revealed that she was doomed, she would die knowing that for a too-short, too-sweet time she'd had everything: A home. Contentment. Love.

A hand stroked down her arm. She flinched, aware of the impossibility that anyone could have joined her inside the scanner. Groaning, she opened one eye.

She wasn't in the scanner anymore. She was stretched out on a cot in a dimly lit room. A nurse leaned over her, patting her arm. "Beth?"

She vaguely recognized the nurse. She had gotten to know most of the oncology staff in the past two years, and this must have been one of the regulars. If only she could clear the lint out of her skull and get her other eye open—

"Beth, it's time to wake up."

"Why?" she mumbled. She didn't want to wake up. Sleeping felt too pleasant.

"You've been out for nearly an hour. That sedative really knocked you cold. Come on, honey—can you wake up?"

"No." But her other eye opened, and she laughed at her own stubbornness. Her cheek itched, imprinted with marks from the wrinkled pillowcase. Her hair felt heavy against her cheek.

"There's someone who wants to see you."

The doctor. Or maybe Evelyn. She must have come to the hospital. She had offered to cab over with Beth that morning, but Beth had told her not to bother.

"He's been waiting a long time."

He? Okay, her doctor, then. He was waiting for her.

"Would you like me to send him in?"

"Sure," she said, bewildered. If she had been admitted to the hospital and given a real bed, she would expect her doctor to visit her. But this was just a lounge somewhere, one of the rooms nurses used when they were assigned to the overnight shift and wanted to catch forty winks between emergencies.

Groggy, she tried to sit. But when she glimpsed Ryan Walker in the doorway, she knew she was still asleep, dreaming. She sank back against the pillow and shut her eyes.

"Beth."

Dear God, it sounded just like Ryan. Even the clomp of his boots on the hard floor sounded like Ryan's footsteps. His scent—soap and spice—was Ryan's. His deep, rich, brown eyes peering down at her when she opened her eyes again were Ryan's.

He hadn't shaved. A dark bristle colored his chin, and his hair was wind tossed. He grabbed a chair, slapped it down beside the cot with a loud thud and straddled it. "How are you?" he asked.

She still wasn't sure this was actually happening. "Ryan?"

"Damn it, Beth—" He caught his breath, then began again, his voice subdued. "I've been driving since five this morning. How are you?"

Confused, that was how she was. She couldn't believe Ryan had actually driven all the way to New York, so she concentrated on the side issues. "Who's looking after Chuck? The Millers?"

"No."

"No, of course not," she agreed. "Erica loves him, but it would be too much for them to have to take care of her and Chuck, too. Mitzi? Did you leave him with Mitzi?''

''No, I—''

''Or Larry? I know he loves bugs. I guess he could handle a dog.''

''Lynne,'' Ryan said.

''Lynne?''

''Your obnoxious know-it-all secretary. I called her before dawn and she said, 'I'll take care of Chuck. You go be with Beth.' ''

If anything, Beth was even more confused. She couldn't imagine Lynne saying such a thing. ''Ryan?'' Her voice sounded as fragile as crystal.

''All right.'' He smiled halfheartedly. ''What she said was, no one could take care of a dog as well as she could. She said that commuter flights had a statistically higher average of fatal crashes and if I paid attention to such things I would never have let you fly down. She said the least I could do was drive down so you wouldn't have to get on one of those rickety little prop planes when it was time to come home.''

''Oh.'' Then he'd driven down only because he didn't want her to take a plane. There was nothing more to it than that.

''So.'' He lifted her right hand and sandwiched it between his. His palms were toasty, thawing her chilly fingers. ''How are you?''

''You shouldn't have come,'' she said. Hearing herself say it proved that she was at last fully awake.

''I *had* to come.''

She gazed into his eyes. They were as dark as night, as eternal as time. ''I wanted to spare you—''

''I don't want to be spared,'' he said. She heard steel in his voice, and tremulousness. ''I know you don't want me here. You want to hike this trail on your own and leave me behind."

"Not leave you behind, Ryan. I just... You don't have to be noble on my behalf."

"You think that's why I'm here? Because I want to be noble?" He laughed incredulously. "Me? Noble?"

"Believe me, Ryan, you don't want to go through what I'm going through. It stinks, Ryan. It's hard."

"Hey, I know my life would be a hell of a lot easier without you in it," he agreed. "I didn't bargain for this. I didn't plan on someone like you barging into my world and turning it upside down." He caressed her hand, exploring her knuckles, her nails, the tapered length of each finger. Then he lifted it to his mouth and pressed a kiss into the hollow of her palm. "Last night, after I took you to the airport, I went back to your house and talked to Chuck. You told me he likes to be talked to, so he and I took a long walk—and no, I didn't use a choke chain," he added with a flash of a smile. "We walked and we talked. Well, *I* talked."

"That must have made Chuck happy."

"Nah. He was depressed. He missed you. We both did."

She smiled politely, not believing him.

"More than missed you," he elaborated. "There was this hole in our lives because you had left. I know you're pushing me away, Beth. You don't want to share this with me. You think I can't take it."

"Ryan—"

"Damn it, Beth—I can take anything except losing you. You're right—I don't want to go through all this. Neither do you. But that's not our choice right now. And you can't push me away."

"Ryan—"

"I want to be with you, to go through whatever I have to with you. No matter what it is. Maybe you don't need me right now. But I need you."

"Are you sure?"

"I love you, Beth," he murmured, his eyes shining with unspent tears. "I want as much of you as you'll let me have." His voice cracked slightly. "Don't shut me out."

"I love you, too," she whispered, curling her fingers around his and squeezing tight. "And I *do* need you."

"Then we'll get through this together."

"Yes."

"We'll do everything together, whatever it turns out to be."

"If you're sure that's what you want."

"It's what has to be. Because my life is on the line, too. Okay?"

Her own eyes overflowed. "Okay," she mouthed, holding on to his hand so tightly, she couldn't imagine anything ever pulling her from him. Not fear. Not death. Not anything.

The door cracked open and the nurse poked her head in. "Beth? The doctor would like to talk to you if you're ready."

Beth exchanged a long, intense gaze with Ryan. He clung to her as tightly as she clung to him. His eyes, his smile, his love reached out to her, giving her the strength she needed.

She sat up and nodded at the nurse, then returned her gaze to Ryan, drinking in his healing love. "I'm ready," she said.

EPILOGUE

THE DECK WAS LARGE enough to hold everybody, although only the adults occupied it at the moment. The children had departed for the open space of the backyard. Erica was busy chasing and being chased by Chuck, bossing around her two-year-old brother, Michael, and fussing over Anne Pendleton Walker, who had clearly taken her name to heart and learned how to walk a full month before her first birthday, which was today. She toddled across the lawn, attempting without success to keep up with her gargantuan pet dog and the Miller children.

"Don't keep sitting down whenever you lose your balance," Erica instructed her.

"Eee!" Annie gurgled, and sat down with a diaper-padded thump.

Beth relaxed in the upholstered chair by the table, which was festooned with a pink paper tablecloth. The balmy May breeze tugged at the paper, but it was pinned down securely by the half-eaten birthday cake on a platter squarely at the center of the table. Pink paper plates sat in a jumble of chocolate crumbs and smears of white butter-cream frosting. As much as the children loved chocolate, they loved running around the yard even more.

There were times—many, many times—that Beth had to pause, to absorb the world around her and reassure herself that it was true, she was here, alive and happy and surrounded by love. Just as once she was in denial about her wretched bad luck, she still sometimes found herself in denial about her awesome good luck.

But her luck had changed one day, four years ago, when Ryan had found her in a darkened lounge in a hospital and confronted her with the discovery that he loved her, loved her so much he would not let her push him away, loved her so much he was willing to give up his comfortable existence and join her in the fight. Beth had awakened to him in the dimly lit room, and she'd felt as if she'd awakened to the future she was destined to have, a future that would include a full life and a full heart. A future that would include Ryan.

It had seemed almost anticlimactic, after Ryan's declaration, to go into the doctor's office and hear that her scans looked absolutely fine. "It's something we'll always want to keep an eye on," her doctor had said, "and the fellow up in New Hampshire was correct to err on the side of caution. Better to investigate than to make assumptions. But as far as we can see right now, you look great."

Beth had felt great. She'd been feeling great ever since.

"Erica!" Cindy shouted over the balloon-laden deck railing. "Stop teasing your brother!"

"I'm not teasing him," Erica hollered back. "I'm teaching him how to jog."

"He's too young to jog."

"I want him to stay healthy."

"Great," Cindy grunted, then chuckled. "I swear, I'm going to fire Lynne for explaining cardiovascular fitness to Erica the last time I brought her to the office."

"She's right, you know," Mitzi remarked, strutting over to the railing and waving at Erica. "Fitness is a good way to keep your body sexy." She was wearing so many diamonds on various fingers that her moving hand sprayed sparks of blinding light into Beth's eyes.

One of those rings, the smallest, was the solitaire diamond Larry had given Mitzi at Christmas. Their wedding would be in June, one month from today, and it promised to be the most gala event Devon, New Hampshire, had ever known. Mitzi had rented Devon Hill and two other inns in the area to house her out-of-town guests. The party itself was going to be in the solarium of her estate. "I'm going to sweep down the bridal staircase in the two-story entry," she'd rhapsodized, describing her dramatic entrance to Beth and Cindy. "Thank God Ryan built such a gorgeous staircase. My cream silk gown will look magnificent against the imported marble tiles...."

Beth was looking forward to the wedding. She had been invited to serve as a bridesmaid, but the strapless gowns Mitzi was having designed for her bridal party were a style Beth couldn't wear, and although Mitzi insisted she wouldn't mind having a gown altered for Beth, Beth had begged off. It was enough that Ryan would be standing up for his cousin Larry.

More than enough. Ryan hadn't stopped complaining about having to wear tails. "This is Devon! The only people who wear tails in Devon are kids dressed as the devil for Halloween."

But he would wear tails, because Mitzi wanted the groom and his groomsmen to wear tails and Larry couldn't refuse Mitzi anything. He was as besotted with her as he'd been the day she'd sauntered into the office of Walker Construction Company four years ago with her magazine clippings and her dazzling charisma.

He looked besotted with her now. As she and Cindy leaned against the railing, watching the children, Larry stood near the cooler chest, holding a chilled bottle of beer and beaming at his bride-to-be. His eyes glowed with admiration and adoration. "Isn't she something?" he said to Jeff, who stood next to him, also chugging beer.

"That's exactly what I said the first time I met Mitzi. 'Isn't she something,'" Jeff joked. Larry was too smitten to hear the playful irony in Jeff's tone.

Beth's gaze circled from Jeff and Larry to Mitzi and Cindy, and from them to the children romping across the lawn. Despite his hulking size, Chuck was as gentle as a nursemaid with the young ones, especially Annie. Her chubby little feet seemed planted too firmly in the grass, and she started to topple forward, but before she could fall Chuck rushed to the rescue, wedging his head under her torso and straightening her back up.

"Eee!" she squealed.

She was beautiful. Golden curls danced around her face, and her eyes, as dark as Ryan's but fringed by long, flirty eyelashes, seemed to embrace the world. She had a definite predilection for smiling, even when she was upset, and her smiles poked dimples into her chubby cheeks.

More than beautiful, she was perfect. Even when she was teething, when she needed a new diaper, when she was storming through the house screeching, "No! No! No!"—her second favorite word, after "Da," for Daddy—she was perfect. When she slept, her perfect little thumb tucked into her perfect little mouth. When she splashed in her bath. When she stumbled across the grass on her plump little feet. When she pressed her downy-soft cheek to Beth's and sighed a milky breath against Beth's chin... she was perfect. A miracle. The greatest luck Beth had ever known.

Beth and Ryan.

He swept out of the kitchen, carrying a bottle of champagne. "Oh, no!" Jeff protested when he spotted the curving green bottle in Ryan's hands. "Come on! The kids are too young for that!"

"This isn't for the kids," Ryan announced, setting a handful of disposable plastic champagne glasses on the table. "This is for the adults."

"*I'm* too young for that," Jeff warned.

"Then grow up. We've got something to celebrate."

Curious, Cindy and Mitzi turned from the railing. Beth was curious, too. Every day was a celebration for her, but she didn't know what in particular had prompted Ryan to include champagne in what was supposed to be their daughter's party.

"We're celebrating Annie's first birthday," Cindy said unnecessarily. "And champagne's fine with me. *I'm* old enough," she added, shooting her husband a teasing look.

"We're celebrating something more than just Annie's first birthday," Ryan announced. He radiated energy, enthusiasm, abundant humor. His thick hair blew in the spring breeze as he aimed the bottle toward the side of the house and removed the cork with a festive pop. Then he filled six glasses with champagne.

"What's this all about?" Beth asked, peering up at him.

He smiled, a devastatingly handsome smile. It was exactly the same smile that had hijacked her heart even before she'd realized it, the smile he'd smiled on Main

Street when he'd had to give her an impromptu lesson in how to tell boy dogs from girl dogs. It was the smile he'd worn long before he had even considered the possibility of falling in love with her, let alone understood what falling in love with her would demand of him—a smile he wore today, still in love with her.

"My wife has some excellent news," he announced once all the glasses were distributed. "Go ahead, tell everyone."

"Tell everyone what?" She frowned, perplexed. "That you're going to build a breezeway between the garage barn and the house so I don't have to carry groceries through the rain?"

"That's old news," Ryan scoffed. "Tell them what day it is."

"They know what day it is. Annie's first birthday."

"And it's five years," he said, his smile intended for all their guests but his gaze only on her. "Five years of negative scans. Five years of healthy tests. Five years of good news." He turned to the others, lifting his glass in a toast. "This lady is officially cured."

"Hear, hear!" Larry bellowed, clicking his plastic glass against Jeff's.

"I've been cured all along," Beth muttered, embarrassed and delighted at the same time. She had mentioned the five-year anniversary to Ryan yesterday at dinner, because her doctor had phoned her with the happy results of her most recent physical.

"Five years makes it real," he said, sipping his champagne and then setting down his glass and leaning over his wife's chair. Without a shred of modesty, he covered her mouth with his and gave her a deep, lusty kiss.

"Isn't that sweet?" Mitzi purred.

"Why don't you ever kiss me like that?" Cindy asked Jeff.

Beth tuned them out, closing her eyes and losing herself in Ryan's kiss, his passion, his love. Just that morning, before they'd gone into the nursery to get Annie out of her crib, Ryan had gathered Beth to himself and murmured, "Thank you."

"For last night?" she'd questioned. "Believe me, it was more fun for me than it was for you."

"We could argue that for a long time," he'd noted with a wicked smile. Then he'd grown abruptly serious. "Thank you for Annie. Thank you for marrying me. Thank you for giving me the chance to be a better man than I was."

"You were always a better man," Beth had asserted.

"No. Not until I met you and you forced me to recognize it. So...thank you."

"Well." She'd contemplated all the things she could thank him for and decided that if she began to list them all, Annie would be ready to start kindergarten by the time they got her out of her crib. "I feel like I should thank you for something."

His smile had returned, more roguish than ever. "You could thank me for last night."

She'd pretended to give his suggestion some thought, then said, "Thanks for building that twenty-by-thirty-foot deck. If the weather holds, we can have the party outside this afternoon."

The weather had held. The sky was a pure New England blue. The day was warm, and Beth was more in love with Ryan than she'd been yesterday, which was more than she'd been the day before, which was more than she'd ever believed possible.

She let him pull her out of her chair and wrap her in his arms. They stood on the deck she had thanked him for, grateful for the party, for their friends, for their beloved child, for their rambunctious dog, for each other. For the luck that had brought them together. For the luck that promised them a long, healthy future.

You're okay, Beth whispered to herself. *You're better than you ever dreamed of being. You've got Ryan, and Annie, and any other children luck might bring your way. You've got a home, a dog, and health, and love.*

She smiled. She was doing just fine.